A STARLESS CLAN

WARRIORS

RIVER

A STARLESS CLAN

Book One: River

A STARLESS CLAN

WARRIORS

RIVER

ERIN HUNTER

HARPER

An Imprint of HarperCollinsPublishers

ISBN 978-0-06-305008-2

Typography by Jessie Gang

22 23 24 25 26   PC/LSCH   10 9 8 7 6 5 4 3 2 1

❖

First Edition

Special thanks to Cherith Baldry

ALLEGIANCES

THUNDERCLAN

LEADER BRAMBLESTAR—dark brown tabby tom with amber eyes

DEPUTY SQUIRRELFLIGHT—dark ginger she-cat with green eyes and one white paw

MEDICINE CATS JAYFEATHER—gray tabby tom with blind blue eyes

ALDERHEART—dark ginger tom with amber eyes

WARRIORS (toms and she-cats without kits)

WHITEWING—white she-cat with green eyes

BIRCHFALL—light brown tabby tom

MOUSEWHISKER—gray-and-white tom
APPRENTICE, BAYPAW (golden tabby tom)

POPPYFROST—pale tortoiseshell-and-white she-cat

LILYHEART—small, dark tabby she-cat with white patches and blue eyes
APPRENTICE, FLAMEPAW (black tom)

BUMBLESTRIPE—very pale gray tom with black stripes

CHERRYFALL—ginger she-cat

MOLEWHISKER—brown-and-cream tom

CINDERHEART—gray tabby she-cat
APPRENTICE, FINCHPAW (tortoiseshell she-cat)

BLOSSOMFALL—tortoiseshell-and-white she-cat with petal-shaped white patches

IVYPOOL—silver-and-white tabby she-cat with dark blue eyes

EAGLEWING—ginger she-cat
APPRENTICE, MYRTLEPAW (pale brown she-cat)

DEWNOSE—gray-and-white tom

THRIFTEAR—dark gray she-cat

STORMCLOUD—gray tabby tom

HOLLYTUFT—black she-cat

FERNSONG—yellow tabby tom

HONEYFUR—white she-cat with yellow splotches

SPARKPELT—orange tabby she-cat

SORRELSTRIPE—dark brown she-cat

TWIGBRANCH—gray she-cat with green eyes

FINLEAP—brown tom

SHELLFUR—tortoiseshell tom

PLUMSTONE—black-and-ginger she-cat

FLIPCLAW—brown tabby tom

LEAFSHADE—tortoiseshell she-cat

LIONBLAZE—golden tabby tom with amber eyes

QUEENS

(she-cats expecting or nursing kits)

DAISY—cream long-furred cat from the horseplace

SPOTFUR—spotted tabby she-cat (mother to Bristlekit, an orange-and-white tabby she-kit; Stemkit, an orange tabby tom; and Graykit, a white tom with gray spots)

ELDERS   (former warriors and queens, now retired)

THORNCLAW—golden-brown tabby tom

CLOUDTAIL—long-haired white tom with blue eyes

BRIGHTHEART—white she-cat with ginger patches

BRACKENFUR—golden-brown tabby tom

SHADOWCLAN

LEADER   TIGERSTAR—dark brown tabby tom

DEPUTY   CLOVERFOOT—gray tabby she-cat

MEDICINE CATS   PUDDLESHINE—brown tom with white splotches

SHADOWSIGHT—gray tabby tom

WARRIORS   TAWNYPELT—tortoiseshell she-cat with green eyes

STONEWING—white tom

SCORCHFUR—dark gray tom with slashed ears

FLAXFOOT—brown tabby tom

SPARROWTAIL—large brown tabby tom

SNOWBIRD—pure white she-cat with green eyes

YARROWLEAF—ginger she-cat with yellow eyes

BERRYHEART—black-and-white she-cat

GRASSHEART—pale brown tabby she-cat

WHORLPELT—gray-and-white tom

HOPWHISKER—calico she-cat

BLAZEFIRE—white-and-ginger tom

FLOWERSTEM—silver she-cat

SNAKETOOTH—honey-colored tabby she-cat

SLATEFUR—sleek gray tom

POUNCESTEP—gray tabby she-cat

LIGHTLEAP—brown tabby she-cat

GULLSWOOP—white she-cat

SPIRECLAW—black-and-white tom

HOLLOWSPRING—black tom

SUNBEAM—brown-and-white tabby she-cat

QUEENS   **DOVEWING**—pale gray she-cat with green eyes (mother to Rowankit, a dark gray tabby she-kit, and Birchkit, a light brown tom)

CINNAMONTAIL—brown tabby she-cat with white paws (mother to Firkit, a brown tabby tom, Streamkit, a gray tabby she-kit, Bloomkit, a black she-kit, and Whisperkit, a gray tom)

ELDERS   **OAKFUR**—small brown tom

SKYCLAN

LEADER   **LEAFSTAR**—brown-and-cream tabby she-cat with amber eyes

DEPUTY   **HAWKWING**—dark gray tom with yellow eyes

MEDICINE CATS   **FRECKLEWISH**—mottled light brown tabby she-cat with spotted legs

FIDGETFLAKE—black-and-white tom

MEDIATOR   **TREE**—yellow tom with amber eyes

WARRIORS **SPARROWPELT**—dark brown tabby tom

MACGYVER—black-and-white tom

DEWSPRING—sturdy gray tom

ROOTSPRING—yellow tom

NEEDLECLAW—black-and-white she-cat

PLUMWILLOW—dark gray she-cat

SAGENOSE—pale gray tom

KITESCRATCH—reddish-brown tom

HARRYBROOK—gray tom

CHERRYTAIL—fluffy tortoiseshell-and-white she-cat

CLOUDMIST—white she-cat with yellow eyes

FRINGEWHISKER—white she-cat with brown splotches

TURTLECRAWL—tortoiseshell she-cat

RABBITLEAP—brown tom

WRENFLIGHT—golden tabby she-cat

REEDCLAW—small pale tabby she-cat
APPRENTICE, BEETLEPAW (white-and-black tom)

MINTFUR—gray tabby she-cat with blue eyes

NETTLESPLASH—pale brown tom

TINYCLOUD—small white she-cat

PALESKY—black-and-white she-cat

VIOLETSHINE—black-and-white she-cat with yellow eyes

BELLALEAF—pale orange she-cat with green eyes

QUAILFEATHER—white tom with crow-black ears

PIGEONFOOT—gray-and-white she-cat

GRAVELNOSE—tan tom

SUNNYPELT—ginger she-cat
APPRENTICE, BEEPAW (white-and-tabby she-kit)

NECTARSONG—brown she-cat

QUEENS   **BLOSSOMHEART**—ginger-and-white she-cat (mother to Ridgekit, a reddish she-kit with a white nose, and Duskkit, a white tom with brown paws and ears)

ELDERS   **FALLOWFERN**—pale brown she-cat who has lost her hearing

WINDCLAN

LEADER   **HARESTAR**—brown-and-white tom

DEPUTY   **CROWFEATHER**—dark gray tom

MEDICINE CATS   **KESTRELFLIGHT**—mottled gray tom with white splotches like kestrel feathers
APPRENTICE, WHISTLEPAW (gray tabby she-cat)

WARRIORS   **NIGHTCLOUD**—black she-cat

BRINDLEWING—mottled brown she-cat

APPLESHINE—yellow tabby she-cat

LEAFTAIL—dark tabby tom with amber eyes

WOODSONG—brown she-cat

EMBERFOOT—gray tom with two dark paws

BREEZEPELT—black tom with amber eyes

HEATHERTAIL—light brown tabby she-cat with blue eyes

FEATHERPELT—gray tabby she-cat

CROUCHFOOT—ginger tom

SONGLEAP—tortoiseshell she-cat

SEDGEWHISKER—light brown tabby she-cat

FLUTTERFOOT—brown-and-white tom

SLIGHTFOOT—black tom with white flash on his chest

OATCLAW—pale brown tabby tom

HOOTWHISKER—dark gray tom

FERNSTRIPE—gray tabby she-cat

QUEENS   **LARKWING**—pale brown tabby she-cat (mother to Stripekit, a gray tabby tom, and Brookkit, a black-and-white tom)

ELDERS   **WHISKERNOSE**—light brown tom

GORSETAIL—very pale gray-and-white she-cat with blue eyes

RIVERCLAN

LEADER   **MISTYSTAR**—gray she-cat with blue eyes

DEPUTY   **REEDWHISKER**—black tom

MEDICINE CATS   **MOTHWING**—dappled golden she-cat
APPRENTICE, FROSTPAW (light gray she-cat)

WARRIORS

DUSKFUR—brown tabby she-cat

MINNOWTAIL—dark gray-and-white she-cat

MALLOWNOSE—light brown tabby tom

HAVENPELT—black-and-white she-cat

PODLIGHT—gray-and-white tom

SHIMMERPELT—silver she-cat

LIZARDTAIL—light brown tom

SNEEZECLOUD—gray-and-white tom

BRACKENPELT—tortoiseshell she-cat

SPLASHTAIL—brown tabby tom

FOGNOSE—gray-and-white she-cat

HARELIGHT—white tom

ICEWING—white she-cat with blue eyes
APPRENTICE, MISTPAW (tortoiseshell-and-white tabby she-cat)

CURLFEATHER—pale brown she-cat

OWLNOSE—brown tabby tom

GORSECLAW—white tom with gray ears

NIGHTSKY—dark gray she-cat with blue eyes

BREEZEHEART—brown-and-white she-cat
APPRENTICE, GRAYPAW (silver tabby tom)

ELDERS

MOSSPELT—tortoiseshell-and-white she-cat

A STARLESS CLAN

WARRIORS

RIVER

GREENLEAF
TWOLEGPLAC
TWOLEG NEST
TWOLEG PATH
TWOLEG PATH
CLEARI
SHADOWCLAN
CAMP
SMALL
THUNDERPATH
HALFBRIDGE
GREENLEAF
TWOLEGPLACE
HALFBRIDGE
CAT VIEW
ISLAND
STREAM
RIVERCLAN
CAMP
HORSEPLACE

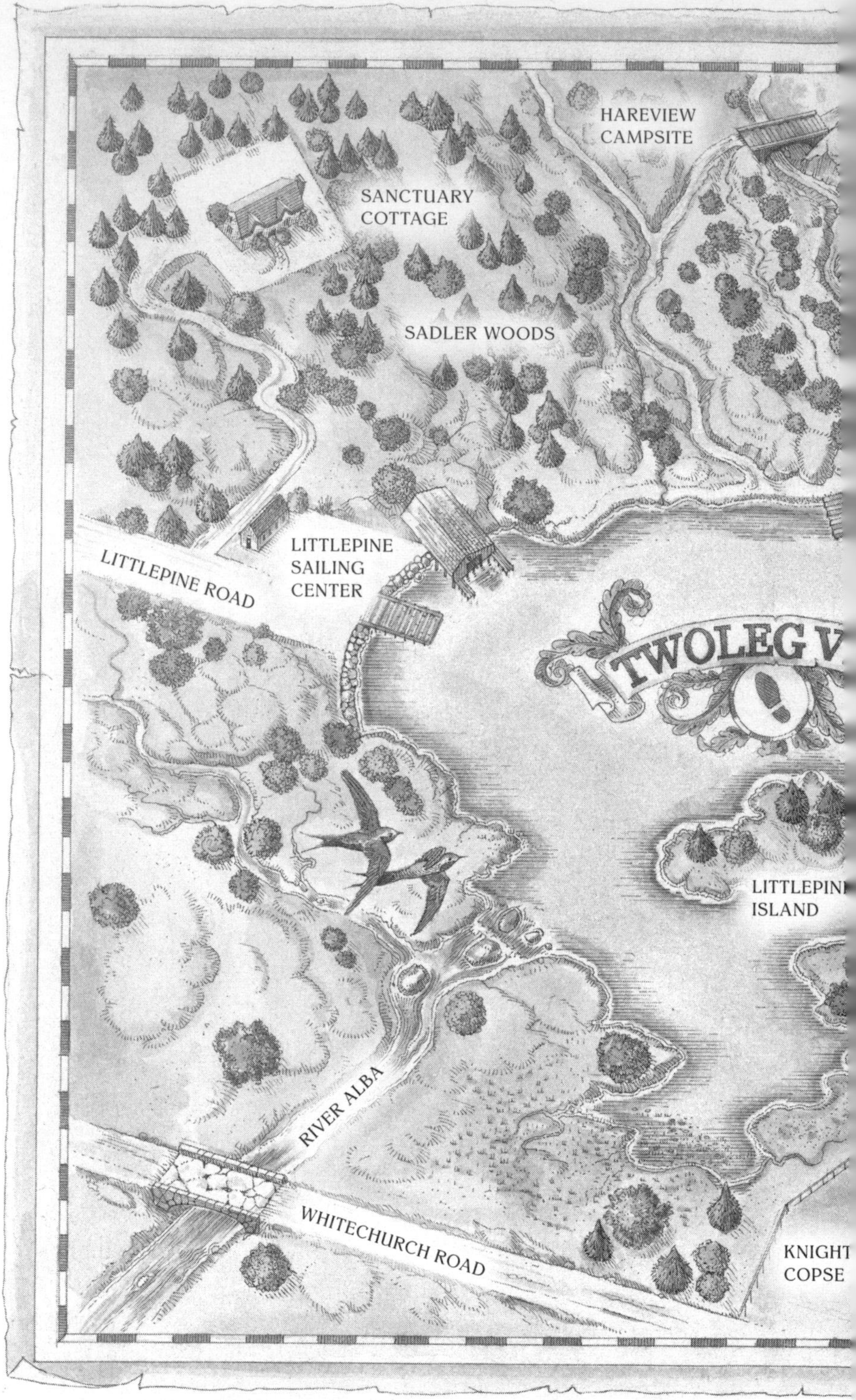
HAREVIEW CAMPSITE
SANCTUARY COTTAGE
SADLER WOODS
LITTLEPINE SAILING CENTER
LITTLEPINE ROAD
TWOLEG V
LITTLEPIN
ISLAND
RIVER ALBA
WHITECHURCH ROAD
KNIGHT
COPSE

PROLOGUE

A full moon drifted above the treetops, shedding a chilly light over the Gathering. Cats crowded around the Great Oak; in its branches, their leaders crouched, half hidden by leaves tinged with the gold and brown of early leaf-fall. Only their eyes, glowing like tiny moons, betrayed their presence.

ShadowClan had been the last to arrive, the cats still wriggling through the crowd to find places. One, a black-and-white tom, stood back, his gaze raking the assembled cats until it fell upon a SkyClan she-cat. Her white pelt, blotched with brown, glimmered in the moonlight. A purr gathered in his throat.

The she-cat raised her head slightly as her gaze met his, and she slid quietly backward until she found a space in the shadow of a bush at the very edge of the clearing. The tom joined her there, and they sat side by side.

"I thought you were never coming," the she-cat murmured.

The tom shivered at the warmth of her breath near his ear. "Tigerstar likes to make an entrance," he responded.

He had barely finished speaking when the ShadowClan leader let out a loud yowl, standing tall on a branch of the

Great Oak. "Cats of all Clans," he meowed as the sound of chatter died away. "Welcome to the Gathering."

Bramblestar, the leader of ThunderClan, was the first of the leaders to give his news, but his words washed over the ShadowClan tom like a warm breeze that barely ruffled his fur. All his attention was on the she-cat at his side.

His delight at being with her was almost like pain. He remembered how long they had loved each other, how they had begun with shared glances and short chats at Gatherings, then managed to snatch a few meetings on their shared Clan border by the lakeside. Every moment they had spent together had felt so precious, and yet so disloyal.

What would our kin and our Clanmates say if they knew?

Sometimes the ShadowClan tom had hoped that everything would work out. After all, his Clan leader, Tigerstar, had fallen in love with a ThunderClan cat, and she had left her birth Clan to be with him. But he still remembered how long it had taken before ShadowClan had accepted Dovewing.

We're both loyal to our Clans, he thought, with a loving glance at the SkyClan she-cat. *We don't want to lose our kin, or our friends.*

His gaze drinking in the graceful curve of her neck, he remembered too how she had come to ShadowClan to help guard the impostor, Ashfur, when he was imprisoned there. The tom shuddered to remember the evil spirit cat who had taken over Bramblestar's body and led ThunderClan until his deception was discovered. While he'd held on to power, he had almost wrecked the Clans in his determination to root out codebreakers.

That had been a terrible experience for the Clans, and the tom felt a pang of guilt at how wonderful it had been for him and for the brown-and-white she-cat. Once, all they could have hoped for were snatched moments beside their shared border. But once Ashfur was a prisoner in ShadowClan, guarded in turn by warriors from the other Clans, her duties had brought her to the ShadowClan camp. Then they'd had a rare opportunity to sit side by side and talk, to be together without feeling they were stealing time away from their Clans.

Best of all, in the end their terrible fear that they might be branded as codebreakers had been washed away like a twig in the floods of greenleaf. The warrior code would change. StarClan would no longer forbid them from being together.

The tom's thoughts were interrupted as the SkyClan she-cat prodded him in the side. "Wake up!" she whispered. Her eyes were glimmering and her tail twitching in excitement. "Mistystar is going to talk about changes to the warrior code. This is what we've come to hear."

When Ashfur had finally been defeated, several living cats had been granted the privilege of setting paw in the hunting grounds of StarClan. When they had returned, they had been given the title of Lights in the Mist, and they had brought back a plan that would change things for all the Clans.

Especially for cats like us, the tom thought, with an affectionate glance at the she-cat.

The tom looked up to see the RiverClan leader slowly making her way toward the end of her branch. For the first time he was struck by how frail she looked; the fur around her muzzle was gray with age, and her blue-gray pelt, once thick and beautiful, was dull and thinning now. But she still gazed down on the assembled cats with all the dignity of a Clan leader as she began to speak.

The ShadowClan tom and the SkyClan she-cat exchanged a glance of anticipation, then focused all their attention on Mistystar. Every other cat was doing the same; no cat was looking at them. Silently they pressed closer and twined their tails together.

The black-and-white tom's heart was pounding so hard that he thought it might burst out of his chest. *Things are changing . . .* , he told himself. *Oh, StarClan, whatever happens, let us be together.*

CHAPTER 1

❧

Crouching beside the fresh-kill pile, Flamepaw tore a bite from the mouse that lay at his paws. But the succulent flesh tasted like dead leaves in his mouth, and when he gulped it down, it settled in his belly like a rock. He couldn't think of anything but his warrior assessment, which was due to start as soon as he and the other apprentices had finished eating.

Beside him, his foster littermate Baypaw, who was sharing his mouse, stopped eating to waggle his hindquarters vigorously, then took off in a massive pounce, landing with his forepaws clasped around a pebble that lay on the ground of the ThunderClan camp.

"Gotcha!" he yowled. "That was my best pounce," he declared as he bounded back to Flamepaw. His eyes sparkled with excitement. "I'm going to catch so much prey. Mice and squirrels, beware! Baypaw is coming for you!"

"Yeah, sure," Flamepaw muttered.

Baypaw crouched beside him and gave him a friendly nudge, his gaze reassuring. "Hey, don't worry," he meowed. "You'll be fine. You're a great hunter."

Flamepaw nodded and forced himself to take another bite

of the mouse. Hoping to distract himself from his upcoming assessment, he angled his ears toward a group of senior warriors who were sharing prey nearby, their heads together in what looked like a serious conversation.

"I don't know what I think about making changes to the warrior code," Birchfall mewed uneasily. "Especially this idea that we could get rid of a leader. It would be like—like telling the sun not to shine!"

Ivypool let out a disapproving snort. "We would have been glad enough to get rid of Ashfur," she pointed out. "Even when we still thought he was Bramblestar. Cats died because we went on accepting him as our leader, even though he was sending cats into exile and suspecting us all of disloyalty, like he had bees in his brain."

"But how often will we have to deal with a cat like Ashfur?" Birchfall asked.

"Once was enough," Thornclaw responded with a flick of his ears. "I think Ivypool is right."

"But Ashfur wasn't a true leader," Birchfall insisted. "If he hadn't stolen Bramblestar's body, no cat would have accepted him. And StarClan never gave him his nine lives and his name. These new rules are all about deposing a leader who has been approved by StarClan. That's quite different."

"You've got a point there," Thornclaw admitted grudgingly.

"Although," Ivypool mewed, "it's not like StarClan is infallible. The first Tigerstar was given nine lives."

"That's true. Though, if a Clan deposed its leader, I don't

understand what would happen to their nine lives," Cherry-fall meowed. "Those lives are given by StarClan; ordinary living cats can't take them away, can they?"

"We could try, if the leader was as vile as Ashfur," Mouse-whisker meowed, sliding out his claws. His eyes shone with anger, and Flamepaw remembered that the warrior had lost two of his siblings as a result of Ashfur's lies.

Shocked gasps came from two or three cats in the group, and Flamepaw exchanged a horrified glance with his foster brother.

"A leader is a leader," Bumblestripe insisted, glaring at the gray-and-white tom. "You don't disobey a leader, you don't depose a leader, and you certainly don't kill a leader. That would get you to the Dark Forest for sure."

"Keep your fur on." Thornclaw flicked his tail at the younger tom, who reared back with an offended expression. "You don't know the Dark Forest—not like Ivypool and I do. And the code has never been that rigid. Many of you are too young to remember, but I'll never forget when ShadowClan drove out their leader Brokenstar, back in the old forest. He deserved it, if ever a cat did. But StarClan didn't take back his nine lives, and they didn't give nine lives to ShadowClan's next leader, Nightstar."

Lionblaze, who had so far listened in silence, rasped his tongue thoughtfully over his golden pelt. "That was a different time, Thornclaw." His voice was a warm rumble in his throat. "Now StarClan might agree to take the nine lives away. After all, they encouraged the Lights in the Mist to make these changes to the code."

Thornclaw flicked an ear in annoyance. "I wish Graystripe were here to explain," he muttered. "He knew how it worked, back in the day. I just don't understand what happened in the Dark Forest, and I wish I did."

"Lots of cats wish that," Lionblaze responded. "But we have to trust that our leaders understand and will do what's right."

Thornclaw's only reply was a grunt.

"What do you think, Flamepaw?" Baypaw mumbled around a mouthful of mouse. "Should we be able to get rid of our leader?"

Flamepaw dragged his attention away from the senior warriors' conversation. "Sure we should," he replied, half hoping that the senior warriors would hear him. "Except I don't think that goes far enough. Maybe the Clans would work better if we changed leaders regularly."

Baypaw's eyes stretched wide with shock, and he choked on his lump of prey, swallowing it with difficulty. "What!"

"Well, what's the alternative?" Flamepaw meowed defensively. "The way it is now, one cat chosen by the previous leader gets to boss every cat around until they've gone through nine whole lives. How is that fair?"

Recovering himself, his foster brother rolled his eyes. "You might not want to say that too loud," he pointed out, "especially considering that our leader, Bramblestar, is your kin."

Flamepaw hunched his shoulders. "It's not like any cat would listen to me, anyway," he muttered sulkily.

Forcing himself to eat more of the mouse, Flamepaw wished silently that every cat would stop judging him because of his kin. His mother was Sparkpelt, daughter of the Clan leader, Bramblestar, and his deputy, Squirrelflight—and Squirrelflight was the daughter of Firestar, the greatest leader the forest had ever known. No cat realized how hard it was, carrying the blood of cats like those in his veins.

I'm even sort of named after Firestar, Flamepaw thought. Gazing at his black paws, he added to himself, *Which is weird, because I'm not at all fire-colored. I guess Firestar was such a great cat, it was more important to Sparkpelt to remind every cat that I'm his kin, instead of looking at what I'm actually like. I wonder if my father would have gone along with it.*

Most cats never mentioned Flamepaw's father, Larksong, who had died before Flamepaw had a chance to know him. Flamepaw's mentor, Lilyheart, was Larksong's mother, and sometimes she told Flamepaw stories about him. *Maybe Larksong would have understood me,* Flamepaw thought wistfully. *Lilyheart says I look like him.*

He swallowed the last mouthful of mouse; Baypaw had already finished eating, and was sitting up, cleaning his whiskers. As Flamepaw swiped his tongue over his jaws, his mother, Sparkpelt, padded over to them.

"Good luck on your assessments," she mewed.

"Thanks, Sparkpelt!" Baypaw responded, bouncing to his paws.

Flamepaw inclined his head politely. "Thank you."

"I'm sure you'll do very well," Sparkpelt told him.

Flamepaw wished that he didn't feel so stiff and awkward around his mother. He knew that Sparkpelt loved him. *Well, she has to, seeing as she's my mother.* But he wasn't sure that she liked him very much. Sometimes he thought she didn't know him well enough to like him.

Sparkpelt hadn't raised him as a young kit; she had been too depressed by the death of his father, Larksong, and his littermate, Flickerkit. Sorrelstripe had stepped in to nurse him instead.

Later, Sparkpelt and Finchpaw—Flamepaw's surviving littermate—had grown close when they had been exiled together by the impostor, leaving Flamepaw behind in the ThunderClan camp. Maybe because he had been separated from her so young, Flamepaw still felt as if he barely knew Sparkpelt. He was not even sure he wanted to know her; he was torn between hoping for her attention because she was his mother, and resenting her for having abandoned him.

Now Sparkpelt didn't seem to know what to say to him. While Flamepaw still stood there in awkward silence, she gave a final dip of her head, then padded across the camp to where Finchpaw was sharing fresh-kill with Myrtlepaw, Baypaw's littermate. At once Flamepaw could see how much more relaxed Sparkpelt became, touching noses with Finchpaw and giving her a loving lick around her ear.

Dragging his gaze away, Flamepaw spotted Baypaw and Myrtlepaw's mother, Sorrelstripe, who had fostered him and Finchpaw. Now she gave him and Baypaw an encouraging wave of her tail. Inclining his head in reply, Flamepaw let out a long sigh. *Sometimes I wish Sorrelstripe were my mother.*

His mentor, Lilyheart, was already waiting near the entrance to the camp. As Flamepaw watched, Baypaw's mentor, Mousewhisker, and Finchpaw's mentor, Cinderheart, padded over to her. A moment later, Eaglewing, Myrtlepaw's mentor, slipped out of the warriors' den and raced across the camp to join the others.

"Come on, Flamepaw!" Lilyheart called. "It's time!"

Flamepaw rose to his paws as the rest of the mentors summoned their apprentices, and followed the other young cats toward the camp entrance. Yowls of "Good luck!" rang in his ears from more of his Clanmates around the clearing. Flamepaw felt his sadness drain away like water into dry ground, replaced by nervous excitement thrilling from his ears to his tail-tip.

Outside the camp, the four mentors and their apprentices headed off in different directions. Before he followed Mousewhisker, Baypaw paused to give Flamepaw a reassuring nudge. "You've got this," he meowed.

"So do you," Flamepaw responded, pressing his muzzle into Baypaw's shoulder. Then he followed Lilyheart into the woods, heading toward the lake.

Once the scents of the other cats and the sound of their paw steps had faded, Lilyheart halted. "Okay, you need to go hunt," she told him. "You won't see me, but I'll be watching you. I expect you to catch loads of prey, so we'll impress all the cats in the camp with what a good hunter you are."

Lilyheart's cheerful tones, and the way she obviously expected him to do well, roused Flamepaw's ambition. *I'm going to make a really spectacular catch!*

Standing still, all his senses alert, he opened his jaws to taste the air. Succulent prey-scents flowed in on him, telling him it would be a good day for hunting.

Almost at once he distinguished the scent of mouse and heard a scuffling. Padding forward, he located the sound among a heap of fallen leaves; he could even see the leaves twitch. *That's where the mouse is hiding—there might even be two!* Briefly he dropped into the hunter's crouch, but then he hesitated; mice weren't particularly impressive prey. *Any daft furball can catch mice!* It wasn't enough for him to pass his assessment by catching just any prey; he wanted Lilyheart to be really impressed.

Straightening up, Flamepaw padded on into the forest, passing over another mouse and a shrew that practically ran into his paws as it scuttled across his path.

Maybe a bird would be good, he thought. *They're harder to hunt.*

A few paces farther on, Flamepaw rounded the edge of a bramble thicket and came upon a squirrel nibbling at something in its forepaws a couple of tail-lengths away from the nearest tree. *It looks so fat and juicy! That would be a great piece of prey to bring back.*

Flamepaw carefully got into position and began to creep forward, checking that he was upwind of the squirrel and setting his paws down as lightly as he could. The squirrel seemed unaware of him, all its attention on what it held between its paws.

But before Flamepaw was close enough to pounce, he remembered a move that he had practiced once or twice with Baypaw. Lilyheart had never seen it. *That would impress her, for sure!*

Flamepaw abandoned his crouch and bounded forward, launching himself into a powerful leap—not at the squirrel but at the tree behind it. He meant to whip around as soon as he hit the tree and ricochet away from it, cutting off the squirrel's escape route as it fled for safety.

But the spectacular move didn't work. Flamepaw hit the tree with one paw crushed under him; pain stabbed up his leg as far as his shoulder. Gasping, he tried to correct his position as he pushed off. But he was tangled up in his own paws and completely misjudged his leap. He thumped to the ground among the tree roots, all the breath driven out of him. The squirrel leaped over him and raced up the trunk, pausing on a low branch to chatter insults at Flamepaw before vanishing among the leaves.

Flamepaw scrambled to his paws, fighting to catch his breath. Debris from among the roots was clinging to his fur. Worse, every hair on his pelt was hot with embarrassment, because he knew that Lilyheart must have been watching. She would have seen how he had messed up the move; worse, the racket he and the squirrel had made must have scared off any other prey within earshot.

Shaking the earth and scraps of leaf out of his pelt, Flamepaw padded on, determined now to make a few good catches—simple catches that any trained warrior could make. *No more showing off,* he told himself sternly.

He paused beside a clump of bracken, ears pricked for the sound of prey hiding in the depths of the fronds. He heard nothing, but when he pushed his way through to the other side, he immediately spotted a magpie pecking at the ground a few fox-lengths away.

Excitement tingled through Flamepaw. This was another outstanding piece of prey! He took up the hunter's crouch again, checking carefully to make sure his paws were properly tucked in and his tail curled along his side. Then, paw step by stealthy paw step, he crept up on the magpie.

I have to catch this one!

He slid one paw forward and almost set it down on a curled-up leaf, but managed to draw back a heartbeat before he would have trod on it and alerted his prey. It took all his strength to keep on sneaking slowly forward, when what he wanted to do was leap on the bird and sink his claws into it.

Flamepaw was sure he hadn't made a noise, but before he reached the best distance for a pounce, the magpie looked up, tilting its head as if it had heard something. *It's going to fly away!* Flamepaw flung himself forward in a massive leap. His claws scraped the magpie's tail; it took off with a clatter of wings and a harsh cry, leaving Flamepaw with his claws slammed down on a single feather.

"Fox dung!" he snarled.

He stared after the bird in utter frustration, then forced himself to concentrate again and peered grimly through the trees. The bird's noisy escape would have scared off most of the nearby prey—again. Flamepaw's belly was churning as he set out once more. He was acutely aware of the sun approaching sunhigh, and expected at any moment to see Lilyheart coming to meet him.

And I haven't caught a single piece of prey. Oh, StarClan, please send me something . . . anything!

Padding onward, Flamepaw drew a huge breath of relief as he picked up the scent of mouse and spotted a skinny specimen scuffling about underneath a holly bush. This time he slid forward carefully, hardly daring to breathe, his paws skimming lightly over the ground. He caught his prey with a neat pounce, and at the same moment another mouse shot out of cover; Flamepaw lashed out with claws extended and caught it as well.

"Thank you, StarClan, for this prey," he mewed with heartfelt gratitude.

But he knew he hadn't done well enough, and, even worse, he had lost the squirrel and the magpie because of his own stupidity. *I could have done so much better.* He could only hope that he still had enough time to add more to his pathetic haul.

He began swiftly scratching out a hole to bury the two catches, only to hear Lilyheart's voice behind him, speaking his name. He turned to see his mentor emerging from the undergrowth.

Flamepaw's tail drooped as he saw the look in Lilyheart's eyes: sympathy mingled with disappointment. His pelt was hot with shame. He didn't need her to tell him he had failed his assessment.

I know I have. And I know I deserved to.

Chapter 2

❧

"Stand still," Curlfeather mewed. *Her tongue* rasped over Frostpaw's white-and-brown pelt in long, skillful strokes. "You know you have to look especially clean and neat. This is a very important day."

Frostpaw did as her mother told her, though she felt as though her belly were filled with butterflies. So much excitement was thrilling through her that she wanted to leap and squeal and chase her own tail.

But I can't behave like that anymore, she told herself. *I'm not a kit anymore; by the end of the day, I'll officially be a medicine-cat apprentice!*

For the last quarter moon Frostpaw had been helping Mothwing in the medicine-cat den, and now she was ready to make her first trip to the Moonpool for the half-moon meeting. There she would meet the other medicine cats, the ones from other Clans, and have her apprentice ceremony.

"I can't wait!" she exclaimed, unable to suppress a wriggle of anticipation. "But I'm kind of scared, too."

"Nonsense, you'll be fine," Curlfeather responded, brushing her tail along Frostpaw's side. "Haven't we always known that you're special? Hasn't StarClan chosen you to be a medicine cat for RiverClan?"

"Do you think they really have?" Frostpaw breathed out.

"Of course they have. Remember how you dreamed about Jayclaw leaving you alone in camp? And then he died a few days later?" Curlfeather's voice softened for a moment as she spoke about her mate, Frostpaw's father. Frostpaw ducked her head. She'd been too young when Jayclaw died to remember much about her father, but sometimes she wondered how her life might be different if he had lived. Would her mother be so protective of Frostpaw and her littermates?

A heartbeat later Curlfeather went on more briskly, "You predicted that thunderstorm only a few days ago. And you've been working hard with Mothwing in her den the last few days, learning all about herbs and healing. You even took that thorn out of Podlight's pad. Of course you're going to be a fine medicine cat."

Grateful for the reassurance, Frostpaw leaned into her mother's soft brown fur, a purr rising in her throat. *Curlfeather's such a great cat. If she thinks I can do it, I know I'll be okay.*

As Curlfeather finished grooming her with a swift lick around her ears, Frostpaw saw the RiverClan leader, Mistystar, emerge from her den, followed by her deputy, Reedwhisker.

"The hunting was good today," Mistystar meowed. "The fresh-kill pile is well stocked. But when you send out the border patrol, Reedwhisker, you need to tell them to check if that badger is still hanging around."

"Sure, got it," Reedwhisker responded. He headed off with a swish of his tail, calling to his Clanmates as he went.

Watching her Clan leader, Frostpaw couldn't help thinking how weary her voice had sounded, and how she was beginning to look thin and frail. *I wonder how many lives she has left. Maybe when I'm a medicine cat, I'll know things like that.*

Her thoughts were interrupted by a sharp voice behind her. "Come on, Frostpaw, stop daydreaming. It's time to go."

Frostpaw spun around to see the RiverClan medicine cat, Mothwing, standing behind her. There was a look of impatience in her beautiful amber eyes, though she gave Frostpaw a friendly touch on the shoulder with her tail-tip.

"She's ready," Curlfeather meowed, giving Frostpaw a farewell nuzzle. "I know you'll do well," she purred.

As Frostpaw gave her pelt a shake, she heard a scamper of paws, and RiverClan's newest warrior apprentices—her littermates, Mistpaw and Graypaw—rushed up to her.

"Good luck!" Mistpaw yowled excitedly.

"Yeah, you'll be fine," Graypaw added. "You've been doing a great job helping Mothwing so far. How could the other medicine cats not accept you?"

Frostpaw turned to follow her future mentor out of camp, then glanced back over her shoulder. "Oh, I hope you're right!" she mewed fervently.

The sun was going down as Mothwing led the way through RiverClan territory toward the horseplace, and then along the WindClan lakeshore. Frostpaw padded along at her shoulder, trying not to feel scared at all the open space around her. This was her first time away from camp, and she had never imagined that the moor could be so steep, or the lake stretch so far, its surface scarlet in the evening light.

"Medicine cats are allowed to pass through other territories," Mothwing informed Frostpaw after a while, "but even so, it's best to stay near the water. WindClan cats can be a touchy lot, and there's no sense in provoking them."

Frostpaw nodded solemnly, beginning to feel really special as Mothwing taught her the ways of medicine cats. *I'm going to learn so much!*

At the border between WindClan and ThunderClan, Mothwing plunged into the stream and Frostpaw followed. Frostpaw flinched at the feeling of cold leaf-fall water soaking her fur, then gradually relaxed. *It's kind of nice, once you get used to it.*

As they headed farther across the moor, Frostpaw realized that she couldn't smell the WindClan border markers anymore. "Why has WindClan stopped marking their border?" she asked Mothwing.

"Because we're outside WindClan territory now," Mothwing replied, "We're outside all the Clan territories."

Frostpaw gasped, hardly able to stop herself bouncing up and down with excitement. *It's not just my first time out of camp,* she told herself. *It's my first time leaving Clan territory. Wait till I tell Mistpaw and Graypaw!*

But Frostpaw soon forgot about bouncing. Her legs were growing tired as she and Mothwing climbed up the long moorland slope, but she didn't dare to ask for a rest. Her mother, she knew, would have stopped before Frostpaw even needed to ask, curling herself around her as a shelter from the wind. Mothwing was concentrating on getting where they were going. Frostpaw found her a bit scary, but at the same time, she liked the way that Mothwing just assumed she could keep up.

She's not treating me like a kit anymore.

"What will happen when we get to the Moonpool?" she asked.

Mothwing gave her a sideways glance. "Well, first you'll meet the other medicine cats," she meowed. "They're a friendly bunch, on the whole. I mean, Shadowsight from ShadowClan is seriously weird, but he's a brave cat, and Jayfeather..." She let her voice trail off, then began again. "Jayfeather is Thunder-Clan's senior medicine cat. He's blind, and don't think that makes him any less skillful. He might be snarky with you, but you mustn't let him upset you. He's snarky with every cat, but if I were sick or in trouble, there's no cat I would rather turn to for help."

Frostpaw privately thought that Jayfeather sounded intimidating, whatever Mothwing might say. "So what happens after that?" she mewed.

"We'll exchange news of our Clans," Mothwing told her, "and then I'll present you to StarClan as a RiverClan medicine-cat apprentice."

Frostpaw let out a gasp. "You mean I'm going to see Star-Clan?"

"Not right then," Mothwing responded. She paused for a moment as they padded around a clump of gorse bushes, then

added, "We just know they're listening, right? After that, all
the cats will gather around the pool, and we'll put our noses
to the water."

"Me too?" Frostpaw's question came out as a squeak, and
she ducked her head in embarrassment.

"You too," Mothwing confirmed. "That's when you might
be able to see StarClan."

"That's so exciting!" Frostpaw breathed out. She had
almost forgotten the weariness in her legs and the harshness
of the stiff grass under her pads "What is it like?"

A couple of heartbeats passed before Mothwing replied. "I
can't tell you. It's different for every cat."

While she was speaking, Frostpaw remembered what she
had overheard some of the RiverClan warriors say. "Is it true
that you don't talk to StarClan?" she asked, then grew hot
with dismay that she had dared to ask the question.

Again Mothwing hesitated before she answered. "Yes, it's
true." Her voice was crisp, but not angry. "The other medicine
cats will help you with that if you need it," she finished.

Frostpaw went on thinking about that as she trudged on
up the moor. She hoped that Mothwing was right, because
she could see that she was going to need a lot of help. She
had always imagined training to be a warrior like her littermates; all three of them had watched the apprentices and
tried to imitate their battle moves. She had never thought
for a single heartbeat that StarClan would choose her to be
a medicine cat.

By now the last of the daylight had died away; the first warriors of StarClan were appearing in the sky, and a half-moon shed its cold light over the moor. The wind had grown chilly, and Frostpaw shivered as it probed deep into her pelt.

Her paws were beginning to feel sore, but Frostpaw didn't want to ask Mothwing how much farther it was to the Moonpool. She gazed up at the crest of the slope they were climbing; it seemed a very long way away. *This has to be the last hill before the Moonpool,* she told herself. But when they reached the top of the rise, all that lay in front of her was more moorland, fold after fold of it, as far as she could see. All that broke up the stretch of tough grass was an occasional outcrop of rocks, and here and there a twisted thornbush.

"It's . . . big," she mewed, her spirits sinking a little.

"It is. But we don't have much farther to go." Mothwing's tone was brisk but comforting. "Why don't I test you on the herbs I showed you yesterday? That should take your mind off it and make the time pass more quickly." Without waiting for Frostpaw to respond, she continued, "What would you use for rubbing on sore paws?"

"Dock leaves," Frostpaw answered. *I wish I had some here.* "Those big, dark green leaves that grow by the stream near your den."

"Very good. And what would you do for a cough?"

"Oh . . . catmint. Tall plants with pale purple flowers. And sometimes, if there's none in our territory, we can find it in Twoleg gardens."

Mothwing let out an approving purr. "You've remembered well. But what if we can't find any catmint? What would you use for a cough then?"

Frostpaw thought hard. She remembered Mothwing telling her this, but she couldn't remember the name of the herb. "Chervil root?" she guessed at last.

Mothwing sighed, with an impatient twitch of her tail. "No, tansy," she meowed. "Or possibly coltsfoot, though catmint is the best. Chervil root is for bellyache. You need to remember these things, Frostpaw. Knowing how to find and use herbs for medicine is the most important thing a medicine cat does."

"Yes, Mothwing," Frostpaw responded. "I'm sorry."

Anyway, communicating with StarClan is actually the most important thing that a medicine cat does, Frostpaw thought. *I'm so looking forward to that!* She was sure it would be more exciting than learning the names and uses of herbs.

She turned to Mothwing, almost ready to argue with her, but when she saw her mentor's forbidding expression, she thought better of it.

To Frostpaw's relief, before Mothwing could continue questioning her, they came to the foot of a steep, rocky slope. Frostpaw could pick up the scent of many unfamiliar cats wafting toward her on the breeze.

"Are we there?" she asked.

Mothwing nodded. "Yes. We just have to climb these rocks, and we'll be above the Moonpool."

Frostpaw scrambled up in Mothwing's paw steps, feeling the slipperiness of the rock beneath her pads and trying not to think about what it would be like if she fell. In one particularly steep place, her short legs wouldn't stretch to the next paw hold; Mothwing had to turn back, grab her by the scruff, and haul her up.

Just as if I were a kit! Frostpaw thought indignantly. *And I'm not a kit anymore!*

At the top of the rocks, Frostpaw found her way blocked by a line of thornbushes. The scent of cats was stronger now, and she could hear the rush of falling water, but she still couldn't see any sign of a pool.

"Follow me," Mothwing meowed, plunging into the bushes.

Frostpaw wriggled after her, trying to ignore the scratching of thorns through her pelt. *I think I'm leaving half my fur behind!*

Tearing herself free from the thorns, Frostpaw emerged from the bushes and halted in awe. In front of her, water poured down from the rocks in a never-ending cascade that glittered with starshine. It fell into a pool at the bottom of a deep hollow; the surface glimmered with the reflection of the half-moon. Frostpaw stood with her jaws gaping; Mothwing had told her about the Moonpool, but she had never imagined it could be so beautiful or so mysterious.

As Frostpaw recovered herself, she realized that several cats were gathered beside the water, and they were all looking up at her. For a moment she wanted to dive back into the bushes and race across the moor to the comfort and safety of the RiverClan camp and her nest in the medicine cats' den.

"Come on," Mothwing meowed, her tone bracing. "Don't stand there like a stunned rabbit! Everything will be fine."

Beckoning with her tail, she set off down the path that led to the water's edge. Frostpaw realized that it formed a spiral, curving gently around the side of the hollow. As she followed her mentor, she felt her paws slipping into other paw marks that dimpled the surface of the stone.

These must have been made long ago, she thought, feeling every hair on her pelt rise in wonder. *Who were the cats who made them? Where did they go?*

Then she and Mothwing reached the bottom of the path, and she had no more time for thinking.

The other medicine cats gathered around Mothwing, greeting her and casting curious glances at Frostpaw, who made herself stand as tall as she could under their scrutiny, even though her legs wanted to fold underneath her and her head wanted to droop.

"This is Frostpaw, my new apprentice," Mothwing announced, laying her tail across Frostpaw's shoulders.

"Excellent!" a mottled brown tabby she-cat exclaimed. "You've been carrying a heavy burden lately, Mothwing, without Willowshine."

Mothwing made no response except for a slight nod. Frostpaw guessed that she was still missing her fellow medicine cat, who had given her life in the fight against the impostor, Ashfur. *And Mothwing can't talk to StarClan.* Frostpaw felt a sudden pang of sympathy. *She'll never see Willowshine again.*

"Frostpaw, these cats are Frecklewish and Fidgetflake from SkyClan," Mothwing began briskly. She gestured with her tail toward the she-cat who had spoken and a black-and-white tom.

Frostpaw dipped her head politely and murmured, "Greetings."

"Then we have Puddleshine and Shadowsight from ShadowClan," Mothwing continued.

Frostpaw examined the ShadowClan cats curiously. Puddleshine was a brown tom with white splotches on his pelt, and Shadowsight—the cat Mothwing had called weird— was a skinny gray tabby tom with dark stripes down his sides.

He doesn't look weird to me, Frostpaw thought, *although he has a lot of scars for a medicine cat. Maybe once I know him better, I'll have a better idea of what Mothwing meant.* Mothwing gave her a nudge, and Frostpaw realized that she had been staring. Embarrassed, she ducked her head and turned with relief to the next cats Mothwing pointed out.

"Here we have Kestrelflight and his apprentice, Whistle- paw, from WindClan," her mentor meowed. "Whistlepaw hasn't been training long."

Frostpaw was relieved that she wouldn't be the only appren- tice. Kestrelflight, a mottled gray tom, gave her a cool nod, but Whistlepaw's glance was warm and friendly. "Welcome," she meowed.

"And last but not least," Mothwing went on, "Alderheart and Jayfeather, from ThunderClan."

Alderheart was a sturdy tom, his dark ginger fur fluffed up against the cold. There was a purr in his voice as he murmured,

"Greetings." Frostpaw instinctively liked him.

She couldn't say the same for the scrawny gray tabby tom standing beside him. Jayfeather stared at her with blind blue eyes that nevertheless seemed to look right through her. It was hard to gaze back at him steadily.

Frostpaw was feeling overwhelmed at being in the presence of so many important cats, even though they had welcomed her. *But I'm important, too!* she realized suddenly. *Or I soon will be.*

Jayfeather was still examining her, his nostrils twitching as if he was committing her scent to memory. "Mothwing," he meowed after a moment, "has StarClan given you some sort of sign that Frostpaw is their choice? RiverClan needs to be able to talk to their ancestors."

Mothwing, who had turned aside to speak to Frecklewish, whipped around to face Jayfeather. "Yes, Frostpaw has had dreams sent by StarClan," she snapped. "Thank you very much for your concern."

Jayfeather's only response was a grunt.

"Frostpaw, I hope you'll follow in Willowshine's paw steps." Alderheart's voice was solemn, but his amber eyes were kind. "And be a thoughtful and good-hearted medicine cat, just like her."

Every cat fell silent for a moment. Frostpaw swallowed hard, remembering gentle Willowshine, who was the medicine cat she had known best all through her kithood. Mothwing had been absent for so long, exiled in the ShadowClan camp because she'd supported the two RiverClan warriors Misty-star had unjustly driven from the Clan.

"I promise I'll try," Frostpaw mewed huskily.

Several cats purred approval.

"So, what news in your Clans?" Jayfeather asked. "Let's get this meeting moving. We're wasting moonlight."

Puddleshine launched into a complaint about Twoleg rubbish abandoned by the lake, and told of how a couple of young warriors had ended up with bellyaches from sampling Twoleg food.

Chervil root for that, Frostpaw thought, and was gratified to hear Mothwing suggest it, though Puddleshine, it turned out, had been treating his Clanmates with watermint.

As a discussion broke out, Frostpaw felt a gentle touch on her shoulder and turned to see Whistlepaw standing beside her. "Are you okay?" the WindClan apprentice asked, keeping her voice low so as not to disturb the others. "It can be a bit scary, your first time."

Frostpaw nodded, feeling shy even with Whistlepaw; the gray tabby she-cat looked so much older and bigger than her. "I'm fine," she whispered.

"It'll be good to have another apprentice here," Whistlepaw continued. "I've only been training for a few moons. I started out as a warrior apprentice."

Frostpaw's eyes widened in surprise. "You didn't know you were chosen by StarClan?"

"Not at first. But then I helped Kestrelflight when he was treating some sick cats, and he offered to train me. That was when I realized that the weird dreams I'd been having were actually StarClan trying to get in touch with me."

"And you get to talk to StarClan now?" Frostpaw asked.

"Yes, at these Moonpool meetings," Whistlepaw replied. "It's so amazing! Barkface, who was Kestrelflight's mentor, has come to me a couple of times, and he's already taught me a lot."

Frostpaw blinked up at her, massively impressed. *Whistlepaw seems so nice. I'm glad we'll be learning together.*

"And do you see—" she began, only to break off as Mothwing padded to her side and patted her on the shoulder with one paw.

"That's enough talk for now," she mewed. "Come on, Frostpaw. It's time for your apprentice ceremony."

Mothwing led Frostpaw to the side of the Moonpool, facing the shimmering cascade of water, while the other medicine cats gathered around.

"Frostpaw," Mothwing began, gazing deep into her eyes, "is it your wish to share the deepest knowledge of StarClan as a RiverClan medicine cat?"

Frostpaw felt as though a tough bit of prey were lodged in her throat. At first she thought that however hard she tried, no words would come; she was so nervous, wondering if Star-Clan was really watching her right now. Then she realized that every cat was waiting for her. She gulped and responded, "It is."

"Warriors of StarClan," Mothwing continued, "I present to you this apprentice. She has chosen the path of a medicine cat. Grant her your wisdom and insight so that she may understand your ways and heal her Clan in accordance with your will." She paused for a moment, her eyes deep with memory, and Frostpaw wondered whether she was thinking about her previous apprentice, Willowshine, and how they could never talk together again. Then Mothwing gave her ears a determined twitch, and announced, "From now on, this cat will be known as Frostpaw."

A thrill of excitement passed through Frostpaw. Mistystar had given her her apprentice name a half moon earlier, when Mothwing had chosen to begin training her, but tonight was the first time she'd heard it spoken outside her Clan. She half expected the other medicine cats to call it out as cats did in the Clans when kits were made warrior apprentices. But instead, all of them stood listening in solemn silence.

"Now, Frostpaw, come to the very edge of the water and crouch down so you can touch the water with your nose."

As Frostpaw took the place on a flat rock her mentor indicated, the other medicine cats found their own places at the edge of the pool. Only Mothwing—and, to Frostpaw's bewilderment, Shadowsight—sat farther back.

Frostpaw still wasn't sure what she should do, until Whistlepaw, who was crouching beside her, gave her a friendly nudge. "Like this," she whispered, craning her neck forward so that she could touch her nose to the water.

Copying her, Frostpaw stretched forward until her nose brushed the surface of the pool. *It's so cold!* For a while she watched the reflections of the stars and the half-moon, until she felt her eyelids drooping.

As her eyes closed, she began to see the faces of other cats, swirling past her as if they were caught up in a river. At first she didn't recognize any of them, until she spotted a gray she-cat she was sure was Willowshine.

Warm happiness flooded through her; she was relieved, too, because she knew how important it was to be able to talk to StarClan—especially for her, since Mothwing couldn't. Now she would really be able to help her Clan.

I'm going to be a real medicine cat! The medicine cat RiverClan needs!

CHAPTER 3

Sunbeam stretched herself out on a flat rock in the ShadowClan camp, enjoying the warmth of the sun's rays filtering through the branches of the pine trees. Beside her, Blazefire groomed her shoulder with firm rasps of his tongue.

I feel so happy, so safe, here with Blazefire, she thought, looking up into his face. *And we'll be mates soon; that will be even better.*

"How was the dawn patrol?" she asked him sleepily. "Any sign of trouble?"

Blazefire shrugged, his ginger-and-white pelt rippling. "Not a whisker. So you can go on sunning yourself as long as you like. You know," he added teasingly, "you've got the right name, Sunbeam. I've never known a cat who liked lazing in the sun as much as you do!"

Sunbeam flicked his nose with her tail. "I'm sure I'll get an apprentice soon," she meowed. "Then I'll have to run around after them all the time." When Blazefire did not respond, she continued, "It's still a ways off, but in a few moons, Dovewing and Tigerstar's kits will need mentors. And Cinnamontail will have her kits with Slatefur any day now."

"Well, I hope it's a good long time before I get an

apprentice," Blazefire declared. "I like being able to do what I want, when I want."

"Oh, you're such a rebel!" Sunbeam let out a small *mrrow* of laughter. "But still," she added more seriously, "we'll be helping the Clan by training apprentices, and that's important."

"That's exactly what Tigerstar would want you to say," Blazefire meowed, nudging her with his shoulder. "What a perfect little ShadowClan warrior you are!"

Sunbeam's pelt prickled with embarrassment; she wasn't sure whether Blazefire was teasing or not. Sometimes she worried that she *was* too caught up in following the rules. And when Blazefire teased her, she was never sure how serious he was being. To her relief, before the awkward moment could stretch out further, Lightleap bounced over to them, her tail waving enthusiastically.

"Do you want to go hunting?" she asked.

"Sure," Sunbeam replied, springing eagerly to her paws.

Blazefire stayed where he was. "No, I've just gotten back from the dawn patrol. You two go, and let me rest my legs."

For a moment Sunbeam was tempted to change her mind and stay with him here on the sun-warmed rock, but after spending the whole morning lazing around, she thought hunting with Lightleap sounded fun.

Almost as soon as they left the camp, they spotted a starling pecking at the ground among fallen pinecones. With her tail, Lightleap gestured for Sunbeam to circle around and come upon the prey from the opposite direction.

Sunbeam obeyed, keeping well away from the starling as

she crept along with her belly fur brushing the ground. Light-leap crouched down behind a tussock of longer grass. Once Sunbeam was in position, she rose to her paws and sprang at the bird, which let out a cry of alarm and fluttered upward. Lightleap leaped into the air with a yowl of triumph and snatched the starling out of the air as it tried to fly away.

"Great catch!" Sunbeam mewed as she ran up to inspect the prey.

"We're a good team," Lightleap responded, scratching a hole to bury the bird for collection later. "Let's see what else we can find."

"Did you hear Oakfur last night?" Sunbeam asked as they padded further into the trees. "Going on all about life in the old forest, and how much better ShadowClan's territory was there."

Lightleap let out a snort of amusement. "Yeah, for about the tenth time! But he's an elder. That's what elders do. Things were always better when they were young cats."

"Things were better *because* they were young cats," Sunbeam pointed out. "Wait until we're elders, Lightleap. We'll have some stories to tell!"

"There are some stories I don't want to tell," Lightleap meowed with a shiver.

Seeing the depth of fear in her friend's eyes, Sunbeam could guess what stories she meant. Lightleap must have been remembering the terrible time when Ashfur had stolen Bramblestar's body and trapped spirit cats in the Dark Forest to carry out his commands and invade the living world.

Lightleap had volunteered to go into the Dark Forest to fight Ashfur, but at the last moment her courage had failed her. Now she not only had to wrestle with the memory of the danger all the Clans had shared, but her own failure, too.

"You shouldn't—" Sunbeam began, then broke off as she heard the sound of scuffling coming from underneath a rotting log. She angled her ears in that direction. "Over there," she whispered.

Lightleap headed for one end of the log while Sunbeam took the other. Then both of them crept toward the middle, where the sound was coming from. When there was barely a tail-length between them, several mice exploded from a nest of pine needles. Sunbeam leaped forward, trapping two, one beneath each forepaw. Lightleap caught a third; the rest of them escaped.

"Not bad," Sunbeam mewed with satisfaction. She prodded a mouse with her nose. "Thank you, StarClan, for this prey."

Lightleap was looking cheerful again as they buried the mice and continued on their way. "You heard what happened to Pouncestep, right?" she asked. "How she was chased by a dog near the greenleaf Twolegplace?"

"Some of it," Sunbeam replied. She remembered how Lightleap's sister had returned to camp, her fur ruffled but a look of triumph in her eyes. But she had only heard the bare outline of the story. "She must have been so scared!"

"She was clever," Lightleap responded. "She fooled that stupid flea-brain: She climbed a tree, and then ran along a branch and leaped into another tree. She left the dog barking at the bottom of the wrong tree, and took her sweet time heading back to camp."

"Great StarClan, that was brave!" Sunbeam commented, her belly lurching as she imagined the dog's gaping jaws and sharp teeth. "I probably wouldn't have been calm enough to think of that with a dog chasing me."

Lightleap gave a disdainful sniff. "It's not all that brave," she mewed, her eyes gleaming. "Any warrior could have done it. I wouldn't have run. I would have scratched that dog's eyes until it ran away."

Sunbeam felt as if her heart were sinking right down into her paws. Ever since Lightleap had lost her nerve and backed out of crossing into the Dark Forest, and the Sisters had sent Lightleap's brother, Shadowsight, instead, she had been taking a lot of unnecessary risks to prove how brave she was. She had been in trouble with her father, Tigerstar, a half-moon before, for sneaking across the border with RiverClan because Hopwhisker had dared her. The scolding she'd gotten from Tigerstar had echoed all around the camp, and Lightleap had been punished by having to do all the apprentice duties by herself for a half-moon.

"Have we caught enough, do you think?" Sunbeam asked, hoping to distract Lightleap from the story of her sister's bravery.

But Lightleap was watching two squirrels chase each other in the branches of a nearby tree. "Watch this!" she exclaimed, bolting up the trunk of the tree next to it. Sunbeam's heart sank a little as Lightleap glanced down at her and she saw the look of reckless eagerness in her friend's eyes.

As Lightleap ran out along a branch, looking as nimble as a squirrel herself, Sunbeam struggled between admiration and horror at the risks her friend was taking. She realized that Lightleap meant to jump into the next tree and catch one of the squirrels as it tried to escape. But it was a long jump, and the branches of the other tree weren't very thick.

Will they even hold a cat's weight? Lightleap is much heavier than a squirrel!

Her pelt bristling with anxiety, Sunbeam ran underneath the branch where Lightleap was balancing. She couldn't believe how dangerous it looked now that she was closer.

Lightleap jumped, and for a heartbeat Sunbeam thought she was going to make it. Her body soared through the air and she landed with all four paws on the branch she was aiming for.

Great leap! Sunbeam thought, her legs quivering with relief as she bounded forward, tracking Lightleap from the ground.

But almost at once, Lightleap's branch sagged under her weight. Lightleap dug her claws into it, dangling briefly, then let out a screech of terror as she fell.

Sunbeam felt as though horror had frozen her paws to the spot. She saw Lightleap plummeting toward her, and braced herself for the impact. With a painful jolt Lightleap landed on top of her, forcing her to the ground with a thump that drove all the breath out of her body. She lay on her side, struggling for air, while Lightleap scrambled to her paws, not seeming to be hurt at all.

"Oh, Sunbeam, I'm so sorry!" she exclaimed. "Are you okay?"

Managing at last to get her breath, Sunbeam tried to get up; but as soon as she moved, she realized she had wrenched something in her back, and she couldn't put one of her forepaws to the ground.

"No, I'm not okay," she panted. "You'll have to help me back to camp."

"I'm so sorry!" Lightleap repeated. "But please, Sunbeam, don't tell any cat what happened. I've only just stopped being in trouble."

"Okay," Sunbeam agreed, though she wasn't sure she should. *Why should she get away with being so stupid?* Stifling a sigh, she added to herself, *Because she's my friend, I guess.* "But you have to stop taking risks," she told Lightleap.

Lightleap's only response was to roll her eyes.

She could try being a bit grateful! Sunbeam thought.

Leaving their prey to be collected later, the two she-cats headed straight back to camp, Sunbeam leaning heavily on Lightleap's shoulder. She was dizzy with pain by the time they thrust their way through the bushes that guarded the ShadowClan camp.

"Take me straight to Puddleshine," she meowed through gritted teeth.

But before they reached the medicine cats' den, more of their Clanmates began to gather around, letting out worried exclamations as they saw Sunbeam's injuries.

"What happened to you?" Pouncestep asked anxiously.

"Was it foxes?" Slatefur demanded.

"No, nothing to worry about," Lightleap told them. "Sunbeam fell and hurt her back, that's all. Right, Sunbeam?"

Sunbeam stared at her friend. It pained her to lie, but she also didn't want to get Lightleap in trouble. Still, it bothered her to be put in this position. "Yeah, I wasn't looking where I was putting my paws," Sunbeam responded, trying hard not to let her annoyance show.

"We caught some good prey, though," Lightleap continued. "I just need to go back and collect it. And Sunbeam will be fine," she added with a dismissive flick of her tail.

Maybe, but right now it really hurts. Sunbeam couldn't see any sign that Lightleap really cared about her, or felt at all guilty about what she had done. Instead she just looked smug about their successful hunt. "Please can we go to the medicine cats' den?" she begged.

The group of concerned cats parted to let Sunbeam and Lightleap through, and, leaning on her friend's shoulder, Sunbeam was able to totter across the camp and into the den.

At least she's helping, she thought, her irritation softening a little.

Shadowsight was the only cat there; he looked up from sniffing at a bunch of wilting leaves as the two she-cats appeared. "Now what happened?" he asked.

Lightleap explained once again that Sunbeam had fallen and hurt herself. "You'll be okay now," she meowed, turning back to Sunbeam. "If you have to stay here, I'll bring you some fresh-kill later." She whisked out of the den without waiting for Sunbeam's reply.

Yeah, sure, I'm perfectly fine, Sunbeam thought, her annoyance rising again. *No need for you to stick around, not at all!*

Meanwhile, Shadowsight had disappeared into the herb store at the back of the den, and now he came back with something folded into a leaf. When he set it on the ground in front of Sunbeam, he pulled the wrapping back to reveal two poppy seeds. "Lick those up," he told her. "They'll help with the pain."

Gratefully, Sunbeam obeyed him. *At least some cat cares that I'm hurting!*

She lay still while Shadowsight examined her, feeling her back with a gentle paw and giving her a good sniff from neck to tail. "Well, you've wrenched your back," he mewed, "and your shoulder is dislocated. I can fix that, but it will hurt."

Sunbeam clenched her teeth. "Okay, go ahead." She lay still, closing her eyes and trying to imagine how good it would be when all this was over and she could share tongues with Blazefire again as they sunned themselves at the edge of the camp.

Shadowsight lay half across her, clamping her uninjured foreleg to the ground with one paw, while with his teeth and his other forepaw he wrenched at her injured shoulder. Sunbeam let out a screech of agony; for a heartbeat, it felt as if burning claws were ripping through her. She sagged against the ground, trembling. But as the pain ebbed, she realized that she felt much better.

"Thanks, Shadowsight," she gasped.

"Your back should heal by itself, with rest," Shadowsight mewed. "I'd like you to stay here for a day or two, so we can keep an eye on you." Gazing down at her with narrowed eyes, he added, "What really happened?"

"Oh, I . . . I guess I tripped," Sunbeam replied.

"Yeah, and hedgehogs fly," Shadowsight retorted, glancing toward the entrance to the den where Lightleap had vanished. "Come on, a healthy she-cat like you doesn't get injuries like these just from tripping." He paused, then added, "Are you sure Lightleap didn't have anything to do with this?"

Sunbeam hesitated. She had agreed not to tell their Clanmates anything that would get Lightleap into trouble, but it was obvious that Shadowsight already suspected part of the truth. *Besides, I'm so worried about the way Lightleap is behaving. I tried to talk to her about how reckless she's being, but she didn't listen.*

I can tell Shadowsight, she decided. *It's not like I'm betraying her to Tigerstar or Cloverfoot.* Shadowsight was Lightleap's brother; maybe he'd be able to talk to her and get her to calm down.

Her mind made up, Sunbeam launched into the story of how Lightleap had fallen from a tree when she was trying to chase squirrels. Shadowsight listened quietly, concern in his eyes.

"She never used to be like this," Sunbeam finished, massively relieved to be sharing her worries. "It's like she doesn't care whether she gets hurt or not."

"You're right—she has seemed reckless and unhappy lately," Shadowsight mewed thoughtfully. "I think she feels like she failed because she couldn't make herself go into the Dark Forest." He heaved a deep sigh. "There's no need for her to feel that way; she was brave even to have tried."

Sunbeam murmured agreement. The poppy seeds were starting to take effect, and she felt as if she were sinking into a comforting dark pelt. Shadowsight's final words seemed to come from a great distance.

"Don't worry. I'll try to figure out what to do."

CHAPTER 4

Padding along the lakeshore on the way to the Gathering, Flamepaw couldn't take any pleasure in the clear, moonlit night, or in the excited chatter of his Clanmates.

"I can't wait to hear what the leaders have decided," Thrift-ear mewed eagerly. "Changes to the warrior code . . . Things will be so different!"

"Yeah," her brother, Flipclaw, agreed. "We'll be able to make up our own minds about what we want to do."

Birchfall, who was walking just ahead of the younger cats, glanced back over his shoulder. "Have you got bees in your brain?" he asked. "For seasons, the Clans have gotten along very well with the warrior code, until Ashfur turned it against us. We need to follow the code, not start meddling with it. Not all changes are for the better."

Flipclaw rolled his eyes at his sister, but didn't respond.

Flamepaw couldn't take any interest in the argument. He had a feeling that he had only been chosen to go to the Gathering because Lilyheart had suggested it to Bramblestar. He knew she felt bad for him; more than once he had caught her giving him a hopeful look as they traveled together beside the lake.

She wants me to cheer up, even though I failed my assessment, he thought. *All my kin want me to be happy in ThunderClan, too. But I don't feel that, and I can't make myself feel it!*

Ever since the impostor Ashfur had been defeated, his Clanmates had congratulated themselves on living in the most amazing Clan in the whole forest. But that wasn't how Flamepaw saw it at all.

No cat understands.

When Flamepaw pushed his way through the bushes that surrounded the clearing on the island, he found that the other Clans had already arrived, and were clustered around the Great Oak, where the leaders sat in the branches. The air was filled with their mingled scents; moonlight glimmered on their pelts and reflected in their eyes.

Flamepaw spotted a group of apprentices from different Clans, and padded across to join them, mumbling, "Greetings," before finding a spot to sit on the outer edge. The new ThunderClan warriors and a few ShadowClan cats were sitting nearby; Flamepaw didn't want to join them and have to listen to his Clanmates describing how they had passed their assessments.

A few tail-lengths away, a cat was slowly making his way over to Ivypool; Flamepaw recognized Rootspring, the weird cat from SkyClan. He dipped his head in greeting to Ivypool, who nuzzled him warmly as he sat beside her.

Rootspring, Flamepaw remembered, was one of the cats who had traveled to the Dark Forest with Bristlefrost. They and other living cats had ventured there to save the real Bramblestar and recover the connection between the forest Clans and StarClan.

If you ask me, it all sounds very strange.

It wasn't that Flamepaw didn't believe the stories, exactly; just from watching Rootspring—his withdrawn demeanor and his tension as he spoke to Ivypool—he could see that the SkyClan tom had been through something horrible And Bristlefrost had never returned, lost to the living Clans and to StarClan through her death in the Dark Forest. But Flamepaw found it all really hard to understand.

Why would the fate of all the Clans be placed in just a few cats' paws?

He had been so young when Bramblestar had begun to act strangely: too young to remember what the Clan leader had been like before. But had he really been possessed by a totally different cat?

Part of Flamepaw wondered if ThunderClan had just needed some cat to blame for the way everything had gone wrong. But he would never dare to say that out loud. *My kin would kill me if I let out a single squeak!*

He tried to push away these dark thoughts as Tigerstar let out a loud yowl, standing tall on a branch of the Great Oak. "Cats of all Clans," he meowed as the sound of chatter died away. "Welcome to the Gathering."

Every cat settled down quietly, though Flamepaw could still feel the excitement in the air. The ShadowClan leader purred as he announced, "ShadowClan has four brand-new kits, born to Cinnamontail just days ago: Firkit, Streamkit, Bloomkit, and Whisperkit. They join my young kits, Birchkit and Rowankit, in the nursery. Puddleshine and Shadowsight have been very busy!"

Flamepaw glanced over at Birchfall, whose eyes shone with pride. Every cat assumed that Birchkit had been named in honor of the senior warrior. As the gathered cats purred their amusement, Tigerstar waved his tail to give up his place to Bramblestar; Flamepaw wondered if this was the moment when the changes to the warrior code would be announced.

When Bramblestar began, however, it was only to pass on the usual Clan news. "ThunderClan has three new warriors," he meowed proudly. "Myrtlebloom, Bayshine, and Finchlight. We wish them well as they take up their new duties in their Clan."

Flamepaw's sister and his foster kin stood up, their eyes shining with a mixture of pride and embarrassment. "Myrtlebloom! Bayshine! Finchlight!" their Clanmates yowled, and after a moment Flamepaw joined in, along with the cats from the other Clans.

But even while he cheered for his Clanmates, he felt as if every cat were staring at him, and he wished he could crawl away into a hole. Sudden anger with Lilyheart stabbed at him. Why had she made him come and witness the triumph of the cats who had been his fellow apprentices?

One of the young cats he was sitting with turned to give him a curious stare. "What happened?" she asked. "Shouldn't you be a warrior along with them?"

"Yeah, what did you do?" another apprentice asked.

"It's what I didn't do," Flamepaw explained bitterly, knowing that they would go on nagging him unless he told them something. "I was trying to catch a squirrel, and I failed my assessment because I couldn't ricochet off a tree."

Several snorts and *mrrows* of laughter greeted his words.

"Yeah, mouse-brain," Graypaw, a RiverClan tom, scoffed. "You have to hunt the prey you can catch. Didn't your mentor teach you that?"

"For StarClan's sake, shut up!" A new voice broke into the conversation, sharp with annoyance.

Flamepaw turned his head to see a young brown-and-white tabby she-cat glaring at the apprentices. He didn't recognize her, though he could pick up her ShadowClan scent.

"Just be quiet," she went on. "Important things are happening in the Clans, and you'll miss it all if you keep on teasing poor . . ." She shot Flamepaw an inquiring glance.

"Flamepaw," he supplied.

The she-cat tilted her head, looking him up and down. "That's a lovely name," she mewed, "but you don't really look like a Flamepaw, do you?"

Flamepaw's gratitude to her abruptly died. He was about to say, *I'm aware of that,* in freezing tones, but the she-cat had already turned away and was paying attention to the Gathering again.

Bramblestar had ceded his place to Mistystar, who had padded almost to the end of her branch to address the Clans.

Flamepaw hadn't ever seen her as close as this, and he realized with a pang how old she was looking.

She's one of the cats who fought in the Dark Forest, too, he thought wonderingly. *How did she survive that?*

In spite of her age, Mistystar's voice was strong, ringing out across the clearing. "StarClan has sent RiverClan a new medicine-cat apprentice. Please welcome Frostpaw."

Flamepaw looked across the clearing to where Mothwing sat among the other medicine cats; she was nudging a small light gray she-cat to her paws. The apprentice looked terrified at the clamor as the assembled cats called her name. "Frostpaw! Frostpaw!"

When the yowling had died down, Mistystar let her gaze travel around the clearing. "Cats of all Clans," she began, "I know that we are all still reeling from the damage caused by Ashfur. But we must move on, and that brings me to an important matter. The Clan leaders and medicine cats have agreed on changes to the warrior code. The medicine cats will present the changes to StarClan at the next half-moon meeting."

Flamepaw's ears perked up; he was interested in spite of how miserable he felt. All of ThunderClan had talked about nothing but the code ever since the Lights in the Mist came back from speaking with StarClan. One of the changes, he knew, was to let cats change their Clan if they wanted to be mates with a cat from another Clan. Flamepaw barely knew any cats from the other Clans—certainly not well enough to want to be mates with them—but he still realized that this was a big deal.

"Any cat will now be able to change their Clan to live with a mate," Mistystar continued. "I know some cats have done this before, but it often led to much conflict and heartbreak. Now there will be an official process to have their union accepted, by StarClan and the living Clans."

"What sort of process?" some cat called from the crowd.

"I'm coming to that." Mistystar's tail twitched with impatience at the interruption. "First, the two cats must declare their intention at a Gathering. Then the cat who wishes to change Clans must perform a task of their intended Clan's choosing, to prove that they are serious. If they succeed in this task, they will be allowed to change Clans."

Mistystar had hardly finished speaking when a clamor broke out among the assembled cats.

"That's too easy!" Flaxfoot of ShadowClan called out.

"Yeah!" Emberfoot of WindClan agreed. "We'll end up with cats changing Clans if they just like the look of another cat. What if it doesn't work out when they have to live together?"

A chorus of agreement greeted Emberfoot's words, interrupted almost at once by Flamepaw's Clanmate Poppyfrost.

"I don't think the code should be changed at all," she declared. "Cats from our own Clan should be good enough."

"The Clan leaders have discussed this thoroughly," Mistystar reminded the ThunderClan she-cat, an edge to her voice. "We have decided the code will be changed."

More clamor, of agreement and protest, rose from the crowd of cats, only to die away as Rootspring sprang to his paws, his yellow pelt bristling.

"We need this change, and it's right," he meowed, his voice shaking with passion. "It might cause pain, sure, but it will prevent much more pain than it causes."

The voices of the other cats gradually stilled. Every cat knew what Rootspring had suffered when Bristlefrost, the cat he loved, had died in the Dark Forest, with even her spirit lost forever so he could never hope to meet her again in StarClan. If changing Clans had been possible for them, they might have had moons to live together as mates, instead of wasting that time because neither cat could face betraying their Clan. They might even have had kits. Every cat felt massive respect for Rootspring, left behind to grieve after the horror he and Bristlefrost had endured.

A sudden idea darted into Flamepaw's mind. "I know what we should do!" he called out. "What if it were harder for the cat leaving their Clan? What if they had to be demoted to apprentice or something?"

One of the apprentices sitting nearby turned to give Flamepaw a mocking look. "Sure, that's the worst thing that can happen to any cat—right, Flamepaw?" he mewed snarkily.

The whole group descended into unkind snorts of laughter, while Flamepaw sat burning with shame and embarrassment.

"That's enough," Mistystar called from the Great Oak, authority in her voice. "The decision has been made. Moving on, we need to talk about how the Clans might depose a leader."

She didn't even acknowledge my suggestion, Flamepaw thought, feeling even more miserable. *Why did I come to this Gathering at all?*

"This is what the leaders and medicine cats decided," Mistystar continued. "First, three-quarters of the Clan members must agree that the leader is harmful, and that number must include the Clan's medicine cats. They will then present their case to the other leaders. If they agree, then the medicine cats will present the case to StarClan. If StarClan agrees, the leader's remaining lives will be taken away, and nine lives will be given to the deputy, who will become the new leader."

"Always the deputy?" some cat called.

"Of course," Mistystar replied. "Who else should be chosen? This will not be a way for some ambitious cat to seize power. And," she added, "for that reason, no deputy can be the cat who begins this process."

Discussion broke out, mostly about the part StarClan would play and the transfer of the nine lives, but no cat seemed to be as passionately against it as they'd been about cats changing Clans. Flamepaw guessed the memory of Ashfur was too strong.

Losing interest, Flamepaw stopped listening. He thought the whole thing was pointless. How could you ever get that many cats to agree on anything? Even when Bramblestar, under the control of the impostor, had been at his worst, there'd still been cats in ThunderClan who'd defended him. Flamepaw wasn't sure that three-quarters of the Clan would have agreed to get rid of him.

At last the Gathering drew to an end. Flamepaw realized

that the proposed changes were going to be presented to Star-Clan in the way that Mistystar had outlined, even though many cats had objected.

Typical, he thought. *The leaders want all the warriors to believe they matter, but the big decisions are always made by the five of them.*

As the cats began to head out of the clearing toward the tree-bridge and their own territories, Flamepaw found Lily-heart padding along by his side. "Just so you know," she murmured into his ear, "apprentices don't usually speak at a Gathering."

Flamepaw realized that she was embarrassed that he had spoken up with his idea about changing Clans. *How mouse-brained is that! How are we supposed to solve any problem if only the older cats can speak?*

But Flamepaw didn't dare say any of that. Instead he just ducked his head. "Okay," he muttered.

"I'll see you tomorrow, then," Lilyheart meowed. "We'll do some battle training." She whisked away through the bushes that surrounded the clearing.

Flamepaw lingered, hoping to avoid her and the new warriors who had been his denmates. When the clearing was almost empty and he thought it was safe to leave, he spotted Bramblestar, still standing at the foot of the Great Oak, gazing around as if he were lost.

It was hard for Flamepaw to understand his Clan leader, even though they were kin. Mostly Flamepaw had known him when he was possessed by the impostor Ashfur, and now that

Bramblestar had returned to his own body, he seemed more plodding and pensive than a Clan leader ought to be.

After a moment, when Bramblestar still didn't move, Flamepaw padded over to him. "Are you okay?" he asked hesitantly.

Bramblestar blinked slowly, as if he had just awoken from sleep. "What? Oh—yes, Flamepaw, I'm fine. Absolutely fine."

Flamepaw thought he sounded as if he was trying to convince himself as much as any cat. "Alderheart was here," he meowed. "I could fetch him for you."

The ThunderClan leader gave his pelt a rapid shake. "No, thank you, Flamepaw. I really am fine. It's just strange sometimes—being back. I find myself disappearing into memory."

"Yeah," Flamepaw agreed. "Sometimes it's strange even when you've been here the whole time."

Bramblestar's whiskers twitched with amusement. "I suppose it must be. Come on, let's go home."

He and Flamepaw were the last two cats to cross the treebridge. Flamepaw was surprised that his leader kept walking beside him as they headed around the lake, laying his tail over Flamepaw's back.

"You will try your hardest at your next assessment, won't you?" Bramblestar asked. "I know you have what it takes to be a strong ThunderClan warrior. For one thing," he added with a sidelong, teasing glance, "it's in your blood."

"I will try," Flamepaw promised. "I really want to be strong for my Clan." His voice broke on the last few words, and he realized it was true. Despite all his problems, he still wanted very much for ThunderClan to be the Clan that most of his Clanmates seemed to think it was. And he wanted to be an important part of it.

"I know you do," Bramblestar purred, his paw steps suddenly seeming lighter. "And I'm sure you will."

CHAPTER 5

Frostpaw crouched outside the warriors' den, sharing a vole with her mother, Curlfeather. A stiff breeze was blowing across the RiverClan camp, sending puffs of white cloud scudding across the sky. The air was filled with the scent of water and the soft gurgling of the streams that surrounded the camp.

"I was so proud of you last night," Curlfeather mewed between bites. "My daughter, a real medicine cat! All the Clans were cheering for you."

"It was a little scary," Frostpaw confessed.

"Nonsense!" Curlfeather's tone was bracing. "You deserved it."

Frostpaw didn't reply, just tucked into her vole. She knew that her mother didn't like it when she seemed nervous about her new place in the Clan. *She expects so much of me,* she thought. *I hope I can make her proud.*

While they were eating, Reedwhisker emerged from the warriors' den and bounded over to the group of warriors lounging around the fresh-kill pile. "Hunting patrol," he announced cheerfully. "Fognose, Podlight, Splashtail, you're with me."

The cats he had named rose to their paws and headed toward the camp entrance.

"Curlfeather, I'll take you, too," Reedwhisker added as he passed the spot where Frostpaw and her mother were eating together.

"Okay." Curlfeather took a last bite of vole and rose to her paws, swiping her tongue around her jaws. "Lead on, Reedwhisker."

Frostpaw watched her mother as she joined the patrol, and didn't realize that Mothwing had padded up to join her until the medicine cat spoke.

"Why do I have to come looking for you?" she asked. "You shouldn't be dawdling over your prey when there could be cats in our den who need healing."

"I wasn't—" Frostpaw began to defend herself.

"Mothwing is right," Curlfeather turned back to interrupt. "Off you go. Your skills are important, and your Clan needs you!"

Feeling a bit ruffled, Frostpaw abandoned the rest of the vole and began following Mothwing. Mistystar, sitting outside her den with her paws tucked under her, gave Frostpaw an encouraging nod as she and Mothwing padded in front of her.

But before the two cats could reach the top of the bank above the medicine-cat den, Brackenpelt brushed angrily past them, almost knocking Frostpaw off her paws. Turning back, Frostpaw saw her halt in front of Mistystar, her tortoiseshell fur fluffed out in annoyance.

"Mistystar, tell us how you *really* feel about changes to the code," she demanded. "If StarClan made you leader," she continued when Mistystar did not respond, "how can any cat take that away? After all that you've led the Clan through, how does it feel to know that we could start conspiring to get rid of you?"

"Yes," the elder Mosspelt, who was grooming herself nearby, agreed. "It all sounds very odd. Are we supposed to believe that what happened in the Dark Forest justifies all these changes?"

Mothwing had not moved, watching the scene with a disturbed look in her amber eyes. Frostpaw stayed by her side; she had thought this had been settled at the Gathering the night before, but obviously she had been wrong. *That's really weird,* she thought. *Are cats really allowed to argue with our leader like this?*

Mistystar rose to her paws and lashed her tail at her Clanmates' complaints, clearly struggling to hold on to her composure. Instead of answering Brackenpelt and Mosspelt, she leaped up onto the tree stump she used to address the Clan and opened her jaws in a commanding yowl.

"Let all cats old enough to swim gather to hear my words!"

Most of the Clan was already in the clearing; more cats appeared from the warriors' den, and one or two brushed through the brambles that surrounded the camp, coming from the direction of the lake.

"It's a pity Reedwhisker just left on that patrol," Mothwing murmured to Frostpaw. "Mistystar might need his support."

When the rest of the Clan was assembled, sitting in a ragged circle around the Highstump, Mistystar continued. "We must discuss this," she told her Clan. "Mosspelt, I understand this is a lot to take in, but I've explained to you many times what took place in the Dark Forest. Is it that you and the others don't understand what happened? Or don't you believe me?"

Frostpaw saw Mosspelt hunch her shoulders, the tip of her tail twitching uneasily. She thought that the elder didn't like being put on the spot like that, in front of so many of her Clanmates. "It's just . . . too big a change," she mewed, glancing around at the others.

"It's not that we don't trust you, Mistystar," Duskfur spoke up. "But in the past, when something so important happened that we changed the warrior code because of it, it was in the open for all cats to see. It's hard to understand how this happened and only five living cats saw it."

"Why do you think I would lie to you?" Mistystar asked, her voice strained.

"Not lie . . . ," Mosspelt protested. "We know you're not a liar. But . . . maybe the other cats had their own ideas, and convinced you that changes were needed."

"That's possible," Havenpelt pointed out. "Rootspring and Crowfeather both loved cats outside their own Clans. As did Graystripe, when he was alive."

"Yes, and Shadowsight's parents started life in separate Clans," Owlnose added. "If it comes to that, Mistystar, you're a half-Clan cat yourself."

Mistystar swiveled her head around and fixed Owlnose with a blue glare. "I refuse to take responsibility for something that happened before I was born," she snapped. "My parentage was never a problem for Leopardstar when she made me her deputy. And clearly it was not a problem for StarClan when they gave me my nine lives and my name. Or do you think you know better than StarClan, Owlnose?"

"Mistystar, I never said—" Owlnose began to protest.

Frostpaw could see that Mistystar was growing upset, her shoulder fur rising and her tail beginning to twitch. She was also panting a bit, as though she were struggling to get air. Frostpaw opened her jaws to interrupt, but Duskfur spoke before she could get started.

"Is it possible that some of these changes weren't needed, but were only wanted by some of these cats?" the brown tabby she-cat suggested.

Mistystar's blue eyes flashed with anger. "Are you including me?" she demanded. "Do you think I've been lying to you? Or are you questioning my judgment? Haven't I always been a loyal warrior, living my life by the code and leading my Clan accordingly?"

"Of course," Shimmerpelt mewed in a soothing tone. "But look at ThunderClan, for example. That whole mess they got into with Ashfur and Bramblestar. Of course they would think they need a way to get rid of a leader. But that would never happen in RiverClan, because you are a true and just leader, Mistystar, with StarClan's blessing!"

Mistystar flicked an ear, looking uncomfortable. "That is kind of you," she said, "but I'm not sure I agree that River-Clan is above this sort of trouble. If we'd had a rule like this, perhaps Leopardstar would never have succeeded in joining us to TigerClan."

Shimmerpelt shifted awkwardly. "Well, yes. But that was *then*. We've learned our lessons, haven't we?"

"Yes," Owlnose agreed, his brown tabby fur beginning to bristle. "And if the Clans make these changes for Thunder-Clan, they might endanger RiverClan sometime in the future. What's to stop one Clan deposing another Clan's leader, to grab power?"

"That's not how it's supposed to work at all," Mistystar began, but by now no cat was listening to her.

"It's a definite risk," Mosspelt meowed, fluffing out her neck fur. "What does being a leader even mean anymore, if ordinary Clan cats can take it away?" She snorted in exas-peration. "Don't get me started on how the code tells us the leader's word *is* the warrior code. How is that true if Clan cats can get rid of their leader?"

Frostpaw could see that Mistystar was at the end of her patience as she lowered her head and drew her lips back in a snarl. With an exclamation of alarm, Mothwing darted for-ward to stand beside the Highstump.

"I didn't travel to the Dark Forest," she declared, raising her voice so that every cat could hear her. "But I sat beside the Moonpool waiting for the cats who did go, and treating some of their injuries. I know that everything Mistystar has told us is true. Look . . . ," she wheezed, letting her gaze travel over the assembled cats. "I haven't always had the best relation-ship with StarClan. But I fully believe that Mistystar and the other Lights in the Mist spoke to StarClan about this. And they all agreed these changes were needed."

Silence spread throughout the clearing, and for a moment Frostpaw thought that the gathered cats might be convinced. But then Duskfur thrust her way to the front of the crowd and turned to address the Clan.

"If you ask me," she began, "it seems like more living cats should help decide the rules we live by. I'm not saying that Mistystar is trying to mislead us. But what's so special about the Lights in the Mist? Who are they? Mistystar, Crowfeather, Shadowsight, Rootspring, and Violetshine. Why should *they* get to decide the rules for all the Clan cats? At least you're a leader, Mistystar, but Shadowsight's the cat who got us *into* the whole Ashfur mess, Crowfeather was a codebreaker himself, and I'm not sure I know enough yet about the SkyClan cats to trust them."

Frostpaw had always known SkyClan as one of the lake Clans, but Duskfur's words reminded her that they had only arrived a few seasons ago, during the time when Darktail invaded the forest. *I suppose no cat really knows very much about them yet.*

Mistystar lashed her tail in anger. "The Lights in the Mist were the cats brave enough to travel to the Dark Forest," she hissed. "Which is more than some of you did. They battled Ashfur and saved all of us: StarClan, the Dark Forest, and the living world. After all the Lights in the Mist did and sacrificed, what right have you, Duskfur, to doubt their intentions? Bristlefrost and Graystripe gave their lives."

Frostpaw could hear how upset the Clan leader was getting, but Duskfur didn't seem aware of it, or she didn't care.

"I'm not convinced the living world needed saving," the brown tabby she-cat meowed. "There was fighting over the impostor, sure, but I seem to remember a time, Mistystar, when you had us fighting to defend him. Now you're convinced that what he did was enough to upend the whole code?"

Mistystar's fur was bushed up in fury, and Frostpaw could see her working her claws into the top of the stump, as if she were tearing apart a piece of prey. "Yes," she admitted at last, an odd strain to her mew, "I was wrong to defend Ashfur when he was posing as Bramblestar. But, can't you see, that's why—"

The Clan leader broke off. Horrified, Frostpaw saw her face change as she lunged forward, fell from the Highstump, and collapsed in a heap on the ground.

Instantly Mothwing was by her side. "Mistystar, what's wrong?" she asked, running her paws over Mistystar's throat and chest.

"I need help." Mistystar's voice was such a feeble rasp that Frostpaw could barely make out the words.

"I'm here," Mothwing mewed reassuringly. "Just lie still. Here—" She glanced around and spoke to the nearest cat. "Sneezecloud! Go and fetch water."

Sneezecloud dashed off.

"What have you eaten lately?" Mothwing asked Mistystar. "Have you eaten?"

Mistystar turned her head a little and fixed her blue gaze on the medicine cat. "This isn't about prey," she murmured. Then her eyes closed and her whole body went limp.

"Where's my apprentice?" Mothwing asked.

Frostpaw could hear the panic in her voice. Her own heart beating wildly, she wriggled her way through the crowd of cats. "Here I am, Mothwing. What do you want me to do?"

"Press down on her chest. Like this." Mothwing demonstrated, her forepaws thrusting down so strongly that Frostpaw wondered if she might break the Clan leader's ribs. Quickly she took Mothwing's place and copied what she had done, putting out all her strength as she pressed Mistystar's chest. Anxiety filled her as she remembered how Mothwing had shown her the technique just a few days before.

But I've never done it on a living cat before, she thought, anguished. *Oh, StarClan, please let me get it right!*

"That's right," Mothwing meowed, stooping over Mistystar's head and parting her jaws to check that her throat was clear so she could breathe. "Again. And again. Keep at it. Hard—as hard as you can."

Frostpaw did as she was told, her forelegs already beginning to ache. There was no sign that Mistystar was rousing. Her breathing was so shallow that Frostpaw wondered if each breath would be her last.

Meanwhile the alarm in Mothwing's voice had spread to the other cats.

"What happened?" Brackenpelt asked.

Owlnose's voice shook with anxiety. "Will she be all right?"

Minnowtail, who had listened to the whole argument in silence, rounded on Duskfur. "How could you?" she demanded, her voice filled with outrage.

"Step back a bit. Give her space to breathe," Mothwing ordered. She was looking more and more distraught, her claws working in the ground and her ears lying flat.

"Can I fetch any herbs?" Frostpaw asked, pressing down again. "Maybe chervil?"

Mothwing shook her head. "It's too late for herbs," she whispered. "Mistystar is dying. You can stop pressing now," she added to Frostpaw. "There's nothing we can do to save her."

Frostpaw stood back, trembling from the effort. Mistystar's chest still rose and fell, but the movements now were so tiny that Frostpaw expected each one to be the last. *Mistystar can't be dying,* she told herself, grief beginning to creep up on her like a cat stalking its prey. *StarClan gave her nine lives.* She tried to remember stories about when her Clan leader had lost lives in the past, but her brain was whirling too much to count. "Does she have any lives left?" she asked in a small voice.

Mothwing just shook her head. Frostpaw didn't know whether she was saying *No* or *I don't know.* A shudder passed through Mistystar's body; as it faded away, Frostpaw waited for her to take her next breath. But it didn't come. Heartbeats dragged by like seasons, and still it didn't come. Gasps of horror could be heard from the assembled warriors, and some cat let out a drawn-out wail that echoed all around the camp. Sneezecloud returned with a mouthful of dripping moss and halted, staring at the Clan leader.

Duskfur and Owlnose exchanged a horrified glance. "She's just getting her next life," Duskfur meowed, though her voice was hollow, and Frostpaw could tell she didn't really believe it.

"She'll wake up soon. You just wait and see."

Mothwing stood motionless for a few moments, her gaze fixed on Mistystar. Then, finally, she stepped away, heaving a deep sigh. "She's not coming back. I couldn't help hoping, even though I was pretty sure she was on her last life. But she would have taken up her next one by now."

Sadness enveloped Frostpaw like a dark cloud as she realized that Mistystar was truly dead. It was as though the lake had vanished overnight, leaving a hole in the landscape that could never be filled. Frostpaw had never known another RiverClan leader. She couldn't imagine her Clan led by another cat.

More cats were beginning to wail as they gazed at Mistystar's inert body and realized that she had no more lives left. Mothwing turned to Frostpaw, grief and desperation in her eyes.

"Frostpaw, you've walked with StarClan," she mewed, her voice low and urgent so her Clanmates wouldn't overhear. "You can speak to them, can't you, and make sure Mistystar finds her way to them? Can you help her? It can't just end this way. . . ."

Frostpaw was daunted by the thought that she could do anything for Mistystar or her devastated Clan. "I'll try," she murmured after a moment's hesitation. She could see how upset her mentor was; whatever she could do would help Mothwing as much as Mistystar.

Reaching out to touch Mistystar's still-warm paw, Frostpaw closed her eyes. With all the concentration she could summon, she sent out her mind, trying to reach out to Star-Clan.

At first, all Frostpaw could see were swirls of dark colors fading to lighter ones. After a while, she thought she could make out a glimmer of stars in the distance.

Help her, she thought. *Please take Mistystar into your care.*

For a while she still saw nothing more. Then a pair of bright green eyes appeared in front of her, along with a faint set of ears and whiskers.

"I hear you," the cat mewed. "She is one of us now. Bury her body, and let her spirit walk with her warrior ancestors."

Frostpaw opened her eyes and turned to Mothwing, quivering with joy at her success. "I did it!" she exclaimed. "Mistystar is safe in StarClan."

Relief lit the depths of Mothwing's amber eyes. "Oh, thank StarClan!" she breathed out. "What happened?" she added more forcefully. "Who did you speak with? Was it Misty-star herself? Or Willowshine? She'll take care of Mistystar, I know."

Frostpaw hadn't been able to see the cat clearly, and now the details were blurring in her mind. *Was it Willowshine?* She tried to focus on the hazy image, to see if it matched her memory of the dead medicine cat. She wasn't sure. But she knew how much it would comfort Mothwing to know that her leader was safe with her beloved former apprentice.

"Yes, I'm sure it was Willowshine," she meowed.

Mothwing took a deep breath and leaped up to the top of the Highstump. "Cats of RiverClan," she began, "our leader is dead, and we all grieve for her. But we can comfort ourselves in knowing that Mistystar is now in StarClan."

"Are you sure?" Brackenpelt asked. "Frostpaw might have gotten it wrong."

"Yeah, this is what happens when your medicine cat can't speak to StarClan," Owlnose added. "You have to rely on a half-trained apprentice!"

Several other cats called out their agreement. Frostpaw felt cold claws fastening in her belly at her Clanmates' lack of trust in her.

Mothwing raised a paw to silence her Clanmates. "My apprentice, Frostpaw, is perfectly capable," she announced in a voice like an icy wind off the lake. "She has spoken with Willowshine, who welcomed Mistystar into StarClan. Tonight we will sit vigil for our leader, secure in the knowledge that her spirit hunts with her warrior ancestors."

Frostpaw could see her Clanmates relaxing; they were still sorrowful, but their desperate grief was fading. She felt herself relaxing, too; Mothwing's words had clearly convinced the other cats that they could believe her.

"Well done, youngster," Mosspelt meowed. She heaved a sigh as if it was hard to force the words out, then added, "You're going to be a great medicine cat."

Several others called out her name. "Frostpaw! Frostpaw!"

Conscious of every cat's eyes turned toward her, Frostpaw ducked her head and gave her chest fur a few embarrassed licks. Even so, their praise warmed her. She looked around for Curlfeather, partly wanting her mother's comfort after their leader's death, and partly wanting her to see how well she had carried out her first real task as a medicine cat.

But Curlfeather was nowhere to be seen. Then Frostpaw remembered that she had gone out earlier with the hunting patrol. *This is terrible,* she thought. *She'll be so upset when she comes back and finds that Mistystar is dead.*

"Where is Reedwhisker?" Mallownose asked. "He'll be our leader now. He'll have to travel to the Moonpool tonight to receive his nine lives from StarClan and become Reedstar."

"He left on a hunting patrol," Havenpelt meowed. "They should be back before long."

"What terrible news to return to," Icewing mewed, her blue eyes troubled. "Do you think we should send some cat to look for them?"

Mothwing shook her head. "We could spend all day looking and not find them. There's nothing we can do now except wait."

A pang of compassion for Reedwhisker pierced Frostpaw like a thorn. Mistystar was his mother; he would have to come to terms with her loss at the same time as taking on the responsibilities of leader.

But he's a good cat, Frostpaw thought as she listened to the senior warriors and how they spoke of Reedwhisker with respect. *He's always been so kind to me. He will make a good leader.*

CHAPTER 6

❧

Sunbeam lay curled up in the medicine cats' den, drowsily grooming herself and wondering when she would be allowed back to her warrior duties. Her foreleg was as strong as it had ever been, and the pain in her back was fading, though it could still startle her with a sharp twinge if she moved carelessly.

Puddleshine had gone out to collect herbs, leaving her with Shadowsight, who had brought in some fresh bedding and now was sorting through it to make sure it was free of thorns.

"How are you feeling?" he asked Sunbeam, not looking up from his task. "Do you want more poppy seed?"

"No, thank you," Sunbeam replied. "When do you think I can go back to the warriors' den?"

"Why, are you tired of me tripping over your tail?" Shadowsight's voice was warm with humor. "Maybe you should keep your tail tucked in."

"My tail is fine, thanks." Sunbeam used the tip to flick a scrap of bracken at the back of Shadowsight's head. "But it's pretty boring here, without anything to do."

"Well, when Puddleshine gets back, I'll make you a fresh poultice of elder leaves," Shadowsight promised. "That should help your wrenched muscles. Then in the morning we'll examine you and make a decision."

"Thanks, Shadowsight." Sunbeam stretched her jaws in a massive yawn. "Do you know what will happen to Lightleap?" she asked after a moment. "You said you told Tigerstar about how I was injured." Her whole pelt prickled with her sense of guilt. *I promised Lightleap I wouldn't tell any cat about what happened. I never thought Shadowsight would pass it on.* "Will she be in trouble?"

"Probably," Shadowsight responded, not sounding particularly worried. "But it's no more than she deserves. If only she would talk more about how she's feeling. When she couldn't . . ." His voice trailed off, and he shook his head, then added more firmly, "She should stop obsessing about how she couldn't go into the Dark Forest."

Is she trying to prove something? This wasn't the first time that the thought had crossed Sunbeam's mind. *To all of us? Or to herself?*

Before she could say more to Shadowsight, she heard paw steps outside the den, and a familiar voice called, "Can I come in?"

"Blazefire!" Sunbeam exclaimed, while Shadowsight replied, "Of course you can."

Full of delight at seeing the white-and-ginger tom, Sunbeam felt herself relaxing. Blazefire always made her feel safe and at home. He padded across the den and dropped a plump mouse at her paws. "I caught it myself," he mewed.

"Oh, thank you! I'm starving." Sunbeam gave Blazefire a glowing look before tearing off a mouthful of the mouse.

When she had taken the edge off her hunger, she asked, "So what exciting things did you do today, with no cat to tell you what to do?"

For a couple of heartbeats, Blazefire was quiet, and Sunbeam was worried that somehow she had said the wrong thing. But then Blazefire let out a *mrrow* of amusement.

"Oh, I ventured into the forest, through fire and flood and dark spirits, battling them all to bring you back a trophy—this magnificent mouse!"

Relief flooded through Sunbeam. She couldn't imagine life without Blazefire, and the last thing she wanted to do was upset him. She thought she had loved him ever since she was a kit, traveling with him and the other cats from the hollow where she was born back to ShadowClan territory.

"Such a brave warrior!" she praised him.

"And how is your back?" Blazefire asked, drawing his tail-tip along her spine.

"Much better," Sunbeam told him. "Shadowsight says—"

She broke off at the sound of racing paw steps outside, and a heartbeat later Lightleap stormed into the den. Her pelt bristled with fury as she stalked across to Sunbeam and stood glaring down at her.

"I know it was you who betrayed me!" she snarled. "You told my parents that I'd been acting stupid because I have some sort of death wish!"

"That's not—" Sunbeam began, but Lightleap just went on raging, not listening to a word she said.

"Tigerstar and Dovewing really gave me a hard time about

my choices yesterday. And it has to be you who told them—they had details that only you knew."

As Sunbeam took a breath to defend herself, Shadowsight thrust himself between the two she-cats. "It wasn't Sunbeam who told them," he mewed. "It was me."

For a moment, Lightleap just stared at him, jaws gaping, giving her brother the chance to explain.

"No cat is angry with you, Lightleap," he told her. "We're just worried. You shouldn't be working so hard to prove yourself to the Clan. I've done the same thing in the past—you know that as well as I do—and it caused me to make some pretty serious mistakes. You're a strong ShadowClan warrior and a valued member of our family. Can't you be content with that?"

Sunbeam was impressed with Shadowsight's wisdom; she could remember how unsure of himself he had been when he was younger. He had grown much stronger after the way he had suffered in the Dark Forest. But Lightleap clearly didn't see him that way; his words only made her angrier.

"That's big talk from you," she sneered. "You're the cat who allowed Ashfur into the Clans and then set him free!"

Shadowsight took a step back, a hurt look in his eyes. Sunbeam knew that Lightleap had been one of his few supporters during the darkest days of Ashfur's reign. It must hurt terribly to see that she was angry enough to blame him for this.

"I don't need your pity, or your advice," Lightleap continued. "I'm perfectly capable of living my own life." She whipped around and stalked out of the den.

Shadowsight cast an awkward glance at Sunbeam and Blazefire, then followed her.

Sunbeam gazed after him, then let her head rest on Blaze-fire's shoulder. "This is terrible," she meowed. "When I told Shadowsight the truth about how I got injured, I didn't expect him to pass it on to Tigerstar. I know it's not really my fault, but I still feel so guilty. Lightleap is my best friend!"

Blazefire turned his head to give her ear a comforting lick. "Don't worry," he told her. "Lightleap is just going through a difficult time."

"I wish I could go after her," Sunbeam responded. "If I could just leave the medicine-cat den . . ." Then she straightened up, gazing into Blazefire's eyes. "Do you think you could go and talk to Lightleap for me?" she asked.

"Me?" Blazefire looked doubtful. "I'm not sure I would know what to say."

"Oh, please," Sunbeam begged. "You know me well enough—just tell Lightleap what I would want to tell her. You're the only cat I would trust to help."

Blazefire hesitated a moment longer, then nodded. "Okay, I'll try. But I can't promise it will do any good."

"Thank you!" Sunbeam pressed her nose into Blazefire's shoulder fur. "You're the greatest, Blazefire."

"Yeah, I know," the tom grumbled good-humoredly. "I'll talk to her later. Right now I have to go out on patrol. I only came by to see how you were doing before we set out." He leaned over to touch noses with Sunbeam, then left with a word of farewell.

Still anxious, Sunbeam slowly finished the mouse Blaze-fire had brought; she was swallowing the last mouthful when Shadowsight returned, looking thoroughly uncomfortable.

"How is Lightleap?" Sunbeam asked.

"Still very upset," Shadowsight replied. "And I'm afraid she's worked out that it must have been you who told me about her behavior the other day."

"Oh, I guess I should have seen that coming," Sunbeam moaned, then added, "Lightleap isn't stupid."

"I'm sorry, but there's something else," Shadowsight mewed gently. "As soon as you're well enough, Tigerstar wants to speak to you about the part you played in what happened."

Sunbeam winced. *This is getting worse and worse,* she thought. *First I'm injured, then my best friend is mad at me, even though it was her fault . . . and now I'm in trouble with the Clan leader. Where will it end?*

CHAPTER 7

"Okay, let's try it again," Lilyheart meowed.

Flamepaw and his mentor were practicing fighting moves in a clearing just outside the ThunderClan camp. Lilyheart was teaching Flamepaw to dive under his opponent's out-stretched paws and knock his legs from under him.

Like I haven't done this so many times before, he grumbled to himself. *I could do it in my sleep!*

"See that low branch?" Lilyheart went on. "Pretend it's a cat attacking you. Now let's see the move."

Flamepaw suppressed a sigh. *It was a lot more fun training with the other apprentices,* he thought. *Then I had a real opponent, not some stupid branch.* It was just one more reminder that his fellow apprentices were warriors now, and he wasn't.

"Come on." Lilyheart twitched her whiskers impatiently. "The other cat would have ripped your fur off by now."

Gritting his teeth, Flamepaw bounded forward, dived under the branch, and swiped at where the imaginary cat's paws would be. Then he rolled away, bounced up again, and turned back to Lilyheart.

"That was very good," she commented. "Though you might

be quicker off the mark with your roll. The one drawback to this move is that you risk getting squashed under your enemy as they fall. Try it again."

Flamepaw tried it again, making sure to roll as soon as he had delivered his swipe.

"Yes, much better," Lilyheart praised him. "Except that your tail was waving around all over the place. Keep it tucked in. Now have another try."

Flamepaw's patience abruptly deserted him. "I know all this stuff already!" he complained.

Lilyheart's eyes narrowed. "Clearly you don't," she snapped, "or you would be a full warrior by now."

Flamepaw couldn't suppress a gasp. He would never have expected Lilyheart to say something that stung like that.

Lilyheart blinked apologetically, seeming to regret her harsh words. "Look, we're going to have to work together if you're going to pass your assessment this time," she mewed, her voice softer. "And you have to remember, whatever you feel about how fair or unfair all this is, you're still my apprentice. That means what I say goes."

Flamepaw nodded, reluctantly accepting that his mentor was right. "I know. I'm sorry, Lilyheart. Should I do the move again?"

"No, I think we're done for now," Lilyheart replied, glancing at the sky. "It's coming up to sunhigh, and I have to do a border patrol. Sorry, Flamepaw, not you," she added when Flamepaw suddenly brightened. "The elders' bedding needs changing, so you can stay behind and do that."

That's so not fair! Flamepaw thought, biting back a groan. Since he was now the only apprentice in the camp, all the boring, unpleasant tasks fell to him, and they took even longer than usual. He would much rather patrol the WindClan border with Lilyheart, but having just been scolded for complaining, he knew better than to risk it again.

"Okay, Lilyheart, I'll take care of it," he meowed, his tail drooping.

Slipping back into camp through the thorn tunnel, Flamepaw headed for the elders' den beneath the hazel bushes. Brackenfur was the only cat there; he moved out of the way while Flamepaw began to gather up all the soiled moss and bracken.

"Thanks, Flamepaw." The old cat stifled a yawn. "It will be good to sleep on fresh bedding." He paused briefly, then added, "So . . . your sister, Finchlight, is a warrior now."

"That's right." Flamepaw kept his answer short. *I really don't want to talk about this.*

But Brackenfur seemed not to realize that he was uncomfortable. "You didn't make it this time around," he went on. "Why was that?"

"I failed my assessment."

"Yes, I heard that." Brackenfur raised one hind leg to scratch his ear. "Tough luck. But what went wrong?"

Oh, great, so we get to go through all this again. Please, StarClan, help me not rip this mouse-brain's ears off! "I messed up my hunting," Flamepaw told the elder.

"Well, I'm sure you'll pass next time," Brackenfur mewed

amiably. "It takes some young cats a while to grow into their fur."

Oh . . . just stop talking, will you?

"You certainly come from a line of great cats," Brackenfur declared. "I know you'll live up to them."

Flamepaw just gave him a brusque nod. He knew that the old cat meant to be kind, but everything Brackenfur said just made him more upset. He was relieved when a chorus of excited squeaks broke out behind him; he turned to see Spotfur's kits, Stemkit, Bristlekit, and Graykit, bouncing up out of nowhere.

"What are you doing?" Stemkit asked.

Bristlekit sniffed curiously at the bedding. "Oh, that's all yucky!" she exclaimed, jumping back.

"We want to help!" Graykit exclaimed.

Looking around for their mother, Flamepaw noticed Spotfur dozing outside the nursery. He wondered if he ought to wake her up, then thought she probably needed the rest, and the kits were fun to be around.

"You're an apprentice, aren't you?" Bristlekit asked, gazing up at Flamepaw with wide eyes. "That's so cool!"

Well, at least some cat thinks an apprentice is an exciting thing to be, Flamepaw thought, amusement replacing his annoyance.

"We want to be apprentices," Stemkit informed Flamepaw. "But Spotfur says we have to wait until we're six moons old."

"That's forever!" Graykit groaned. "We want to be apprentices *now.*"

"Then we'll be apprentices now," Bristlekit announced.

"Flamepaw, you get to be our mentor."

"Okay, then," Flamepaw mewed, entering into the spirit of the game. "If you're apprentices, you have to help me clear out this old bedding."

"Sure! We can do that," Graykit agreed enthusiastically.

Stemkit and Graykit plunged into the elders' den and began to shovel the bedding into heaps with their tiny paws. Bristlekit hesitated for a moment, her nose wrinkling, then cheerfully bounced into the heaps with her littermates. Flamepaw thought they were getting more of it stuck in their pelts than they gathered up, but at least they were trying.

Brackenfur let out a chuckle from deep within his chest. "You've got your paws full there," he remarked.

With Flamepaw helping and directing, the kits had soon cleared two of the three elders' nests. Flamepaw was beginning to roll the moss and bracken into balls ready to carry out of camp, when he heard a cat yowling from the middle of the clearing.

"Kits! Kits, where are you?"

Turning, Flamepaw saw Daisy, the cream-colored she-cat who helped in the nursery, spinning around with an agitated air as she looked for the kits. He waved his tail to attract her attention.

"Hey, Daisy! They're over here."

Daisy came bounding across the camp to the elders' den, staring in amazement as her gaze fell on the kits. "Flamepaw, what do you think you're doing?" she demanded. "Graykit, put that down!"

Turning back into the den, Flamepaw saw that Graykit had found a twig somewhere and was gripping it in his jaws. He was waving it around; Stemkit had to leap back to avoid having it poked into his eye. Hearing Daisy's voice, Graykit dropped the twig and stood there looking guilty.

"They're just playing at being apprentices," Flamepaw explained. "They wanted to help."

"There's a reason kits aren't apprenticed until they're six moons old," Daisy meowed, flicking her ears irritably. "They're too young to help safely."

"I guess . . . ," Flamepaw muttered, beginning to feel as guilty as Graykit looked. *She's talking to me like I'm a kit!*

"In the future," Daisy continued, "if you see the kits running around unsupervised, you should find me or Spotfur. Come on, kits, time for your nap."

The three kits trailed out of the den, stopping to give their pelts a good shake, spraying the older cats with scraps of moss and debris. "We never get to have any fun!" Graykit complained.

"Poking your eye out is not fun!" Daisy exclaimed, sweeping her tail around the kits to herd them back to the nursery.

Flamepaw watched them go, then began to gather up the rest of the bedding. He flicked his tail in frustration. *I can't do anything right,* he thought. *Not even play with kits.*

The sun had gone down behind the trees, but there was still light in the sky when Sparkpelt, who was eating a squirrel beside the fresh-kill pile, called Flamepaw over to her with a wave of her tail. "Come and share," she invited him.

Flamepaw felt a warm pulse of surprise that his mother had singled him out. As he padded over, he wondered if she was going to ask about his failed assessment. Even though it had happened several days ago, they still hadn't talked about it. *Because we never do talk about difficult stuff.*

Sparkpelt was clearly not going to discuss it now. "Have you had a good day?" she asked; Flamepaw thought she sounded as polite and formal as if she were speaking to a cat from another Clan.

"Fine, thank you," Flamepaw replied, equally polite. "I did battle training with Lilyheart."

"I'm sure you did well." Sparkpelt nudged the squirrel toward him. "Come on, eat."

Flamepaw relaxed a little as he sank his teeth into the succulent flesh, only to look up warily as Lilyheart came striding across to him, her dark tabby fur bushed up and her tail-tip twitching.

Oh no! Flamepaw groaned inwardly. *What have I done now?*

"I just spoke to Daisy," Lilyheart meowed, halting beside him. "Were you using Spotfur's kits to help you with your apprentice tasks?"

"No, I was not!" Flamepaw retorted indignantly. "They came to me when I was clearing out the elders' den, and they wanted to play at being apprentices. I just let them—I didn't mean any harm."

Lilyheart stared at him for several heartbeats, her eyes narrowed. "There's nothing wrong with playing with the kits," she declared at last. "But you have to be careful. They shouldn't be doing tasks meant for apprentices."

Flamepaw could feel frustration rising inside him and struggled to hold on to his temper. Then, to his surprise, his mother looked up from her prey and faced Lilyheart.

"Really, Lilyheart!" she mewed. "It sounds like an honest misunderstanding. The kits are very cute, and they don't take no for an answer when they've got an idea in their little furry heads. I'm sure Flamepaw has learned his lesson and won't make the same mistake again—right, Flamepaw?"

"Of course not," Flamepaw agreed, grateful that his mother understood.

Lilyheart hesitated for a moment, then gave a satisfied nod. "Okay, I'll see you for more training in the morning." She walked off to the fresh-kill pile to choose a piece of prey for herself.

"Thank you, Sparkpelt," Flamepaw meowed.

"You're welcome. I'm sure you meant well. Now stop worrying about it and enjoy your squirrel."

Flamepaw was happy to do just that.

Sparkpelt ate quietly for a few moments, then raised her head, giving Flamepaw an awkward look. "I've noticed—well, I really couldn't miss it—that you seem to be struggling with your apprenticeship."

While she was speaking, Flamepaw felt his pelt begin to burn with shame and discomfort. It had felt really good when Sparkpelt had stood up for him. *And now she's nagging me, just like every other cat!*

"It must be hard for you," his mother went on, "that Finch-light was made a full warrior and you weren't. Is it making you anxious?"

"What do you care?" Flamepaw blurted, the old anger building inside him.

Sparkpelt looked even more awkward, clearly finding it hard to meet Flamepaw's gaze. "I care because you're my kit."

"Oh, sure!" Flamepaw scoffed.

"There are high expectations of you because of your kin," Sparkpelt went on, ignoring the interruption. "You belong to a family that's done great things for our Clan: Alderheart, Squirrelflight, Bramblestar, all the way back to—"

"Firestar," Flamepaw finished bitterly.

"Yes. And I can understand that you wouldn't want that pressure—Alderheart and I struggled under it, too—but we can't control who we are. We can't control what our Clan-mates think when they look at us, or how they chatter when one of us is . . . well, struggling. But it's a gift, really, having Firestar in our blood."

"I don't want it!" Flamepaw snapped. He hadn't planned to say that, but when he saw Sparkpelt staring at him in surprise, he knew he had to justify himself. "I never asked to be Firestar's kin. I don't *feel* like Firestar's kin. Every cat says that *you* look just like him, and maybe Finchlight at least has a bit of orange in her pelt, but I'm an all-black cat!"

As he spoke, something began swelling inside Flamepaw, perhaps because the weight of his mother's expectations had become too much to bear, or perhaps because—at last—he was talking about serious things with his mother.

"Besides," he added, striving to keep his voice steady, "I don't feel connected to you, either, because you left me when I needed you. Even Finchlight left me when you joined the exiles' camp!"

"I didn't have a choice—" Sparkpelt began.

"That may be true, but you didn't even check on me!" Flamepaw interrupted, his resentment overflowing.

Sparkpelt's eyes widened, and her ears flicked up; clearly, she was stung by his words. After a few heartbeats she mewed softly, "You are all black, just like your father."

Flamepaw stared at his paws. "Maybe Larksong would have understood me," he murmured. "But I'll never know."

Sparkpelt shook her head helplessly, seeming not to know what more to say. Flamepaw couldn't even remember what he'd wanted when he'd said those things to his mother. Every hair on his pelt burning, he rose to his paws and stumbled away, acutely aware of the stares of a few nearby Clanmates.

He passed Alderheart, who was watching him with kind curiosity, and almost stopped to speak to him. Alderheart had never been anything but kind. But he wasn't a father.

Flamepaw padded on, out through the thorn tunnel, and came to a halt beneath a cluster of trees, trying to calm himself. *I feel like such a stupid furball,* he told himself, wondering why he always felt like that when he tried to explain his problems. *What did I want Sparkpelt to say? What could she say?*

"Flamepaw?"

Sorrelstripe's voice sounded from somewhere behind him;

Flamepaw turned and saw, approaching from the direction of the camp, the gentle dark-brown she-cat who had nursed him when Sparkpelt was grieving.

"You seemed upset back there," she meowed. "I'm so sorry. Is there anything I can do to help?"

Though Flamepaw still struggled to find the words that would express what he was feeling, it had always been easier to talk to Sorrelstripe than to his own mother. "It's just . . . I let the kits help me today, just for fun, and Lilyheart scolded me about it. Why do I always feel that I'm doing things right, but every other cat thinks I'm wrong? I thought I was a good apprentice. I thought I would make a good warrior. . . ."

"You are, and you will," Sorrelstripe assured him, pressing her nose comfortingly against his cheek. "If you're sure you're ready, you should ask Lilyheart for another assessment. You don't have to wait until she thinks you're ready. You can prove it to her—to every cat. Especially to yourself, Flamepaw. I believe in you," she purred.

Flamepaw was so touched by her words that for several heartbeats he couldn't speak. At last, he touched his nose to hers. "Thank you, Sorrelstripe."

"Don't thank me," his foster mother mewed. "Prove it to me instead."

Suddenly full of resolution, Flamepaw drew himself up straight. "I will!" he promised. "I'll do whatever it takes to make you proud of me."

CHAPTER 8

The sun was going down over the RiverClan camp as the Clan waited for Reedwhisker and his hunting patrol to return. Every cat had found some reason to be in the clearing; Frostpaw could taste the nervous anticipation in the air, and feel her heart thumping against her rib cage. Her pelt tingled with expectation, yet she dreaded the moment when Reedwhisker would hear the terrible news.

Beside her, Mothwing was standing, thoughts swimming like minnows in her amber eyes. She had agreed to be the cat who would announce Mistystar's death to the Clan leader's son.

The mingled scents of cats and prey announced the return of the hunting party. A buzz of excitement and apprehension ran through the assembled cats, as if a swarm of bees had suddenly descended on the clearing. Frostpaw watched as the warriors straggled in through the clumps of hazel and bramble that surrounded the camp. Podlight was in the lead, followed by Fognose, Splashtail, and then Curlfeather. Frostpaw waited a few heartbeats, expecting to see Reedwhisker bringing up the rear, but he didn't appear. The other four cats were dragging in an enormous amount of prey, but the Clan deputy wasn't with them.

Mothwing stepped forward. "Where's Reedwhisker?" she demanded bluntly.

Podlight halted, flicking his tail as he dropped the two voles he was carrying. "Nice to see you too, Mothwing," he meowed, amusement in his eyes. "Isn't Reedwhisker here with you?"

Mothwing shook her head, while a confused muttering rose from the Clan. Frostpaw's pads prickled with a sudden sense that something was wrong.

"I'm sure he'll be back soon," Fognose meowed. "Have you noticed all the prey we brought home? It was a fantastic day's hunting!"

Mothwing let her gaze travel slowly over the patrol. "There's terrible news," she announced. "Mistystar is dead."

The amusement fled from Podlight's eyes and he stared at Mothwing in disbelief. "How?" he asked eventually. "Surely she wasn't on her last life!"

"It was sudden," Mothwing explained, "and I don't believe she felt much pain. But this was her last life. She has joined StarClan now; Frostpaw spoke to Willowshine, who welcomed Mistystar into their hunting grounds."

The four cats of the patrol stood looking at each other in stunned silence for a few moments. Frostpaw thought that her mother looked particularly shocked, her eyes wide and disbelieving. It was she who spoke at last. "She was a great leader."

Her gaze rested for a moment on Frostpaw, warm and

sympathetic, as if asking whether she was okay. Frostpaw gave her a tiny nod.

"Mistystar was amazing," Curlfeather went on, her whiskers drooping sadly. "Remember how she pulled the Clan back together after Darktail almost destroyed us?"

"And after that she was so brave, to go into the Dark Forest to defeat Ashfur," Podlight mewed, his voice full of awe. "She must have known she was on her last life then."

"She sacrificed so much for her Clan," Splashtail declared.

Murmurs of the same awe rose from the assembled cats as they joined in with memories of Mistystar, huddling together as if they felt the loss of their leader like a cold wind sweeping through the Clan.

Finally Mothwing interrupted. "About Reedwhisker . . . He's needed urgently. He will need to go to the Moonpool soon, to claim his nine lives and become Reedstar."

Podlight shook his head in bewilderment. "I don't know where he went. We lost track of him; I thought he'd just wandered off, chasing a rabbit or something."

"That's right," Curlfeather meowed. "We tried looking for him—we followed his scent trail, but there was rain last night, and the ground is too wet to hold a scent. In the end we thought he would be waiting for us back here in camp."

"Well, he isn't here," Mallownose stated.

Nightsky blinked anxiously. "Do you think we should be worried?" she asked.

"It's a bit early for that. But Reedwhisker is a responsible warrior," Mothwing muttered, half to herself. "He wouldn't just wander off." Frostpaw saw panic flash across her mentor's eyes, though within a heartbeat she drew herself up, clearly struggling to stay calm. "No," she declared. "Podlight is probably right. Most likely he got distracted chasing some prey and followed it into a ravine that he's having trouble getting out of, or he got lost."

Really? Frostpaw couldn't suppress her doubts. *When he knows our territory so well?* Though she hoped Mothwing was right, she began to believe something might have happened to Reedwhisker. Maybe he had had an accident, or run into a fox or badger. *But I can't say so. That will just make every cat more worried.*

"The light is fading," Mothwing continued, standing straighter with apparent confidence. "We need to send out search parties now if we're to have any hope of finding him tonight."

"Yes, we must find him soon," Curlfeather pointed out.

"It's the worst possible time for this to happen," Duskfur stated, ruffling her pelt.

"What was he thinking?" Owlnose grumbled. "He was supposed to be leading the patrol, not wandering off like some daft apprentice!"

Some cat spoke from the back of the crowd, their voice hollow with anxiety. "What if we never find him?"

"Of course we'll find him," Curlfeather mewed briskly. "We have to. Or else . . ." She let her voice trail off.

Frostpaw saw Mothwing wince, though she said nothing. But the medicine cat did not need to speak for Frostpaw to understand what her mother meant. *Or else RiverClan will be without a leader.* And then what would happen? *Has this ever happened before?*

"Mothwing, are you going to choose the search parties?" Curlfeather asked.

For a moment Mothwing hesitated. Frostpaw saw her glancing around, and suddenly realized that there was no obvious cat who should make the decision. Was it Mothwing's place as a medicine cat to do that, or should it be a senior warrior?

Then the golden tabby she-cat gave her pelt a shake. "Yes, thank you, Curlfeather. Owlnose, Havenpelt, Lizardtail, you can lead. Take whichever cats you want with you. Podlight, you and your patrol don't need to go out again, but organize a guard here, in case there's trouble we don't know about."

"We'll make sure the camp is safe," Curlfeather promised.

"What should we do if we run into a ShadowClan or Wind-Clan border patrol?" Owlnose asked as the cats split up into groups. "Should we mention . . . ?"

"Not yet," Mothwing mewed decisively. "The last thing we need is the other Clans tangling their paws in our business. But if Reedwhisker is still missing in the morning, we'll have no choice."

The camp seemed desolate once the search parties had left. The hunting patrol added their catch to the fresh-kill pile, making it as huge as Frostpaw had ever seen it, but no cat could do more than pick halfheartedly at the prey.

"We must prepare for Mistystar's vigil," Mothwing declared.

Frostpaw felt exhausted at the very thought. The shock of

Reedwhisker's disappearance had driven the thought of the Clan's farewell to their leader out of her mind.

"It won't be difficult to pay tribute to Mistystar," Shimmerpelt mewed. "She was such an important cat to us here in RiverClan. She did so much for so many. . . ."

A choking sound came from Mothwing's throat. Spinning around, she fled across the clearing and disappeared in the direction of her den.

"She must be really exhausted," Frostpaw murmured to her mother. "She tried to save Mistystar, and then she had to be strong for the rest of the Clan. I guess, now that the patrols are out, she can't hide her grief anymore."

Curlfeather shook her head, letting out a sigh of sorrow and compassion. "Mothwing and Mistystar were close for a very long time," she mewed. "Maybe closer still since they resolved their quarrel over the rebels, and Mothwing returned from ShadowClan."

Fognose nodded agreement. "How will we ever manage without Mistystar? She led our Clan through such difficult times."

"Reedwhisker will be a good leader," Podlight declared sadly. "But it won't be the same."

As her Clanmates continued to discuss the loss of Mistystar, Frostpaw rose slowly to her paws. At her mother's questioning look, she murmured, "I should go help Mothwing."

Frostpaw dipped her head to the rest of the cats, then headed out of the clearing and leaped down onto the stretch of pebbles between the stream and the medicine cats' den. Brushing aside the hanging vegetation that covered the entrance, she saw Mothwing curled deeply into her nest, her paws and tail over her face. Deep shudders coursed through her body.

"Mothwing?" Frostpaw mewed gently. There was no response from the medicine cat. Padding into the den, Frostpaw laid a paw on her mentor's shoulder. "I'm so sorry," she continued. "I know you were close to her."

"I can't believe that I'll never speak to her again." Mothwing's voice was stifled; she didn't move or look up at Frostpaw. "We lost so much time while I stayed with Shadow-Clan. Maybe I was too proud."

"Mistystar was proud, too." Frostpaw settled down beside the nest, her pelt brushing Mothwing's. "But she admitted that it was wrong to fight on Ashfur's side. And I know she understood why you stayed away," she mewed.

Mothwing let out a long sigh and turned her head to look sideways at Frostpaw. "Do you think Mistystar would be ready to talk to me?" she asked. "Could you check on her in StarClan?"

"I'm not sure it works like that," Frostpaw replied. It felt strange, having to explain this to her mentor, when she had only just been made an apprentice. *Who is there to explain things to me?* "From what I understand, StarClan cats communicate with us, not the other way around. You don't get to choose who you speak to."

"But you could try." Mothwing's amber gaze burned with eagerness. "I don't know how it works. I've always been shut off from StarClan—or I cut myself off. But . . . couldn't you try, Frostpaw?"

Frostpaw wasn't at all sure that it would work; she had only made contact with StarClan twice. And even then she hadn't been able to talk with the spirit cat. But she cared about her mentor, so desperately grief-stricken, and she wanted to ease her pain. "Of course," she responded.

Please, StarClan, don't let me fail, she prayed. *That would only hurt Mothwing more.*

She stretched out her paws, laid them on Mothwing's, and closed her eyes, trying to remember what she had done to ease Mistystar's passage into StarClan. *Please,* she thought, trying to cast her mind up through unmeasurable distance to the stars. *Please, Mistystar . . .*

For a long time Frostpaw could see nothing, only surging gray mist. Little memories of the day flickered through her mind: Mistystar falling; Curlfeather warning that they would have to find Reedwhisker soon; the huge fresh-kill pile.

Then a voice sounded in her head. *We must move on.*

Frostpaw's heart began to beat faster as she recognized Mistystar's voice, ringing out as clearly as when the leader would summon her Clan to a meeting. Focusing to remember every detail of Mistystar's face, she caught a sudden flash of her ice-blue eyes.

Mistystar! she thought fiercely. *Is that you? Are you all right?*

But the blue flash had vanished. Over and over again

Frostpaw tried to recover it, the silence growing heavier as she waited anxiously for the contact to be renewed. But she could see nothing except the swirling gray fog. Now even her memories had left her; she had to accept that for now it was over.

At last Frostpaw opened her eyes to see Mothwing gazing hopefully at her.

"Did you see anything?" the medicine cat asked.

Frostpaw nodded. "I did," she replied softly. "Mistystar told me that we must move on."

Mothwing drew in a wondering breath. "I knew she would speak to us," she murmured. "She knows that I will miss her terribly. . . . But she's right. We must all move on." She stretched out a paw and laid it on Frostpaw's. "Thank you," she mewed. "Thank you from the bottom of my heart."

Frostpaw still felt weak with grief from the day's terrible events, but warmth spread through her at Mothwing's words.

I helped my mentor, and my Clan.

CHAPTER 9

Sunbeam bounded across the camp, her paws itching to be on the move. At last she had been released from the medicine cats' den and allowed to go back to her warrior duties, and for the first time in days she would be able to join a hunting patrol. She could almost taste the warmth of the prey that she would catch.

Tawnypelt was gathering her patrol together outside the warriors' den. Scorchfur and Whorlpelt were with her; Sunbeam's paw steps slowed when she realized that the fourth cat was Lightleap.

Anxiety surged through Sunbeam, her enthusiasm ebbing, as she remembered how Tigerstar had spoken to her the day before about her part in the accident when Lightleap fell from the tree. He hadn't given her a punishment, but he had blamed her for going along with Lightleap's lie. "Watch your step," he had warned her. "Because I'll be watching you."

That's so unfair! she fumed to herself. *I didn't do anything wrong, and yet I've still ended up in trouble.*

But even more than the memory of the scolding from the Clan leader, Sunbeam was worried about the way Lightleap didn't want to be her friend anymore. *How can I concentrate on patrolling if she's still so hostile?*

Tawnypelt led her patrol toward the lake in the direction of the greenleaf Twolegplace at the border with RiverClan. The scents of the camp had not entirely faded before Sunbeam noticed that Lightleap had fallen to the back of the group, walking listlessly with her head down and her tail drooping.

Slackening her pace, Sunbeam let the rest of the patrol draw a little way ahead so that she could pad alongside Lightleap. *If she'll just let me explain why I told Shadowsight, she'll understand that I was only trying to help. Maybe then we can be real friends again.*

"Lightleap, I have to talk to you," she began. "I never meant to get you into trouble. I told Shadowsight because—"

"Yes, you told Shadowsight," Lightleap hissed, turning her head to glare at Sunbeam. "When you promised not to tell any cat. I trusted you!"

"I'm sorry, but I only wanted to help," Sunbeam defended herself. "I know how unhappy you are, Lightleap. But, honestly, no cat blames you for not going into the Dark Forest. I wouldn't have dared to set paw in there, not for all the mice in the forest. You don't have to—"

"I don't want to talk about the Dark Forest," Lightleap interrupted, her lips drawn back in a snarl. "And I certainly don't want to talk to *you.*"

"But I just want to be friends. . . ."

Sunbeam let her voice trail off as Lightleap picked up speed to catch up with the main patrol. When she was about to reach them, she seemed to realize that she didn't want to be with them, either; she veered away to one side, so that she was still walking alone.

Sunbeam felt an ache in her chest, as if a massive paw were pressing down on her heart. *Lightleap doesn't even want to speak to me!* Then she heard a tiny shriek, cut off as one of her Clanmates caught a mouse. Sunbeam realized that ever since she'd left camp, her thoughts had been full of Lightleap; she hadn't even tried to taste the air or listen for prey. *I'll mess up this whole patrol if I'm not careful.*

Raising her head, Sunbeam called out to Tawnypelt, "I'm going to try down here!" She gestured with her tail to a place where the undergrowth was massed more thickly.

"Okay!" Tawnypelt called back.

Sunbeam followed a narrow grassy track through banks of fern, keeping her ears pricked and stopping to taste the air every few paw steps. Soon she came to a dip where she could crouch unseen beneath the arching fronds and wait for prey. But even now she couldn't concentrate on the scents and tiny movements all around her.

Will Lightleap ever get over this and be my friend again? What if she doesn't?

Distracted by her dark thoughts, Sunbeam didn't notice the squirrel that scampered past her until its tail almost flicked the end of her nose. She charged out of the ferns, grabbing for the squirrel with her forepaws, but she was far too late. She gave chase as her prey headed for the nearest tree, but it raced up the trunk while she was still a couple of fox-lengths behind, and halted above her head, on a branch Sunbeam could tell was far too thin to bear her weight.

"Fox dung!" she snarled, glaring up at the squirrel. "Okay, you got lucky this time. But watch out, that's all!"

Missing what should have been an easy catch made Sunbeam feel even worse. *I've got to snap out of this and start behaving like a warrior!*

As she turned away, determined to put aside her worries and concentrate on hunting, Sunbeam heard a yowl of rage somewhere far ahead of her, as if a cat had been suddenly surprised by an enemy. It was followed—faintly, because of the distance—by the wet growl of a fighting cat.

Sunbeam froze, angling her ears in the direction of the sounds. She heard nothing more; cautiously, she began to head toward the noise, keeping to the shelter of the ferns or the shadows cast by tree trunks as she wove her way among the trees.

Her heart beating unpleasantly, Sunbeam tried to think who might be fighting on ShadowClan territory. *We don't have any enemies right now.* Ever since Bramblestar's return from the Dark Forest, and the defeat of Ashfur, there had been peace among the Clans. *So this must be rogues.*

Sunbeam's courage faltered at the thought. She had never had much dealing with rogues, but the elders around the fresh-kill pile in the evening told terrible stories about them. She tried to imagine herself fighting, going over the best moves and techniques to use, but that just made her realize she had no idea how many cats she would be facing. She was acutely aware that she had broken away from the hunting patrol; now she was quite alone.

Is it really wise for me to get into a fight?

Sunbeam decided that the most sensible thing she could do was to find the rest of her Clanmates and tell them what she had overheard. Tawnypelt, as the most senior warrior, could decide what to do.

Besides, she added to herself, *the noise was really far away. It could even have been coming from RiverClan, and if it was, that's their problem.*

As she turned away, heading for the spot where she had parted from the patrol, a breeze sprang up, fluttering the leaves and setting the fern fronds swaying to and fro. Sunbeam's nose twitched as she picked up a scent. Instantly she identified it as ShadowClan, and felt sudden relief that she must be closer to the patrol than she had expected.

Then the scent grew stronger, and Sunbeam was able to identify the cat it belonged to. Lightleap!

The fern fronds parted and the brown tabby she-cat limped into the open, coming from the direction where Sunbeam had heard the strange sounds. When she saw Sunbeam, she halted, with an awkward expression that rapidly changed to suspicion.

"Have you been following me?" she demanded, her voice harsh. "Are you spying on me?"

"No, I'm not, honestly," Sunbeam responded. "I was trying to spy for prey, but this StarClan-cursed squirrel got away from me."

Her attempt at humor had no effect on Lightleap, who simply turned her back on Sunbeam and limped away.

"What happened?" Sunbeam called after her. *Was it Lightleap I heard, fighting the rogues? Maybe she took another of those crazy risks. Is she badly hurt?*

Lightleap paused, looking back over her shoulder. "Nothing happened," she responded. "I trod on a thorn, that's all. Now leave me alone."

Sunbeam followed her, ready to scold her for dismissing her injury when there could be a threat to the Clan. *If there are rogues on our territory, then Tigerstar should know about it.* Anxiously she scanned Lightleap for any other wounds, but to her relief she couldn't see anything; Lightleap didn't look like a cat who had been in a fight.

She could be telling the truth, Sunbeam thought, *and she'll be even angrier with me if I suggest she's lying.*

She had decided not to say anything when Lightleap suddenly halted, spun around, and confronted her. "Stop trailing after me like you're a dumb kit!" she snapped. "What part of 'leave me alone' don't you understand?"

"I'm trying to be your friend!" Sunbeam protested. "But Great StarClan, Lightleap, you do make it difficult."

For a couple of heartbeats she thought she might have reached Lightleap, who stood rigid, staring at her in silence. But the moment didn't last. Lightleap let out an angry hiss and turned to pad off, leaving Sunbeam feeling even worse than when she had broken away from the rest of the hunting patrol. Somehow, instead of making up with Lightleap after the quarrel, she'd made her friend even more hostile.

I'd better find the others, she thought wearily. *And I don't think I'll tell Tawnypelt about the noise after all. I don't want to get into trouble again. Telling on Lightleap didn't go too well last time. Anyway, I'm sure it was nothing.*

Sunbeam sat outside the warriors' den in the ShadowClan camp, her gaze fixed on Lightleap, who was crouched beside the fresh-kill pile, sharing prey with her sister, Pouncestep. Although Sunbeam had just returned from the dawn patrol, and her belly was full from the mouse she had eaten when she arrived back in camp, she wasn't content. She still felt uneasily that she should have investigated the strange noises she had heard on the day before, or reported them to Tawnypelt.

But she had an even more pressing problem: Would Lightleap ever get over feeling that Sunbeam had betrayed her, so that they could be friends again? After they returned from hunting, Sunbeam had tried several times to speak to her, only to have Lightleap coldly turn her back, or make a great show of ignoring her while she talked with other Clanmates.

And what was she doing all by herself yesterday?

Movement at the camp entrance distracted her from these thoughts; she sat up as she saw the latest hunting patrol escort Sneezecloud and Brackenpelt of RiverClan into the clearing. Their heads were raised and their eyes wide; their legs seemed stiff as they headed into the center of the camp. Sunbeam could tell that something was wrong.

Cloverfoot rose from where she was sharing a squirrel with

Yarrowleaf near the fresh-kill pile and padded across to meet the newcomers. Sunbeam rose, too, and eased herself closer, curious to find out what all this was about. Lightleap followed the Clan deputy, her eyes bright with interest.

She doesn't look worried, or guilty, Sunbeam mused with relief. *This can't be about what happened yesterday.*

"Greetings," Cloverfoot began, with a slight dip of her head; her tone was chilly. "Why are you here?"

"Greetings, Cloverfoot." Brackenpelt halted in front of the Clan deputy. "We wanted to ask if any of your cats have seen Reedwhisker."

Cloverfoot blinked, looking a little bewildered. "I haven't," she stated. Swinging around, she let her gaze travel over the members of the Clan who were out in the clearing. "Reedwhisker? Any cat?"

There was no response except for a few shaken heads.

"What makes you think Reedwhisker would have been on ShadowClan territory?" Cloverfoot asked. "Surely you're not going to admit he might have been trespassing?"

Sneezecloud, standing at Brackenpelt's shoulder, gave his Clanmate an alarmed glance at this, but the tortoiseshell she-cat remained calm. "Of course not, Cloverfoot," she replied. "We have no reason to think he's here. But he went out on a hunt and Mistystar wanted him back in camp. There's nothing to worry about."

"Then I'll say good-bye. My Clanmates will escort you to the border."

Brackenpelt opened her jaws as if to protest that there was

no need, then closed them again, clearly thinking better of it. "Thank you for your help," she mewed at last.

Flanked on either side by their escort, the RiverClan cats headed out of camp. Just before they disappeared into the bushes, Sneezecloud looked back over his shoulder. "If any of you do see him," he called, "tell him that we're looking for him."

Excited chatter broke out among the ShadowClan cats as soon as the RiverClan cats were gone. Blazefire strolled over to stand at Sunbeam's side.

"That was so strange!" she exclaimed, turning to him.

Blazefire shrugged. "You shouldn't think too much about it," he advised her. "RiverClan has always been a weird bunch, right?"

"I suppose so." Though she agreed with Blazefire, Sunbeam remembered the noise of fighting in the forest, and the way Lightleap had appeared, limping, during the hunt. *Is all this somehow connected?*

"There's something I have to tell you," she meowed to Blazefire. "Follow me; we'll go where no cat will overhear us."

Blazefire rolled his eyes good-humoredly, but he followed Lightleap without protest to their favorite flat rock near the edge of the camp.

"I'm still really worried about Lightleap," Sunbeam continued when they were settled. She described how Lightleap had abandoned the hunting patrol, and later she herself had broken away to hunt alone. "And when we met up again, Lightleap accused me of spying. I know she's having a tough time," she finished, "but if she's getting up to something secret—whatever it is—who knows what might happen?"

Sunbeam paused, unwilling to share her worst fears, even with Blazefire. *Suppose Lightleap did see Reedwhisker, and fought with him? She might even have attacked him because he was trespassing—but if so, why didn't she report it? Oh, I can't tell any cat about this! It would make things even worse between me and Lightleap.*

Blazefire was obviously waiting for her to continue; Sunbeam rapidly thought of something to say that didn't sound too mouse-brained. "A distracted warrior could be a liability to her Clanmates, right?"

To her dismay, Blazefire didn't look as worried as she had expected. "You only ran into Lightleap because *you* had wandered off," he pointed out coolly. "Wouldn't you count as a 'distracted warrior,' too?"

"That's different," Sunbeam protested, though she knew she was doing a poor job of convincing Blazefire.

"I know you're concerned about Lightleap," Blazefire continued, resting his tail-tip briefly on Sunbeam's shoulder. "You're a good friend. But you can't be too hard on her, or get too caught up in the rules. Lightleap's father is our leader, remember—not you."

"I know who our leader is!" Sunbeam responded, hurt that Blazefire would scold her instead of sympathizing with her.

"Then maybe you should loosen up a little bit," Blazefire suggested.

"Maybe." Sunbeam could hardly get the word out. She had been so sure that Blazefire would support her. Instead he was dismissing her concerns about Lightleap as if he were flicking a fly off his fresh-kill. Usually he would agree with her, or tease her affectionately about how she was focused on the rules, but he wasn't teasing now.

Sunbeam turned her head away to hide her sense of betrayal. *Oh, Blazefire, I know that something is really, really wrong! And what in StarClan's name am I going to do about it?*

CHAPTER 10

❧

Flamepaw paced back and forth at the bottom of the cliff beneath the Highledge, every so often casting a glance up at the entrance to the Clan leader's den. He startled at the sound of paw steps behind him and spun around to see his sister, Finchlight.

"You scared me out of my fur!" he exclaimed.

"Sorry," Finchlight responded, brushing her tail against his side, "but there's no need to get so worked up."

"That's easy for you to say," Flamepaw grumbled. "You're a warrior already. This new assessment is really important for me."

"Just relax," Finchlight meowed, pushing her muzzle against Flamepaw's shoulder. "Trust your instincts, and don't dwell on how you messed up last time."

Messed up? For a moment Flamepaw was furious with his sister for being so blunt. *But she's right,* he admitted, *so there's no point in getting angry with her. Or with myself . . .*

Flamepaw nodded, trying to let his lingering fury at himself fade like mist under the sun. He knew that he shouldn't have been trying to show off. *If I hadn't been such a stupid furball, I would be a warrior by now.*

"You're right," he told Finchlight. "I have to put all that out of my mind. Bramblestar has agreed to come and watch me today, to support me, because I'm his kin."

Saying the words made Flamepaw feel immensely proud. *My Clan leader is taking trouble especially for me! If I have to live up to the pressure of my famous family, at least I get something out of it,* he added to himself wryly.

"Are you sure?" Finchlight asked, with a doubtful glance up at the Highledge. "No cat has seen much of Bramblestar today. He hasn't come out of his den in ages. And I'm sure I heard him and Squirrelflight arguing up there earlier."

"Bramblestar promised he would be there," Flamepaw assured her. "And our Clan leader doesn't break his promises."

He remembered how Bramblestar had looked when he made the promise: the interest and approval glowing in his amber eyes. For a long time Flamepaw hadn't believed that he belonged in his Clan, but finally, under that warm gaze, he could see a way to prove himself.

Now he flexed his claws impatiently; he felt as though every hair on his pelt were straining to begin the assessment.

Should I tell Bramblestar I'm going to get started? Would that make him get a move on?

Flamepaw took a few uncertain paces toward the bottom of the tumbled rocks that led up to the Highledge, only to halt as a cry came up from Twigbranch, who was on guard at the camp entrance.

"RiverClan cats!"

Turning toward the sound, Flamepaw saw four cats emerging from the thorn tunnel. Poppyfrost was in the lead, followed by two RiverClan warriors—Flamepaw thought he recognized Minnowtail and Havenpelt. Molewhisker brought up the rear.

"We came across these cats while we were patrolling the border," Molewhisker announced to his Clanmates. With a glance at the newcomers, he asked, "Do you want to see Bramblestar?"

The two she-cats both shook their head. "Oh, we wouldn't want to disturb him," Minnowtail meowed. "We just wanted to know if any cat had seen Reedwhisker. Has he been here at all?"

Flamepaw shot Finchlight a confused glance. "Reedwhisker, here? Have they got bees in their brain?" he muttered.

All the ThunderClan cats were staring at the newcomers with identical blank expressions. "Why would Reedwhisker have come so far away from RiverClan?" Molewhisker asked. "Especially when he would have to cross other territories to get here? Did he need to meet with Squirrelflight or Bramblestar?"

"Oh, no reason." Flamepaw noticed how swiftly Minnowtail replied: so swiftly that he began to wonder whether she was hiding something. "It's not important."

"Except he went off without telling any cat where," Havenpelt explained. "While we were on patrol, we just thought we'd drop by and ask if any cat had seen him."

"No. We haven't." Bumblestripe's voice was cold.

Minnowtail dipped her head politely. "Thanks, anyway. We'll be going, then."

"Sorry for intruding," Havenpelt added.

The two she-cats turned and bounded out through the thorn tunnel. Their ThunderClan escort, taken by surprise at their abrupt departure, had to race to catch up with them.

"That was weird," Flamepaw remarked, padding forward with Finchlight to join the cats who were beginning to gather near the camp entrance.

Bumblestripe, pressing up behind him, let out a derisive snort. "RiverClan has always been weird."

"It must be all that fish they eat," Cherryfall added. "And now they seem to have lost their deputy. How did they manage that?"

Thriftear shrugged. "Who knows?"

"What I'd like to know is this," Thornclaw began, raising his voice to be heard over the general chatter. "Could those two really have been on a patrol that brought them all the way to the ThunderClan border? They'd have to cross through another Clan's territory. They didn't just 'drop in.' They came here for a reason, and maybe it wasn't to look for Reedwhisker."

"Thornclaw's right," Twigbranch meowed. "Is there any cat who's not worried that they might be up to something? Don't forget, Mistystar sided with the fake Bramblestar. How can we be sure that she has the Clans' best interests at heart now?"

Honeyfur glared at Twigbranch, her shoulder fur bushing

up and the tip of her tail twitching. "So what if Mistystar sided with the impostor?" she snapped. "Lots of cats did that—even here in ThunderClan!"

An outcry followed her words. Cats who had rebelled when Ashfur was controlling Bramblestar faced up to those who had stayed loyal to the cat they'd believed was their leader. Flamepaw took a pace back, alarmed by the bristling pelts, lashing tails, and lips drawn back in a snarl. He had only been an apprentice when the impostor had ruled ThunderClan, but Sparkpelt had sided against him, and that had separated Flamepaw from his mother and sister. Glancing around, he spotted Sparkpelt in the crowd; her orange fur was bristling as she glared at Honeyfur.

"We'll always be ready for future betrayals," Lionblaze hissed. "No impostor will ever deceive ThunderClan again."

"But surely nothing like that *could* ever happen again." Finleap was obviously trying to sound reasonable. "How many cats like Ashfur could there be?"

Lionblaze's only response was a growl from deep in his throat.

"They're not actually going to fight, are they?" Flamepaw muttered to Finchlight.

His sister blinked uneasily. "Some cat ought to stop them," she responded, with a glance up at the Highledge.

To Flamepaw's relief, Squirrelflight emerged from the leader's den and ran lightly down the tumbled rocks to halt on the fringe of the group of furious cats. "What in StarClan's name is going on here?" she demanded. "No—don't tell me.

I don't want to know. Just break it up. Do none of you have duties you should be doing?"

Her scathing words quieted the angry cats, who stepped away from one another, looking ashamed of themselves. Twigbranch went back to her place at the mouth of the tunnel, while Lionblaze started to call together a hunting patrol.

Squirrelflight watched for a moment with sharp green eyes until she was sure that the stormy exchange was over, then turned to Flamepaw. "Are you ready to start your assessment?" she asked.

Flamepaw jumped; in the midst of all the commotion he had almost forgotten his assessment. At Squirrelflight's words his optimism wavered a little. "Isn't Bramblestar coming?"

Squirrelflight's gaze flicked back toward the Clan leader's den, and a shadow crossed her face. Flamepaw thought she seemed troubled, though she was clearly trying to hide it. "Bramblestar has other things to take care of," she explained, seeming to choose her words carefully. "So I'll be observing you in his place. Go and find Lilyheart, and we'll get going."

Flamepaw nodded. "Sure, Squirrelflight."

All the same, as he trudged across the camp to call Lilyheart from the warriors' den, Flamepaw felt weighed down by disappointment. He had felt special—really important—when he thought that his Clan leader was going to observe his assessment. It had given him confidence, a hope that he was really talented. *Cats are always telling me I'm special, but just for a while I really felt special.*

But now it wasn't going to happen.

Maybe Bramblestar isn't coming because he knows you'll fail, a nagging voice in Flamepaw's mind suggested. He knew how mouse-brained that idea was, but he couldn't quite push it out of his mind.

I should have known, he thought bitterly. *I should have known that Bramblestar wouldn't keep his promise. None of the rest of my kin keep theirs, so why should he?*

Flamepaw crouched in the long grass beside the old Thunderpath, in the shadow of the abandoned Twoleg nest. This time he wasn't looking for something impressive. He was determined to catch anything and everything that crossed his path. It was just his bad luck that so far the prey wasn't running well.

It's like I've been here for moons, he thought. *Lilyheart's going to fail me again because there isn't any prey.*

Tasting the air carefully, Flamepaw picked up a very faint scent of thrush, along with another bird-scent that he couldn't place. It was far away, but it was the only scent he had detected since he came out here.

Suppose this is part of the test? he asked himself. *Suppose Lilyheart told me to start here so I could show initiative?*

Flamepaw slid out of the long grass and padded along the old Thunderpath in the direction of the scent. Soon he spotted the thrush, fluttering from one bush to the next.

Yes!

Flattening his belly to the ground, Flamepaw crept along, moving so silently that he couldn't even hear his own paw steps. He remembered to check the wind direction and scanned the ground for any loose twigs or dead leaves that might give him away if he stepped on them.

I hope Lilyheart is watching this.

The thrush had flown up to a low tree branch. Flamepaw's heart hammered with anticipation as he waited for it to come down again. As the moments passed, he began to feel more and more impatient, wondering what his chances would be if he tried to jump into the tree himself.

Then a shadow swept over him. Looking up, Flamepaw realized what the other bird-scent had been.

A hawk!

Flamepaw got a good view of the barred gray wings, the hooked beak, and the talons as the hawk swooped down over his head, then gained height again. *Has it seen the thrush, or is it just flying?* he wondered.

Watching the hawk carefully, Flamepaw realized it must have seen the prey, otherwise it would have flown off, or found a branch to perch on.

Am I quicker than a hawk?

Flamepaw closed his eyes to think, then opened them again as a throb of panic went through him. That had been a mouse-brained thing to do, he reflected, closing his eyes when a hawk was flying around. But it wouldn't be mouse-brained if he could snatch the thrush from under the fierce bird's beak.

He wondered if his mentor would have to pass him, if he managed to beat a hawk to the prey.

He slid out his claws, digging them deep into the ground. His whole body was curled into a knot of nervous tension. He imagined the Clan deputy herself praising him for his daring. Her green eyes would be wide with amazement at his skill. She would tell him she had never seen such a spectacular catch. She might even tell Bramblestar, and then the Clan leader would be sorry he'd missed seeing it. Letting the scene flow through his mind, Flamepaw convinced himself that he had to go through with it.

He waited until the hawk flew up higher again. Then he gathered his hindquarters under him and pushed off into a massive leap toward the branch where the thrush still perched. Lashing out with one forepaw, he knocked it off balance and pounced on it as it hit the ground.

The thrush was flapping wildly under his claws. Flamepaw picked it up in his mouth and raced back toward his original hiding place. Behind him he could hear the hawk's wings beating angrily, but when he risked a glance over his shoulder, it didn't seem to be following him.

Once Flamepaw felt safe, he slowed down. Instantly the thrush tried to escape his grip, fighting so hard that he was afraid he would lose a tooth. He ducked his head to the ground, opened his jaws, then slammed them shut again to kill the prey. Dropping its limp body, he sat back on his hindquarters. *That went pretty well,* he congratulated himself.

While he was still getting his breath back, his mentor and the Clan deputy emerged from behind the abandoned Twoleg nest.

"That took courage," Lilyheart meowed with a nod of approval.

Flamepaw felt a purr rising in his throat at his mentor's words, only to stifle it a heartbeat later at the sight of Squirrelflight's critical expression.

"Courage, yes," the Clan deputy agreed. "But Flamepaw, how reckless of you was it to put yourself in a position where you might have to fight a hawk? Even seasoned warriors wouldn't do that lightly. What if you'd lost? Where would ThunderClan have been then?"

"But I—" Flamepaw tried to interrupt. His vision of Squirrelflight praising him faded like mist under the morning sun.

Squirrelflight swept on regardless. "If catching a piece of prey carries that much risk, you would do well to think through your options and make better decisions."

Lilyheart was listening to the deputy with a confused look on her face. "Does that mean I shouldn't pass him?" she asked.

"It's your decision, Lilyheart," Squirrelflight replied. "I'm just offering my opinion."

Lilyheart paused, frowning, while Flamepaw felt tension thrilling through him from ears to tail-tip. At last his mentor faced Flamepaw, gazing straight into his eyes.

"I'm sorry, Flamepaw," she mewed, "but I think you need more time, to grow into some more cautious habits."

Flamepaw gaped at her, hardly able to believe what he had just heard. *She's failing me again? I was told to catch prey, and I caught prey—and I outsmarted a hawk! They're going to fail me for that?* Angrily he dug his claws into the ground. *Maybe they just want an apprentice around to do all the horrible jobs.*

Disappointment throbbing through him, Flamepaw couldn't find anything to say. Squirrelflight was his kin, his mother's mother, and that was supposed to be important. That was why he had the name that didn't fit him at all, the name he was struggling to live up to, even though he didn't want to have to live up to it.

It took all Flamepaw's strength to stop his resentment from showing in his face as he turned away and began plodding back to camp.

Flamepaw crouched by himself near the wall of the stone hollow, in the shade of an elder bush that was rooted in a crack above his head. He stared at his paws so that he wouldn't accidentally catch the eye of any of his Clanmates. Since word had gotten around that he had failed his assessment again, everything had been really awkward. His Clanmates seemed quite happy to avoid him, too; he could tell that no cat knew what to say to an apprentice who had failed his warrior assessment twice.

The patter of paw steps broke into his thoughts, followed by his sister Finchlight's voice. "Do you want to come and eat?"

Flamepaw looked up at her. "I'm not hungry," he snapped.

For a heartbeat Finchlight blinked thoughtfully, then sat

beside him, so close that their pelts were brushing. "You'll pass next time," she mewed.

"That's easy for you to say," Flamepaw retorted, turning his head away. "You weren't let down by both of our mother's parents."

"I'm sure Squirrelflight had her reasons," Finchlight insisted. "She was probably doing what she thought was best for the Clan."

Flamepaw let out a snort. "Shouldn't kin be more important than Clan?"

"No!" Finchlight's gazed at him in disbelief. "Nothing is more important than Clan, and ThunderClan has a long way to go before we recover from Ash—"

"How long are we all going to keep talking about Ashfur, and what happened?" Flamepaw demanded, tossing his head as if he wanted to get rid of a troublesome fly. His anger with his sister was swelling; he just wished she would go away. "How long are we going to make that the excuse for everything? I bet the other Clans aren't obsessing over it like we are."

Finchlight's eyes stretched wide with shock, but her voice was calm as she responded. "ThunderClan has always been the natural leader of all the Clans," she pointed out. "For that reason, we have to hold ourselves to a higher standard."

"That's mouse-brained!" Flamepaw let out a *mrrow* of angry laughter. "Try telling that to Tigerstar and see what he says. Or any of the other leaders. Anyway," he added, "Squirrelflight probably hates me now because she doesn't think my name should belong to a failure."

Finchlight's shocked expression intensified, and her tail-tip twitched irritably. "Do you really think that?" she asked.

Flamepaw didn't reply. He just hunched his shoulders and stared at his paws. *Stop meowing on and go away,* he thought.

His sister heaved a heavy sigh and shook her head, rising to her paws. "If you're really so immature that you believe that," she told him, "then maybe it *is* the right thing that you're still an apprentice."

CHAPTER 11

Frostpaw parted her jaws in a massive yawn, then rose to arch her back in a good long stretch. The night before, RiverClan had sat vigil for their dead leader; in spite of Frostpaw's sorrow, it had been a wonderful experience for her to stay up all night and listen to the stories about how great Mistystar had been, how much she had been loved, and events that had happened before Frostpaw was even born. At last, when Mosspelt had taken Mistystar's body out to be buried, helped by Mothwing and Duskfur, and the new day's essential duties had been dealt with, most cats had settled down to sleep, worn out by their grief.

Now the sun was going down over the RiverClan camp and the cats were waking again. Frostpaw could tell that they were still weighed down by the loss of their leader, but what really worried her was the tension she could sense in almost every cat in camp: tension that had gripped the Clan like claws fastening deep in their fur as they wondered what had happened to Reedwhisker.

The cats who'd been sent out to ask the rest of the Clans had come back to report that no cat had seen him. And there was no trace of him anywhere in the territory; while his scent could be picked up here and there, there was no clear trail to show where he had gone.

Where can Reedwhisker be?

Frostpaw had never experienced the change from one leader to another. Few RiverClan cats were old enough to remember their previous leader, Leopardstar, since Mistystar had been their leader for so long. She wondered anxiously what was supposed to happen. Would StarClan be angry if they had to wait for the new leader to journey to the Moonpool?

Will they even let us have a new leader if we can't find Reedwhisker?

Gradually, cats were beginning to congregate around the fresh-kill pile, exchanging worried glances with each other. Frostpaw padded over to join them, stopping beside her mother.

"Should we have an acting leader?" Duskfur suggested, her voice shaking with nervousness. "If Reedwhisker doesn't—"

"Reedwhisker will come back!" Podlight interrupted his mother harshly. "Why would any cat think he won't? We don't want to tempt fate like that, do we?"

"Of course no cat wants to tempt fate," Owlnose responded with more caution, "and we definitely don't want to start a panic, but if we've learned one thing from our recent troubles, it's that we should be prepared to adapt when we have to."

"Owlnose is right," Nightsky agreed, with a flick of her ears toward the brown tabby tom. "If all the Clans are making suggestions to StarClan about how to depose a leader, then surely we should think about the decisions we'll make if we find ourselves without a leader or a deputy."

"Well, some cat has to take responsibility for now," Curl-feather asserted, with a glance around her as if she was wondering which cat might be suitable.

"It seems obvious to me," Duskfur responded. "It should be our medicine cat."

Mallownose nodded agreement. "Yeah, medicine cats are wise."

"But our medicine cat doesn't exactly revere StarClan," Shimmerpelt pointed out. "And Frostpaw is a new apprentice."

Frostpaw felt every hair on her pelt begin to rise in sheer terror. *They wouldn't ask me to lead, would they? They can't! But . . . what if they did?* She stared at her paws, desperate not to catch any cat's gaze. *I'm too young . . . I don't have the experience—and I don't want to!*

An image flashed into her mind of herself sitting on the Highstump, with the Clan gathered around, listening to her. *I guess that would be nice, except I don't have any idea what I would tell them. And what if we were attacked? I couldn't lead the Clan into a fight!* A shiver ran through her, right down to the tips of her claws. *Suppose I had to sort out a border dispute with Tigerstar or Harestar? It would be just awful!*

Frostpaw heaved a deep sigh. She knew that what she really wanted was to help other cats, not tell them what to do. *I'm a medicine cat, not a leader.*

Meanwhile, every cat had turned their head to look at Mothwing. So far she had said nothing, sitting with her paws tucked under her and her amber eyes flicking from one speaker to the next. "Shimmerpelt is right," she meowed, blinking slowly. "Besides, leading a Clan is not the role of a medicine cat."

Frostpaw felt a wave of relief. In the crowd, she spotted her littermate, Mistpaw, watching her with sympathetic eyes. Graypaw stood close by. For a moment, Frostpaw wished she could leave Mothwing's side and go cuddle with her littermates, like they had when they were small, before Curlfeather realized she was having visions. Sometimes she wished she could join them in the warriors' den—both to be close to them, and for the chance to watch discussions like these with no responsibility for solving the problems.

Sometimes being a medicine cat apprentice was very lonely.

"Maybe one day Frostpaw could," Curlfeather declared, "but for now I think it's best that one of our senior warriors take it on."

"I wouldn't mind doing it," Podlight offered.

Mallownose glared at him, his shoulder fur beginning to bristle. "Why you?" he demanded. "I have just as much right— "

"Stupid furballs!" Lizardtail interrupted. "What's the point of arguing about it, when Reedwhisker will be back soon?"

Frostpaw purred her agreement, pleased to see Reedwhisker's former apprentice sticking up for him. But to Frostpaw's dismay, few cats listened to Lizardtail.

"We don't know that," Duskfur retorted, glaring at him.

"And are we supposed to sit around on our tails, waiting

until he does?" Shimmerpelt demanded. "Meanwhile, I'm happy to act as leader—"

A chorus of yowls drowned out what she was saying. Frostpaw tried to ignore the quarreling voices while she wrestled with the tension she could feel growing inside her. She knew that it wouldn't be much longer that they could go on hoping that Reedwhisker would return, and worry wrapped around her like strands of cobweb at the thought that RiverClan would be without a leader.

She startled nervously at the touch of a nose on her ear, and looked up to see Curlfeather gazing down at her sympathetically.

"This is all too much for you, isn't it?" her mother murmured. "Why don't you go to your den and find something useful to do? You don't have to listen to all this nonsense."

Frostpaw gave her mother a grateful purr. "I'll do that," she responded. "There are some fresh herbs that need sorting."

She felt her tension begin to ebb away as she bounded across the clearing, pushed her way through the bushes that surrounded it, and leaped from the bank onto the stretch of pebbles in front of the medicine cats' den.

But as she slipped inside the den to where she and Mothwing had stored the herbs they'd collected earlier, she noticed something odd about her own nest. She had arranged her bedding just how she liked it, with a layer of moss padding the heap of bracken, but now a large dock leaf was lying across the edge.

That wasn't there when we put the herbs away, she thought. She gave the leaf a sniff. But there were so many competing scents inside the den that it told her nothing useful.

It wasn't just an ordinary dock leaf, though, Frostpaw realized. Parts of it had been torn away, so that it looked almost like a star. *A star?* Frostpaw felt a shiver run through her from ears to tail-tip. Something told her it was very important. Was it a message from StarClan, with advice she could give to her Clan? Surely it couldn't mean that she was meant to be a 'star—a leader!*I'm only an apprentice,* she told herself. She was well aware how inexperienced she was, and she just didn't feel ready to deal with all the turmoil in the Clan. *I wish it were all over, and I could just have a normal apprenticeship.*

Frostpaw was reluctant to show the leaf to any other cat, even Mothwing. She was too afraid that they would take it as a sign that she should be leader. But eventually she realized that it was just a leaf, and the only thing she could do was to take it and show it to her mentor and her other Clanmates.

When she returned to the clearing, the argument was still going on, but Curlfeather spotted her as she approached, and rose to her paws. "What do you have there?" she asked.

Frostpaw made her way to her mentor's side and dropped the leaf. "I found this in my nest," she explained. "It wasn't there before."

Her Clanmates' voices died away as they crowded around to see what Frostpaw had brought.

"It looks like a star," some cat murmured.

"Could it be . . . ?"

"Maybe it's a sign."

"Could this mean that StarClan is letting us know we haven't been abandoned?" Curlfeather asked, fixing Mothwing with a pointed stare. "Could it be a sign that we're on the right track?"

"Yes, and that StarClan wants our medicine cats to take on more responsibility," Havenpelt agreed. "That they should collaborate with our senior warriors until we have a StarClan-approved leader."

Mothwing clearly disapproved of Curlfeather's and Havenpelt's words, and of the murmurs of agreement that came from their Clanmates. "I really don't want the responsibility," she grumbled, "and in any case, I wouldn't be StarClan's first choice for leader, would I? And I'm more comfortable healing than leading."

"That may be true," Curlfeather meowed. "But we need some sort of arrangement until we find Reedwhisker."

"Frostpaw can speak to StarClan," Podlight pointed out. "Even though she's not a full medicine cat yet, maybe she can be their messenger, and pass on their wisdom to Mothwing."

A tide of apprehension engulfed Frostpaw at the thought of so much responsibility, but before she could protest, a chorus of approval broke out at Podlight's suggestion. From her Clanmates' eagerness, Frostpaw realized that every cat was sick of arguing, and ready for any solution that would save the Clan if they were left without a leader.

Though Mothwing still didn't look enthusiastic, she seemed to have no choice but to relent. "Very well," she declared. "If we never find Reedwhisker, and if we ever find ourselves in the terrible situation of being leaderless, Frostpaw and I will lead the Clan until StarClan guides us to a new leader. But the thing that worries me most," she continued, "is that we have no experience. What does every cat think of asking one of the other leaders for help?"

Almost before she could finish, the rest of the Clan yowled her down.

"Humble ourselves to another Clan?" Mallownose sounded shocked out of his fur. "Never!"

"It's all speculation, in any case," Mothwing reminded them defensively. "Reedwhisker will be back soon, and we'll all forget that we ever had this discussion."

Once again, Frostpaw drew away, trying not to imagine the dark future in which she would be burdened with the responsibility of leading the Clan. Even though it wasn't happening—and wouldn't ever happen—she could feel the weight of it on her back, pushing her down like an enemy who meant to drive the breath out of her.

Wrapped up in her worries, she jumped as Curlfeather appeared at her side. "What's the matter?" her mother asked gently.

"I'm just afraid that the Clan is asking too much of me," Frostpaw confessed. "I don't know enough! I can't be a leader—I can't even give Mothwing the help she needs."

"You don't have to worry," her mother murmured, giving her ear an affectionate lick. "If it ever comes to it, that you have to take on leadership as well as your medicine-cat duties, you know that I'll always be here to help."

Frostpaw relaxed a little at her mother's loving words. However bad things were, at least she had her mother by her side. And it wasn't as if it was ever likely to happen!

CHAPTER 12

The rising sun had not yet cleared the trees, and the air felt moist and fresh, with mist still lingering in shaded hollows. Sunbeam padded along the ShadowClan border beside Hollowspring and Hopwhisker. Though she had found it hard to wake up for the dawn patrol, she was glad of the distraction from her worries about Lightleap, and her frustration that Blazefire had refused to take her side.

It's hard—Lightleap's avoiding me, and I don't want to talk to Blazefire right now, Sunbeam thought. *I get along fine with Hopwhisker and my brother, but it's not the same.*

"I don't expect we'll run into trouble," Hopwhisker, who was leading the patrol, meowed. "Everything has been so peaceful since we got rid of Ashfur."

A soft growl came from Hollowspring's throat. "We'll never forget what that mange-pelt did to us. But now at least it feels as if the five Clans are closer than ever before."

Hopwhisker nodded agreement. "Who knows?" she murmured. "Maybe one day soon there'll be so much peace and stability, there won't even need to be a border patrol."

Hollowspring let out a *mrrow* of amusement. "You're just

hoping for that so you don't have to leave your nice warm nest at dawn anymore."

The patrol leader gave her Clanmate a playful shove. "I am not!" she insisted. "I wouldn't like it at all. It would be so boring!"

"No," Hollowspring insisted. "There would be more time for hunting and battle training."

"Battle training?" Hopwhisker rolled her eyes. "There would be no point in battle training if everything was peaceful. We would just lie around getting fat and lazy. We might as well go and be kittypets!"

Sunbeam felt too depressed to join in the gentle teasing. "I have a horrible feeling there are always going to be enemies," she declared. "There will always be cats who go bad."

Hopwhisker and Hollowspring fell silent, staring at Sunbeam, before glancing at each other, then swiveling their gaze back to her.

"Great StarClan, you're cheerful this morning!" her littermate Hollowspring meowed.

Sunbeam didn't respond, and a moment later Hopwhisker signaled for silence as they approached the greenleaf Twolegplace that formed the border with RiverClan.

There were no Twolegs about this morning, but plenty of evidence that they had been there. Scanning the halfbridge that jutted out into the lake, and the stretch of open ground covered with hard, black Thunderpath stuff, Sunbeam could see Twoleg garbage strewn everywhere. The stink of it filled her nostrils.

"Just look at that!" Hollowspring explained. "It's disgusting."

"Why do they leave such a mess?" Sunbeam asked. "Do you suppose their dens are like that, too?"

"I wouldn't be surprised," Hopwhisker grumbled. "But we ought to check it out—what if this mess is hiding prey?"

She padded forward to the edge of the open ground and began to nose at a crumpled white object like a huge leaf. A moment later she started back, letting out a yowl of pain and holding up one forepaw. As Sunbeam and Hollowspring raced toward her, she collapsed on one side and curled around herself, whimpering in agony.

When she reached her, Sunbeam noticed blood pouring out of Hopwhisker's paw; looking more closely, she saw an ugly gash across her pads. "What happened?" she asked.

Hopwhisker pointed with her tail. "I cut it on that . . . thing."

Underneath the crumpled leaf thing, Sunbeam spotted something hard and shiny, with an uneven edge sharper than a claw. "Twolegs!" she exclaimed. "I'd like to claw their pelts off. This isn't the first time we've had trouble with their garbage."

"Never mind that," Hollowspring mewed. "We'd better get Hopwhisker to Puddleshine and Shadowsight right away."

Sunbeam glanced back briefly in the direction they had come. "We're closer to RiverClan than we are to our own camp," she pointed out. "We should take Hopwhisker to Mothwing." When Hollowspring gave her a dubious look, she added, "It'll take forever to get her home like this, and there's a good chance the wound will get dirty and infected. That will make it so much harder for the medicine cats to treat her. Mothwing will be quicker."

"Quicker is good," Hopwhisker hissed through clenched teeth. "This is really hurting."

Hollowspring still looked doubtful; he took a couple of paw steps in the direction of RiverClan, scanning the undergrowth. Sunbeam followed him, then halted when a powerful wave of scent washed over her from the far side of the border.

"Smell that?," Sunbeam mewed. "There must be a River-Clan patrol. I could ask them."

"Okay," Hollowspring agreed.

Sunbeam raced across the stretch of Thunderpath stuff. As she ran, she spotted two RiverClan cats facing each other among the undergrowth. "Hi, Lizardtail! Hi, Nightsky!" she called out to them. "Can you help us?"

The RiverClan warriors turned toward her, seeming startled. Sunbeam was puzzled; now that she had gotten closer, they didn't look like cats on patrol. It was as if they had been having a tense conversation, and didn't welcome the interruption.

Halting in front of them, Sunbeam dipped her head politely. "We have an injured warrior," she meowed. "Please may we take her to Mothwing?"

Lizardtail and Nightsky exchanged a glance. "Why can't you just take her back to ShadowClan?" Lizardtail asked.

Sunbeam was briefly disconcerted; she hadn't expected such a cold response, not when the Clans were at peace. "Our camp is so far away," she explained. "Hopwhisker has a deep wound on her paw that could get badly infected." When the two RiverClan cats still hesitated, she added more urgently, "This is medicine-cat business, right? Medicine cats aren't supposed to care about borders."

Nightsky and Lizardtail exchanged a glance. Sunbeam thought that Nightsky in particular seemed agitated; both cats looked as if they would really like to refuse but couldn't think of any way they could argue with what Sunbeam had just said. "Okay," Nightsky meowed curtly.

Sunbeam raced back to where she had left her Clanmates. Between them, she and Hollowspring helped Hopwhisker to rise, and supported her across the border to where the River-Clan cats were waiting.

Lizardtail and Nightsky led them along the edge of the lake, in the direction of the RiverClan camp. Sunbeam was puzzled; she could still sense tension between the RiverClan warriors.

It can't just be because we're here. There was something going on with them before we even arrived.

Their escort led them to the place where one of the streams that surrounded the RiverClan camp flowed out of the lake. Nightsky halted on the bank.

"You can wait here," she directed. "I'll fetch Mothwing." She bounded off before any cat could object.

"That doesn't make sense," Hollowspring meowed, looking after the dark gray she-cat with a confused expression on his face. "Why bring Mothwing out here, where she won't have any supplies?"

Lizardtail's only response was a shrug.

Not many moments had passed before Mothwing appeared, padding along the bank of the stream with her apprentice, Frostpaw, following her. Both cats carried leaf wraps of herbs in their jaws.

"Okay, Hopwhisker," Mothwing mewed as she set her herbs down beside the injured cat. "Let's take a look at this paw. Frostpaw, see if you can find some cobwebs. Among the roots of trees is a good place."

Frostpaw darted off, while Mothwing bent her head over Hopwhisker's wound and gave it a deep sniff. "Okay, lick it clean," she continued. "I'll make you a poultice of horsetail. That should help stop the bleeding."

While Hopwhisker obeyed, Sunbeam exchanged an anxious look with Hollowspring. She could see in his eyes the same suspicion that she herself was feeling. *It's like something is going on in RiverClan—but what? Why don't they want us to go into their camp?*

While Mothwing was preoccupied, Sunbeam silently crept away, then leaped across the stream and climbed the bank. At the top she dived into the bushes and slid forward until she could peer into the RiverClan camp.

Not many of the Clan were out in the clearing, and they all seemed to have the same air of tension as Nightsky and Lizardtail. One or two were pacing to and fro, their tails flicking and their shoulder fur bristling. Others had their heads together, as if they were in serious discussion about something. No cat was doing anything useful, and there was no sign of Mistystar or her deputy.

This is all really weird . . .

As cautiously as if she were stalking a mouse, Sunbeam backed out of the bushes, then fled down the bank and back across the stream. Breathing a sigh of relief that no RiverClan cat had spotted her, she rounded a clump of ferns and almost collided with Frostpaw, who was tottering along on three legs with a thick wad of cobwebs clutched in her fourth paw.

Sunbeam fought back a flash of panic. "Sorry," she mewed, steadying the apprentice and hoping that she wouldn't ask her where she had been. As they padded together back to the lakeside, she went on, "Did it take Sneezecloud long to find Reedwhisker?"

Frostpaw gave her a startled look, as if she didn't know what Sunbeam was meowing about—or maybe she did know, but had no idea how to answer.

"Oh, Reedwhisker is all good, thanks," she replied at last. "We all are," she added politely, "and I hope you are in ShadowClan, too."

But that isn't the question I asked, Sunbeam thought. If she hadn't already suspected something odd was going on in RiverClan, she certainly did now.

When she returned to her Clanmates beside the lake, Mothwing had already applied the horsetail poultice to Hopwhisker's paw.

"Oh, Frostpaw, that's great," the medicine cat mewed.

"More than enough to bind up the wound. This will do for today," she continued to Hopwhisker as she wrapped the injured paw, "but tell Puddleshine to take the cobweb off tomorrow and apply a new dressing. You'll need to stay off it for a while."

"Thank you, Mothwing," Hopwhisker responded, struggling to her paws. "It feels better already."

Sunbeam repeated her Clanmate's gratitude. "And give our thanks to Mistystar, too, for allowing us on your territory," she added. "You've been a great help."

"Yeah—sure, Sunbeam." Mothwing sounded unusually awkward, and the other RiverClan cats exchanged uneasy glances. "You're very welcome."

Padding back along the lakeside, helping Hollowspring to support Hopwhisker and keep her injured paw off the ground, Sunbeam was even more convinced that something was wrong in RiverClan. All the cats had seemed really edgy; surely they couldn't still be feeling the effects of dealing with Ashfur. It was more like they were hiding something.

I wonder if I ought to tell Tigerstar, she asked herself. *I feel like I should—but if I don't know what the problem is, will I just be making more trouble? Besides, Tigerstar told me to watch my step. If I'm not careful, I'll be making trouble for myself.*

CHAPTER 13

❧

Flamepaw padded through the thorn tunnel behind Lilyheart and the other two cats—Stormcloud and Twigbranch—who made up the hunting patrol. It was a cold, damp day, and the prey had all been hiding down in their holes; Flamepaw had only managed to catch a single vole. Stormcloud and Lilyheart had brought down a squirrel with a clever bit of teamwork, while Twigbranch had caught a mouse after stalking it patiently through the outskirts of a bramble thicket.

All that work, and not much to show for it!

Stormcloud led the patrol over to the fresh-kill pile to deposit their prey. The pile looked pretty scanty at this early hour of the morning; Flamepaw could only hope that the other patrols would have better luck.

"That's not much of a haul."

The voice was Bramblestar's; Flamepaw turned around to see the Clan leader standing a few tail-lengths away, gazing disapprovingly at their catch.

"The prey wasn't running well today," Lilyheart explained, dipping her head to her leader.

Bramblestar didn't look impressed. "The Clan still needs

to eat," he meowed. "Twigbranch—one mouse? Come on, you can do better than that!"

To Flamepaw's surprise, Twigbranch crouched down in front of Bramblestar. Her ears lay flat and her eyes were wide and scared. "I'm—I'm sorry, Bramblestar," she stammered. "I'll go out again. I'll do better next time, I promise."

Without waiting for a response, she scurried off and disappeared into the thorn tunnel.

Stormcloud blinked nervously at Bramblestar. "It wasn't her fault," he protested. "None of us could—" He broke off, then added, "I'm going with her," and bounded across the camp after Twigbranch.

Lilyheart, however, wasn't at all intimidated by her Clan leader. "We can't catch prey if there's no prey to be caught," she snapped, her claws flexing. "And Twigbranch got that mouse with the best bit of stalking I've seen in moons!"

"I wasn't trying to—" Bramblestar began.

Lilyheart's furious gaze told Flamepaw she was in no mood to listen. "Come on, Flamepaw," she ordered, flicking her tail to beckon him. "We'll go too." As he followed her across the camp, she added, "We'll try the abandoned Twoleg den. That's usually good for a mouse or two."

Before he plunged into the tunnel, Flamepaw glanced back over his shoulder. Bramblestar was gazing after them, a depressed droop to his tail. As Flamepaw watched, he turned away and began to trudge slowly up the tumbled rocks toward his den.

That's seriously weird, Flamepaw thought. *That's no way for a*

Clan leader to behave. *It's almost like he's forgotten how to lead.* A pang of anxiety shook him from ears to tail-tip. *Great StarClan, don't let there be anything wrong with Bramblestar!*

"Let's think it through," Finchlight meowed encouragingly. "What do you do when you want to catch prey?"

Flamepaw heaved a long sigh. He knew that his sister was trying to help, coaxing him to be more patient and to assess everything about his surroundings before creeping up on his prey. It was good to spend time with her, too. But even though she didn't mean to, Finchlight was stirring up all his frustrations about his last assessment and how he had failed for the second time.

He and Finchlight were sitting together in the stone hollow, not far from the tumbled rocks that led up to the Highledge. Now and again the sun peeped out from between the clouds, but a chilly breeze had sprung up, rattling the branches of the trees at the top of the cliffs. Dead leaves whirled in the air; Flamepaw fluffed out his pelt against the cold.

"Is this going to be my life from now on?" he grumbled, half to himself. "Am I always going to be practicing for an assessment I'm never going to pass?"

Finchlight nuzzled his ear. "Of course you're going to pass this time," she told him, her voice bracing.

"Easy for you to say." Flamepaw sighed. "It feels like ThunderClan just takes itself so seriously. I bet cats in other Clans aren't as miserable as I am."

His sister looked slightly taken aback, pausing for a moment before she responded. "It's a good thing that ThunderClan standards are so high," she insisted at last. "It's what makes us the best Clan!"

"Huh!" Flamepaw grumbled. "Probably every Clan thinks they're the best Clan." He stopped himself from voicing his doubts that ThunderClan really was the best; he didn't want to argue with Finchlight, not when she was trying to help him. But when she asked gently, "What's wrong?" he realized that he hadn't been able to hide how he felt.

For a few moments Flamepaw hesitated, trying to find the right words. "I guess I'm sad," he confessed at last. "And confused. I'm supposed to be this brilliant ThunderClan warrior, from a line of important ThunderClan warriors—so why do I feel so out of place? Am I just not a good fit for this Clan? Is that why my mother wasn't there for me when I was a kit cowering in the nursery, worrying about the bad cat who'd taken over the Clan?"

Finchlight listened in silence, her eyes wide and glimmering with sympathy. "Our mother was heartbroken after Larksong died," she murmured, touching her nose to Flamepaw's ear. "It's not that she didn't want to be there for you; she just couldn't. And then she was exiled—she couldn't help that, either. She feels so wretched about it now."

But surely the Clan could have stopped cats being sent into exile? If ThunderClan is so perfect, why did they let the false Bramblestar take over in the first place? Flamepaw asked himself resentfully. *They should have realized he was no good when he started throwing cats out of the Clan.*

He turned his head away, trying not to let his doubts show, but he was well aware it was impossible to hide anything from Finchlight; she knew him too well.

"It wasn't Sparkpelt's fault," she repeated, with a firm but gentle prod in his flank. "We were exiled, after all."

"I get that," Flamepaw responded, then added with a stab of jealousy, "I wonder if you're so much better than me because you got to spend that time with our mother." Sparkpelt would have taught Finchlight all her hunting moves, and how to defend herself . . . It would have been so great.

"Hey, which cat says I'm better than you?" Finchlight asked with a comforting *mrrow*. "I passed my assessment first, that's all. Anyway, I suppose being with Sparkpelt might have helped me learn my warrior skills, but she talked about you all the time while we were in exile. She missed you with every heartbeat. And I know that you will get closer in time. Just be patient."

"I hope that's true." Flamepaw sighed again. "I just can't imagine how it can happen."

"Let's not worry about that now," Finchlight meowed. "Let's concentrate on getting you through your assessment. Imagine that you're—"

Whatever she might have said was cut off by an angry yowl from above their heads. Looking up, Flamepaw saw that Squirrelflight had just appeared from the leader's den. She took a pace along the Highledge, then turned back to speak to Bramblestar.

"Your decision could leave ThunderClan vulnerable!"

"What decision?" Flamepaw whispered into Finchlight's ear. "What is she talking about?"

As Bramblestar emerged onto the Highledge to join his deputy, he said something to Squirrelflight, his voice too low for Flamepaw to make out the words. Prickling with curiosity, Flamepaw began to creep cautiously up the tumbled rocks so that he could overhear better. Finchlight hissed, "Don't be so nosy!" But Flamepaw ignored her, flattening himself behind a jutting rock so that he could listen without being spotted.

"Okay, a WindClan patrol strayed into our territory when they were chasing prey," Bramblestar meowed. "But it was Crowfeather who was leading it, so what's the big deal?"

"'Strayed into our territory'?" Squirrelflight growled. "Their warrior leaped over the stream, for StarClan's sake!"

"Crowfeather explained," Bramblestar replied curtly. "It was a WindClan vole that swam the stream and climbed out on the ThunderClan side. It—"

"At which point it became a ThunderClan vole," Squirrelflight interrupted. "But Hootwhisker jumped across and caught it. If our patrol hadn't spotted them, do you think we would ever have found out about it?"

Bramblestar let out a deep sigh. "We've shared a bond with Crowfeather ever since we traveled to the sun-drown-place to find Midnight. And now he ventured into the Dark Forest to help drive out Ashfur. We know we can trust him; we don't have to be suspicious about his intentions. If Crowfeather says it was a genuine mistake, I for one don't doubt him."

"They still kept the vole, though," Squirrelflight snapped. "That was our prey, and they should have given it back. Honestly, Bramblestar, are you going to let them get away with it?"

Bramblestar heaved another sigh that seemed to come right from the bottom of his chest. "I had hoped we might enjoy a bit of peace, after all the trouble Ashfur caused."

"There's peace, and there's letting another Clan walk all over us!" Squirrelflight snapped. When Bramblestar didn't respond, she continued, "I think we should go to WindClan and at least let them know that this can't happen again. It's more important than ever to defend our territory after everything ThunderClan has been through. We can't let other Clans think we're so weak that we allow WindClan to steal our prey!"

Bramblestar gave an uneasy shrug. "I don't want to fight with a cat who went to the Dark Forest for us," he insisted. "Crowfeather is one of the Lights in the Mist. It would be wrong to forget the risks and sacrifices those cats made."

"No cat who traveled to that terrible place will ever forget it," Squirrelflight pointed out. She sounded as if her patience was rapidly running out. "I'm not at all worried about that," she went on. "What we need is just a friendly—and firm— reminder to WindClan to respect our boundaries. Borders are important; we can't have confusion over that. Don't worry, Bramblestar. It won't turn into a battle."

The Clan leader still looked torn, as if balancing his deputy's advice against their friendship with Crowfeather was just too hard. "I'm tired," he mewed. "I'm going to get some rest.

Honestly, Squirrelflight, it will all work out. I trust Crow-feather."

His head bowed and his tail drooping, he retreated into his den. Flamepaw was irresistibly reminded of his retreat earlier that day, after his unfair criticism of the hunting patrol. *This isn't right,* he thought, more worried than ever. *And Squirrelflight knows it, too.*

Squirrelflight stared after her leader and mate for a moment, flexing her claws in frustration, then gave her pelt a shake and padded along the Highledge to the top of the tumbled rocks. Flamepaw had just enough time to scramble back to ground level beside Finchlight before the deputy bounded swiftly down to join a group of senior warriors near the fresh-kill pile.

"I suppose you all heard that?" she began.

The warriors—Lionblaze and Sparkpelt among them—glanced at each other and shuffled their paws in embarrassment, as if they weren't sure they should have been listening either.

"It's no secret," Squirrelflight went on. "I imagine the whole Clan knows about that stolen vole. Cherryfall, you were on the patrol, weren't you?"

The ginger she-cat nodded. "I couldn't believe my eyes when Hootwhisker leaped the stream," she meowed. "Like, what are borders for?"

"Exactly," Squirrelflight agreed. "So I'm taking a patrol to go to WindClan at dawn tomorrow. I need to talk to Hare-star about that vole. He can't think WindClan is going to get away with it, just because Bramblestar and I are friendly with

Crowfeather." She gave an exasperated flick of her tail.

Lionblaze's eyes gleamed approval, and he let out a low growl from his throat.

"But we have to be careful, and not too aggressive," Squirrelflight reminded him. "We don't want to start a war with WindClan. I'll do all the talking."

As she spoke, Molewhisker cast an uncertain look up at the Highledge, where the Clan leader had disappeared. "Are you sure about this?" he asked Squirrelflight. "It didn't sound like Bramblestar wanted us to confront WindClan."

"It won't be a confrontation," Squirrelflight informed him crisply. "It will be a discussion. I don't want a large group," she continued. "Just one or two other cats, not enough to be threatening. Sparkpelt, I'll take you."

Sparkpelt straightened up, blinking with pleasure at being chosen. "I'll be ready, Squirrelflight," she mewed.

Lionblaze looked hopefully at the deputy, but Flamepaw guessed that Squirrelflight wouldn't want him on this delicate mission. *He doesn't look like he'd be okay not fighting.*

But he was surprised a moment later when Squirrelflight swung around and fixed him with her green gaze. "I'll take you, too, Flamepaw," she told him. "It'll be good experience for you, to see how we conduct serious Clan business. It might help you pass your next assessment."

Flamepaw felt a thrill of excitement shivering through his pelt. He had kept a few paw steps away from the senior warriors, sure that Squirrelflight would send him away if she spotted him listening. He had never imagined that she would choose him for an important patrol. "Thanks, Squirrelflight!" he blurted, straightening up and doing his best to look brisk and competent.

A moment later, all his old doubts crowded up on him. *What if I mess up again? And should we really be going to WindClan when our Clan leader doesn't approve?*

The group split up, and Lionblaze began calling cats together for a hunting patrol. Flamepaw lingered to talk to Squirrelflight.

"Is Bramblestar okay?" he asked.

"Of course he is," Squirrelflight insisted.

But her gaze flicked back toward the leader's den, and worry prickled beneath Flamepaw's pelt. He didn't think she was sure about her answer. *And what's going to happen to Thunder-Clan if our leader isn't okay?*

CHAPTER 14

Wisps of cloud drifted over the half-moon, but the light was bright enough for Mothwing and Frostpaw to see their way as they trekked across the moor to meet the other medicine cats at the Moonpool. Far ahead, Frostpaw could just make out the figures of Alderheart and Jayfeather.

"What are we going to tell the other medicine cats?" Frostpaw asked her mentor. Mothwing and the senior warriors had been huddled in discussion earlier that day; Frostpaw had been quite relieved when her mentor had sent her out of camp to replenish the horsetail stocks. But now she felt just as nervous as the first time she had traveled to the Moonpool, though for a different reason. "About Mistystar being dead and Reedwhisker being missing?" she added when Mothwing didn't reply immediately.

"We don't need to tell them anything," Mothwing replied calmly. "We'll find Reedwhisker soon, so there's no need to involve other Clans in RiverClan's business."

"But what if they see Mistystar in StarClan?" Frostpaw meowed. *What if they see Reedwhisker?* she added silently. She didn't dare suggest to her mentor that Reedwhisker might be dead; she hardly dared think about it herself.

Mothwing looked briefly uncomfortable. "I hadn't thought of that," she admitted. Then she gave her pelt a shake. "From what the others have told me, they mostly meet with ancestral spirits from their own Clan. If they do see Mistystar, I'll answer their questions. You don't need to worry about it."

It's easy to tell me not to worry, Frostpaw thought as her mentor paused for a moment. *That doesn't actually help!*

"In any case," Mothwing continued, "tonight we're going to tell StarClan about the changes to the warrior code that we decided on. That will be the focus of the meeting, and no cat will have time to ask too many questions."

Frostpaw could tell that Mothwing wasn't as confident as she was trying to appear. Her own nervousness was growing with every paw step she took nearer to the Moonpool. StarClan would surely disapprove of lying to the other medicine cats—and not telling them something important was almost the same as lying.

Still, it will all be sorted out soon, she tried to reassure herself. *I just need to get there and talk to StarClan. Maybe our RiverClan ancestors will be able to tell me where Reedwhisker is, and everything will be fine.*

Pushing her way through the bushes at the top of the hollow, Frostpaw saw that almost all the other medicine cats were already gathered around the Moonpool. Puddleshine and Shadowsight were the only ones missing.

She followed Mothwing down the spiral path, dipping her head politely to the other cats as she padded up to them.

"Hi, Frostpaw!" Whistlepaw greeted her, coming up to

touch noses with her. "It's great to see you again."

The other cats murmured words of welcome, the warmth in their eyes showing Frostpaw how happy they were to have her among them. Frostpaw gave her chest fur a few embarrassed licks.

"I hope you're keeping Mothwing in line," Jayfeather meowed. "Mothwing, seeing as Frostpaw is the one who talks to StarClan, does that mean she's in charge?"

Frostpaw didn't know how to respond to that. There was a humorous edge to Jayfeather's tone, but she couldn't be sure whether he was joking or not.

"Frostpaw and I will help each other," Mothwing replied coolly. "Just as Willowshine and I did. It's only toms who get their tails in a twist worrying about who has more power."

At least Mothwing didn't seem to be offended by Jayfeather's words, reassuring Frostpaw that this was just friendly banter. Probably.

But there was a sarcastic edge to Jayfeather's tone as he asked Kestrelflight, "Eaten any good voles lately?"

Kestrelflight didn't reply, though he narrowed his eyes and glared at Jayfeather as if the blind cat could see him.

What's all that about? Frostpaw wondered, then gave an inward shrug. If there was something going on between the WindClan and ThunderClan medicine cats, it was none of her business.

While she was still wondering, there was a stir of movement at the top of the hollow. Frostpaw looked up to see Puddleshine and Shadowsight emerge from the bushes and race down the spiral path.

"Sorry we're late," Puddleshine panted as he halted beside the others. "One of the younger warriors had a bellyache just as we were about to leave."

"Young warriors!" Frecklewish shook her head. "Always in some kind of trouble."

The medicine cats settled themselves comfortably beside the pool and began to exchange Clan news. Frostpaw thought that everything they mentioned sounded really unimportant: an apprentice stung by bees in SkyClan, a wounded paw in ShadowClan.

"Thank you for your help," Puddleshine meowed, dipping his head to Mothwing and Frostpaw.

"Our pleasure," Mothwing responded briefly.

Frostpaw remembered meeting the ShadowClan cats beside the lake, and how she had found cobwebs to bind Hopwhisker's wound. She hoped they hadn't realized why Mothwing had made sure they stayed well away from RiverClan's camp.

She wondered too whether RiverClan was the only troubled Clan in the forest, or whether the other Clans also had more going on than the medicine cats felt like mentioning.

"Did the patrol that came to ShadowClan find Reedwhisker?" Shadowsight asked Mothwing.

"Yes, they did, thank you," Mothwing replied, her tone and her manner perfectly cool as she spoke the lie.

"Wait a moment," Jayfeather meowed. "You sent a patrol to ThunderClan, too. What—"

"And to SkyClan," Fidgetflake interrupted.

"And to us." Kestrelflight's gaze raked around the group of medicine cats before coming to rest on Mothwing. "So you sent patrols to all the Clans, looking for Reedwhisker. What's going on, Mothwing?"

Frostpaw felt an unpleasant fluttering in her belly as she saw Mothwing begin to lose her calm demeanor. "Nothing is going on," she snapped. "The matter is settled. Besides, it was warriors' business, not medicine cats'."

"All business is medicine-cat business," Jayfeather muttered.

Frostpaw waited nervously for the other cats to go on questioning Mothwing, but though they still eyed her suspiciously, they said nothing more. Mothwing sat rigid, her shoulder fur bristling and a challenging look in her amber gaze.

Eventually Alderheart let out a long sigh. "Enough of this. It's time to speak to StarClan." As he and the other cats found their places along the edge of the Moonpool, he continued, "Remember that we will be presenting the changes we've suggested to the warrior code. We are to seek the approval of the spirits of our ancestors, and report back to each other when we're done."

The rest of the medicine cats stretched their necks forward to touch their noses to the surface of the pool, and Mothwing leaned over and whispered to Frostpaw. "Are you ready?"

Frostpaw nodded. "I'll do my best."

As she bent her head to the water, she felt almost overwhelmed by the glitter of the reflected moon and stars, as if she could fall upward into the sky. She was eager to speak with her ancestors, yet for a couple of heartbeats she hesitated, sheer nervousness freezing her.

Am I ready? she asked herself. *Suppose our ancestors don't like our plans for the warrior code? Suppose I don't explain it right? What if I fail?*

Bracing herself, she let her nose touch the water and felt the chill flow through her. She seemed to be enclosed in a shimmering circle, as if the spirits of StarClan were all around, yet not showing themselves to her. She wished that she could ask one of the other medicine cats if she was doing it right, but when she dared to glance aside, she saw that they were all deep in the dreams where they walked with StarClan.

Frostpaw touched the water again and closed her eyes, making a massive effort to concentrate.

"Please speak to me, spirits of RiverClan," she begged, her voice quavering. "Your Clan desperately needs your help." When no cat appeared to her, she added, "Is Mistystar there?"

There was still no response in words, yet now Frostpaw thought that she could see the forms of cats solidifying out of the shining mist. They drifted in and out of her vision, and at first she didn't recognize any of them, though she felt a huge relief that at least they were there. Finally one cat emerged more clearly: a golden tabby she-cat with a spotted pelt and gleaming amber eyes. Frostpaw had never seen her before, but she had heard stories about the time when she led RiverClan.

"Are you Leopardstar?" she ventured, trying to push down her disappointment that Mistystar hadn't come. *But I've seen her once,* she told herself. *Maybe that's enough.*

The golden she-cat dipped her head. "What have you to say to me, young one?"

Hesitant to begin with, Frostpaw gradually gained more confidence as she recounted the suggestions the Clans had made about changes to the code. Leopardstar's expression remained blank; as Frostpaw explained, she couldn't guess what the leader thought.

"Are you okay with that?" Frostpaw asked when she had finished.

Leopardstar nodded, but when she spoke, it was about something completely different. "RiverClan is in trouble," she declared, "But if you act quickly, Frostpaw, it can be saved. I see Reedwhisker in a shadowy place, within your own borders. Listen!"

Frostpaw pricked her ears, and seemed to hear the sound of Twoleg voices in the distance. Then she felt herself falling . . . falling with stars all around her, and the voice of Leopardstar echoing in her ears.

"Careful!" That was Mothwing's voice; Frostpaw's mentor was gripping her shoulder with one forepaw, dragging her backward. "You nearly fell in!"

Frostpaw opened her eyes to find herself sprawled on a flat stone at the water's edge. She was panting for breath, as if she had run all the way from the RiverClan camp.

"Well?" Mothwing asked with an impatient twitch of her whiskers. "Did StarClan say anything? Did you speak to Mistystar?"

"No, but I saw Leopardstar!" Frostpaw gasped, excitement surging through her at the memory.

"And does she agree with the changes to the code?"

Looking around, Frostpaw saw that the other medicine cats were already clustered together, discussing what they had seen. It sounded as if StarClan had approved the proposed changes.

Frostpaw half expected some cat to turn to her and Mothwing and demand why they had never reported that Mistystar was dead. But they all seemed focused on the warrior code. *Mothwing must be right, that StarClan cats only show themselves to their own Clan,* she thought with a breath of relief. She certainly wasn't going to risk revealing any secrets by asking the other medicine cats if that was true.

"Well?" Mothwing repeated, tapping a paw.

"Yes," Frostpaw responded, remembering the way Leopardstar had nodded. "She was fine with that. But I learned something even more important!"

"What?" Mothwing asked.

Frostpaw felt she would burst with excitement, but she managed to keep her voice low so that the other medicine cats wouldn't overhear. "I know where Reedwhisker is!" she announced.

CHAPTER 15

Two blackbirds, a male and a female, were pecking together at something on the ground. Sunbeam gestured with her tail for Gullswoop to sneak around in a wide circle so that she could approach the prey from the opposite side. The white she-cat flattened herself to the ground and disappeared into the long grass.

At a nod from Sunbeam, Yarrowleaf began to work her way around in the other direction. The birds still seemed unaware that a hunting patrol was closing in on them.

"Now!" Sunbeam yowled.

The birds let out panic-stricken squawks as her screech split the silence and three cats leaped out at them from three different directions. They fluttered upward, but it was too late. Sunbeam snagged one claw in a flapping wing and brought one bird down so that Yarrowleaf could snap its neck with a well-aimed paw. Meanwhile, Gullswoop had gripped the other bird by its neck and shook it until it went limp.

"Thank you, StarClan, for this prey," Sunbeam gasped.

The hunting had gone well. Earlier, Yarrowleaf had caught

a squirrel, and the blackbirds were nice and plump, a good addition to the fresh-kill pile.

"I think we can go back to camp," Sunbeam meowed. "Yarrowleaf, if you go and fetch your squirrel, Gullswoop and I will bring these."

"Sure thing, Sunbeam."

Yarrowleaf headed off through the trees, while Sunbeam and Gullswoop padded off side by side.

"You know, Sunbeam, you're a really good hunter," Gullswoop meowed, speaking with difficulty around the wing of the blackbird she was carrying. "You should feel so proud of yourself."

Sunbeam shrugged, a little embarrassed. "We all did well today."

"But you were leading," Gullswoop insisted. "You don't give yourself enough credit. I think you're one of the best hunters in the Clan."

That's going a bit far, Sunbeam thought, wondering why her Clanmate would praise her so highly for a routine catch. It suddenly occurred to her that Gullswoop sounded like she was trying to cheer her up, which in a way was even weirder. *Why does she think I need that?* Sunbeam was sad that Lightleap still wouldn't talk to her, but it was strange that Gullswoop had noticed it. *How many other cats have noticed it?* she asked herself, her fur prickling uneasily. *Is the whole Clan gossiping about me?*

"You know, I'm really fine," she said, responding to what Gullswoop had not said.

"Oh, I'm so glad to hear that." There was relief in Gull-swoop's voice. "Have you made up with Lightleap, then? How is she doing?"

"I'm not sure," Sunbeam replied. "We haven't spent much time together lately."

"Interesting . . . ," Gullswoop murmured with a flick of her ears. "It must bother you that she's spending so much time with Blazefire. I don't blame you. . . ."

Sunbeam halted as abruptly as if a rock had sprung up from the ground and thumped her in the chest. "What do you mean? I haven't talked much with Blazefire recently, but he's still my . . . my special friend."

Gullswoop stared at her, disconcerted. "I—I didn't mean—" she stammered. "Maybe I've got it wrong. It's not like they like each other, not in that way. I'm sure of it."

Sunbeam's only response was a curt nod, but all the way back to camp her belly was shaking, and she felt as if she wanted to crawl out of her pelt. *How long has this been going on?* She remembered how she had asked Blazefire to talk to Lightleap for her, but she hadn't realized the two had been spending so much time together.

Maybe that's why Blazefire wouldn't back me up the other day when I saw Lightleap wander off from the hunting patrol.

When she reached the camp, Sunbeam forced herself to do her duty by taking her blackbird to the fresh-kill pile, then began to look for Blazefire. He wasn't out in the clearing, and his nest in the warriors' den was empty.

Emerging into the open again, Sunbeam spotted Shadowsight at the entrance to the medicine cats' den. Bounding over to him, she asked, "Have you seen Blazefire?"

"I think he went with a hunting patrol toward the SkyClan border," Shadowsight replied, sounding a little reluctant to tell her. "Lightleap was with him, and a couple of others."

Something about the soft way the medicine cat spoke made Sunbeam feel even worse, as if the whole of ShadowClan knew that Blazefire and Lightleap were together.

Her immediate reaction was to head out and try to follow Blazefire's scent trail, but she told herself how stupid that would be; she could easily end up chasing him around the forest and missing him altogether. Or, if she found him, it would be so embarrassing to interrupt a hunting patrol, as if she were trailing after him like a lost kit.

Instead she settled herself on a flat rock from where she could watch the camp entrance. The longer she waited for the hunting patrol to return, the more anger swelled inside her until she felt it like a huge lump of crow-food in her belly.

I wonder if this *is why Lightleap has been avoiding me.* Sunbeam scraped her claws furiously across the rock. *All this trouble started because I was worried about her, and trying to be a good friend. And now she does this to me!*

The sun was going down, casting long shadows across the camp, before Snaketooth and Whorlpelt returned, dragging a large rabbit between them. Sunbeam sprang to her paws and raced over to confront the two warriors.

"Were you on the same patrol with Blazefire and Light-leap?" she demanded.

"That's right," Snaketooth replied, exchanging an uncom-fortable glance with Whorlpelt, "but they went off on their own."

"Yeah, we lost track of them," Whorlpelt confirmed. He hesitated, then added, "Why don't you come and eat with us? I'm sure they'll be back pretty soon."

Somehow the gray-and-white tom being nice to her made Sunbeam angrier still. "Be honest with me," she mewed through gritted teeth, glancing from Whorlpelt to her for-mer mentor. "Has Blazefire been spending a lot of time with Lightleap?"

Once again Whorlpelt glanced uneasily at Snaketooth. "Well—okay—sure, sometimes," he stammered.

"Just as friends." Snaketooth was so eager to get the words out that Sunbeam suspected she didn't really believe what she was saying. Was she just trying to make her former apprentice feel better? "I mean—you're all friends, aren't you?"

Sunbeam wanted to unload her anger on these cats who were trying to hide the truth from her, but as she opened her jaws to speak, a yowl rang out from the forest beyond the camp. In the gathering twilight it sent an eerie chill through every hair on Sunbeam's pelt.

"What was that?" Whorlpelt asked.

Before any cat could reply, the yowl was repeated, and Lightleap burst in through the camp entrance, her ears flattened and her fur bristling.

"Come quickly!" she screeched. "I need help. Blazefire is hurt!"

Sunbeam raced through the forest at Lightleap's side, heading for the SkyClan border. Shadowsight and Snaketooth were hard on their paws.

"What happened?" Sunbeam asked.

"We were hunting among some rocks. We caught lots of mice," Lightleap explained, her words coming in short bursts as she gasped for breath. "There was a kind of tunnel. Some mice were hiding in there. I dared Blazefire to go in and flush them out. He did, but the tunnel was too narrow. He pushed at a rock and the tunnel fell in on him. Two huge rocks are pinning him down!"

Fury surged through Sunbeam; she slid out her claws and might have sprung at Lightleap if Shadowsight hadn't appeared at her side. *How could she put Blazefire in danger like that?*

"Are you both mouse-brained?" Shadowsight turned a shocked look on the brown tabby she-cat. "Why did you do that? You said you'd already caught lots of mice. You didn't need the prey!"

Lightleap gave the medicine cat an anguished glance. "I didn't mean for it to turn out like this!" she wailed. "It was just supposed to be fun! Blazefire is usually so quick! Remember when we were kits in the big Twoleg den and—"

"There's no time for that," Shadowsight meowed sternly;

he flicked a glance at Sunbeam, who guessed he must be see-ing the hurt in her face.

She remembered that Shadowsight, Blazefire, and Light-leap had all known each other when they lived with Tigerstar and Dovewing in the big Twolegplace. It had never occurred to Sunbeam to be jealous that Lightleap had known Blazefire for longer, but now she felt as if jealousy were burning her up, as if each hair on her pelt were a flame.

Lightleap led the way almost to the SkyClan border, to a stretch of the forest where the ground was uneven and rocks poked through the grass. Sunbeam bit back a cry of dismay when she spotted Blazefire lying unmoving beneath two large rocks, pinned by the tail, one hind leg, and part of his flank.

Shadowsight instantly ran up to him, laid a paw on his neck, and gave him a good sniff.

"Is he dead?" Lightleap's voice was quavering. "He was awake when I left him to get help."

"No, just unconscious," Shadowsight replied. "We need to get these rocks off him, and then I can have a better look."

In spite of her earlier anger, Sunbeam was overcome by a rush of worry for Blazefire. Along with Snaketooth, she put all her strength into pushing the rocks away until the ginger-and-white tom was free. She watched anxiously as Shadowsight checked his breathing and ran his paws gently over all of Blazefire's body.

Eventually the medicine cat sat up. "We'll have to carry him back to camp," he announced. "His leg is broken, but I'm not sure what other injuries he might have."

Sunbeam's heart was heavy as she helped carry Blazefire back through the forest. Snaketooth balanced him on her back, while Sunbeam steadied him on one side and Lightleap on the other. Sunbeam didn't want to look at Lightleap or speak to her, much less have to cooperate with her in helping Blazefire.

The sun had gone down, and shadows were gathering under the trees. Every paw step was an effort, and not just because of the weight of their injured Clanmate. *Will he survive?* Sunbeam wondered. And if he did, would he fully recover?

Puddleshine was waiting for them in the medicine cats' den when they returned. Some cat must have told him what had happened, because he had already prepared a nest for Blaze-fire and a leaf with three poppy seeds to relieve his pain.

All the way through the forest Blazefire had remained limp and unresponsive, but as the medicine cats settled him in the nest, he stirred a little and his amber eyes blinked open. "Sunbeam?" he murmured.

"Yes, I'm here," Sunbeam responded, bending over to give his ear a nuzzle. She was aware of Lightleap standing close by, watching them. *He didn't want her,* she thought, and was then ashamed of herself for feeling so petty.

Blazefire let out a purr, then turned his head to lick up the poppy seeds Puddleshine was offering him. Then he sank back into the nest, closing his eyes again.

"We need to find some sticks to set his leg," Puddleshine meowed to Shadowsight. "Best to do it while he's unconscious."

"Sunbeam, you should go now, and come back in the morning," Shadowsight told her. "Blazefire should be awake by then."

"Will he be okay? Will he walk again?" Sunbeam asked, even though she was afraid of what the answer might be.

Shadowsight shot a grave look at Lightleap. "Only time will tell," he replied.

Sunbeam followed Lightleap out of the medicine cats' den. Since she'd seen Blazefire pinned under the rocks, shock and anxiety had filled her with a kind of numbness. That was fading now, allowing her anger to seep back in.

"How could you?" she demanded, letting her shoulder fur bush up as she turned toward the brown tabby she-cat she had thought was her friend.

Lightleap's gaze was full of guilt and sorrow, as if she realized at last how serious this was. "It was just a game," she protested. "I had no idea Blazefire would get hurt."

"I'm not just talking about that." Sunbeam tried to put the icy wind of leaf-bare into her tone. "You know I've loved Blazefire since I was a kit. So why . . ."

Lightleap's eyes widened. "Sure, Blazefire and I have been spending time together," she meowed. "But only as friends! We have a lot in common, that's all. We like to do stupid stuff, and take risks, whereas you . . . Sunbeam, you're all about the rules."

"Sometimes following the rules saves a lot of heartache," Sunbeam pointed out, with a nod in the direction of the medicine cats' den.

Lightleap blinked miserably. "I'm sorry," she murmured.

Part of Sunbeam wanted to forgive her friend, but she had taken all she could for one day. Besides, she wasn't sure she believed Lightleap that she and Blazefire were just friends. With a curt nod she stalked off swiftly to the warriors' den, found her nest, and curled up tight in it with her tail wrapped over her face.

I wish I could wake up and find that all this was just a terrible dream.

Sunbeam roused from her nest to realize that the dawn patrol was leaving. Pushing her way into the open, she shook scraps of debris from her pelt and raced across the camp to the medicine cats' den.

When Sunbeam slipped inside, she saw that Shadowsight was still curled up in his nest, but Puddleshine was awake, bending over Blazefire. He glanced over his shoulder at her and beckoned her with a whisk of his tail.

"He's awake," the medicine cat told her, "but still dazed from the poppy seed. You can see him for a few moments."

He withdrew to the back of the den while Sunbeam hurried up to Blazefire. He lay stretched out on his side; one of his hind legs was kept straight by sticks bound tightly to it with ivy tendrils, and some kind of poultice was plastered to his tail by cobwebs.

Sunbeam had wanted so much to see him, but now that she was here, looking down at the cat she had thought would be her mate, she found she didn't know what to say to him. Every hair on her pelt prickled with relief that he seemed to be recovering, but she still felt angry that he had been so reckless, and along with that a little guilty because she had asked him to talk to Lightleap. *Did that lead them to take risks together?* The cat she'd thought she knew wouldn't have acted like this, and her hurt over whatever was happening between him and Lightleap still roiled in her belly. But she didn't know how to put all that into words.

"You scared me" was all she managed to say.

Blazefire blinked up at her, his amber eyes clouded with pain. "I'm sorry," he mewed.

"It's okay," Sunbeam responded. "I mean, you should have known better than to go into that tunnel! But you'll recover, and then everything will be fine, and we . . ."

Her voice trailed off as she realized that Blazefire was still struggling to talk. "I wanted to tell you . . . ," he mewed, his voice blurred. "I was planning to tell you . . . I do love you, I think I always will, but I don't think we're a good match to be mates."

Sunbeam felt as if some cat had hurled a rock at her chest; for a moment she couldn't breathe. *He can't be saying this! He can't!*

Blazefire paused, as if gathering his strength, and then continued. "We're just too different. And it wouldn't be fair to make you wait while I recover—if I ever do—and then not have it work out."

Sunbeam listened in silence, trying to take in what Blazefire was telling her. She felt stunned, as if her whole world had suddenly vanished and left nothing but a huge, empty pit. All her life, she had thought that she would eventually become

Blazefire's mate. She had believed that she knew him.

And I really didn't know anything.

"Are you okay?" Blazefire asked.

Sunbeam wanted to screech at him, to ask him how she could possibly be okay when she had just lost the cat she loved and the life she'd thought they would have. But Blazefire was sick and in pain, and in spite of everything she still cared for him.

"Yes, I'm okay," she meowed crisply, rising to her paws. "You don't have to worry about me." Then, unable to contain her bitterness, she looked back as she was about to leave the den. "I just thought you were a different cat."

CHAPTER 16

❧

Pale dawn light seeped into the ThunderClan camp. The sky was gray with cloud, and a chilly breeze ruffled Flamepaw's fur as he waited near the thorn tunnel for Squirrelflight and Sparkpelt to join him. He flexed his claws uneasily, digging them into the earth. The day before, when the Clan deputy had chosen him to be part of the patrol to WindClan, he had felt excited. Now it seemed awkward for him to be on a mission with his mother and *her* mother.

They'll both be there to see me when I mess up again.

Across the camp he saw Squirrelflight emerge from the warriors' den, followed almost at once by Sparkpelt. They bounded over to his side.

"Good, you're ready." Squirrelflight gave Flamepaw a brief inspection; he immediately felt as if he must have dust on his pelt or a leaf in his ear. "Let's go."

But before Squirrelflight could lead the way into the tunnel, Flamepaw picked up the sound of another cat brushing through from the outside. A heartbeat later Bramblestar padded into the camp.

Flamepaw froze. He didn't know whether Squirrelflight

had told their Clan leader that she intended to go to Wind-Clan, but he was sure Bramblestar wouldn't approve.

However, the leader's gaze flicked over the three cats with little interest, and he gave Squirrelflight a brief nod. "Good hunting," he meowed, then headed toward his den.

Squirrelflight returned the nod, but made no attempt to tell Bramblestar where they were really going.

Flamepaw's pelt prickled with uneasiness, but he said nothing. All he wanted was to get through this mission to WindClan and prove that he was ready to be a warrior. *Whatever is the matter between Squirrelflight and Bramblestar really isn't any of my business.*

But the three cats had hardly left the stone hollow behind when Sparkpelt picked up her pace to walk beside her mother. "What's going on with Bramblestar?" she asked. "Doesn't he know we're on our way to WindClan?"

A few heartbeats passed before Squirrelflight answered. "Bramblestar just needs time to recover," she mewed at last.

But that doesn't answer Sparkpelt's question, Flamepaw thought, surprised that Squirrelflight wasn't being completely truthful, even with her daughter. He remembered the conversation he had overheard the day before, when the Clan leader had said the confrontation was unnecessary, and he noticed the skeptical look that Sparkpelt gave her mother. It seemed to Flamepaw that Sparkpelt's reaction proved he was right: Squirrelflight was doing something she shouldn't.

"How is Bramblestar?" Sparkpelt asked, her green eyes shadowed with anxiety for her father. "He must have had a terrible time in the Dark Forest."

Squirrelflight let out a long sigh. "Yes, what happened there has affected him deeply," she admitted, then added quickly, "He's fine—completely fine. He's a great leader, and absolutely himself . . . but he's not sleeping well. He keeps having dreams about the Dark Forest."

"That's not surprising," Sparkpelt murmured. "What kind of dreams?"

"Disturbing ones," Squirrelflight replied. "When we were there, Bramblestar's spirit was sometimes under Ashfur's control, like all the spirits who were stranded there. And Ashfur made Bramblestar fight for him." She hesitated, then added, "There was a time when he made him attack me."

Flamepaw bit back a gasp of shock. He had heard about some of the events in the Dark Forest, but nothing as terrible as this. He could hardly imagine what it would be like if he had to fight Finchlight, or even Sparkpelt. It was no wonder that Bramblestar wasn't sleeping well.

"Bramblestar has been dreaming about the time he turned on me," Squirrelflight went on. Flamepaw thought she sounded relieved to have another cat she could talk to, though he couldn't imagine that *he* would ever pick Sparkpelt if he had something important he needed to talk about. *She's hardly the easiest cat to confide in.* "And the others in ThunderClan. He didn't want to hurt me, but he couldn't help himself."

"I think we all know that," Sparkpelt told her, touching her mother on the shoulder with the tip of her tail.

Squirrelflight flashed her a grateful look. "But it's not just that," she said. "Some of the Clan hasn't forgotten the time when Ashfur was leading us in Bramblestar's body, and it disturbed Bramblestar deeply when he heard about some of the things he did. He was absolutely horrified to find out that some of his Clanmates thought he might have been the one doing them. Now he says he can tell that sometimes they're afraid of him."

Flamepaw suddenly understood the weird encounter with Bramblestar beside the fresh-kill pile the day before. Bramblestar had criticized the hunting patrol for their poor result, which was a bit unfair but not unreasonable for a leader who wanted to make sure his Clan would be fed.

He scared Stormcloud, and he terrified Twigbranch.

When the impostor had been in charge of ThunderClan, Flamepaw had been too young to understand everything that happened, but he understood now. He knew how Twigbranch had been exiled as a codebreaker but promised the chance to atone, if she brought back a massive amount of prey.

But when she'd done that, Ashfur still hadn't let her back into the Clan. *No wonder she got scared when Bramblestar scolded her for not catching enough!* She must have felt like she was in danger of being exiled again.

"Really?" Sparkpelt sounded scornful as she responded to what Squirrelflight had told her. "Afraid of our own leader?"

"Not always," Squirrelflight replied. "But whenever Bramblestar is even a little bit forceful. He wants to avoid that, above anything."

"But he's supposed to be forceful," Sparkpelt pointed out.

"Forceful is how Clan leaders are."

Squirrelflight shrugged. "It bothers him, that's all."

Sparkpelt thought about that for a moment. "But if he's afraid of being seen as aggressive, how can you be sure he's making the best decisions for the Clan?"

The Clan deputy didn't answer that question. Instead she was silent as the cats emerged from the trees and began to head along the lakeshore toward the stream that formed the border with WindClan. But Flamepaw knew exactly what she would have answered. *She must agree with Sparkpelt. Why else would she be going to confront WindClan without letting the Clan leader know?*

Anxiety twisted Flamepaw's belly, painful as if he had swallowed a bramble tendril. He knew that no Clan could survive without a strong leader, and yet almost every other cat seemed quite unaware that Bramblestar had problems. Squirrelflight clearly knew, but she had only confided in her own daughter, pretending to the rest of the Clan that everything, including their leader, was fine.

But what else can she do? Flamepaw asked himself. *What can a deputy do, if they can't trust their leader anymore?*

The dawn light had strengthened; somewhere behind the clouds the sun must have risen, but there was no sign of it. In the open the wind was stronger, too, flattening Flamepaw's fur against his sides and ridging the surface of the lake.

"Flamepaw is doing really well," Squirrelflight told Sparkpelt after a few moments, changing the subject entirely. "He's just not quite there yet. He's been struggling with judgment."

Don't mind me, Flamepaw thought, resentful and embarrassed all at once. *Go on talking about me, just as if I were a . . . a tree stump!*

Sparkpelt glanced back at him. "That's always a problem for young cats," she murmured.

"But you've always shown good judgment," Squirrelflight went on. "Why don't you give him some extra help?"

Sparkpelt looked taken aback. "I'd be happy to," she responded after a moment.

Flamepaw could tell that his mother didn't really want to. "I'm already getting help from Lilyheart," he snapped. "That's why I have a mentor."

Sparkpelt's whiskers twitched at his tone. "That's fine, then," she mewed.

Squirrelflight's face fell, and Flamepaw felt even worse. Sparkpelt seemed glad to have an excuse not to help him, maybe because he had been rude to her, or maybe because she really didn't care whether he became a warrior or not. And Squirrelflight could see it, too.

It was a massive relief for Flamepaw when they reached the bank of the border stream and the two she-cats stopped talking about him. The wind carried the scent of the WindClan border markers, but there was no sign of any cat. Flamepaw glanced around for a suitable spot to hide, only to feel his mother's tail touching his shoulder.

"There's no need to sneak," Squirrelflight told him. "We want the WindClan cats to see us. We're here to talk." She sat down and began calmly washing her paws.

Flamepaw sat beside her and Sparkpelt, his nervousness growing with every heartbeat as they waited. *Just keep your mouth shut,* he told himself. *Then you can't get into trouble.*

He felt they had been sitting on the bank for moons, but in fact it was not long before a strong scent of cat washed over him and a WindClan patrol emerged from the undergrowth on the opposite side of the stream.

Nightcloud was in the lead, with Sedgewhisker and Oatclaw padding along at her shoulder. The black she-cat's ears pricked as she spotted the ThunderClan patrol, and her fur bristled as she drew to a halt. "What do you want?" she demanded.

"Greetings, Nightcloud," Squirrelflight responded, dipping her head politely. "We're here to talk to Harestar, if you'll allow us to cross your border."

Nightcloud hesitated for a few heartbeats, sizing up the ThunderClan patrol with a gaze that was unfriendly, if not downright hostile. She was a beautiful cat, Flamepaw thought, with the typical wiry WindClan body and sleek black fur.

Sure, her name suits her perfectly, he told himself, stifling a sigh.

"No," Nightcloud meowed at last. "You stay over there, where you belong. Oatclaw, run back to camp and ask Harestar if he wants to come and talk to the ThunderClan deputy."

Oatclaw raced off at once, his tail streaming out behind him as he disappeared through the trees. When he was gone, the WindClan cats settled down to wait on their own side of the stream. A slightly awkward silence fell.

"How is the prey running in WindClan?" Sparkpelt asked after a moment.

"Well enough," Nightcloud replied curtly.

"And is all well in ThunderClan?" Sedgewhisker added in a softer tone.

Squirrelflight launched into a story about a patrol that had tracked a fox until it had finally decided to leave for the unassigned territory across the border. Flamepaw had to admire her tact: emphasizing ThunderClan's courage and competence without touching on anything that could be interpreted as criticism of WindClan.

The deputy was just finishing her story when Oatclaw reappeared. He was accompanied by Heathertail, and they were escorting not Harestar, but the WindClan deputy, Crowfeather.

"Harestar was busy," he announced brusquely as he drew to a halt at the edge of the stream. "He sent me instead. What can I do for you?"

"Greetings, Crowfeather." Squirrelflight's tone was genuinely warm, and her green gaze was friendly. "Have you recovered from your time in the Dark Forest?"

Crowfeather visibly relaxed. "I have, thank you, Squirrelflight. I hope you have, too, and Bramblestar."

"Yes, every cat is fine," Squirrelflight told him.

Of course, Flamepaw thought. *Even if she is worried about Bramblestar, she would never admit it to a WindClan cat. She would never tell him the things she told Sparkpelt.*

"I think you know why we've come," Squirrelflight continued, sounding briskly efficient now. "Yesterday Hootwhisker leaped the border stream and caught a vole on ThunderClan territory. That vole was ours, Crowfeather. You know that's part of the warrior code."

Crowfeather looked briefly embarrassed, but he met Squirrelflight's gaze squarely. "You surely haven't forgotten that WindClan helped you get your leader back from the Place of No Stars," he meowed. "Maybe a vole or two isn't worth fighting over."

"This isn't a fight," Squirrelflight responded firmly. "It's a simple request."

Her forceful tone impressed Flamepaw; the ThunderClan deputy had made it quite clear that this could be a fight, if that was what WindClan wanted. At the same time, he worried about what might happen if the confrontation really did turn into a fight, and trouble between ThunderClan and Wind-Clan. *What would Bramblestar do then?* he wondered. *He would have to back up Squirrelflight, or let WindClan think they can treat us however they like.*

The air tingled with tension between the two deputies; Squirrelflight's shoulder fur was beginning to rise, while the tip of Crowfeather's tail flicked back and forth irritably.

Then Crowfeather slowly dipped his head. "Very well," he conceded. "I'll arrange to send you some prey, to make up for the vole. After all, I wouldn't want Bramblestar to make himself ill fretting over relations between our two Clans, not while he's weakened from what Ashfur did to him."

Squirrelflight had begun to let her fur lie flat, but at Crowfeather's last words it bristled up again.

"I told you, Bramblestar is fine," she hissed.

The WindClan deputy twitched his whiskers, looking unconvinced. But when he next spoke, there was sincerity in his voice. "I'm not trying to cause trouble. I'm truly worried about Bramblestar," he meowed. "I'll always feel a bond with him, after our journey to the sun-drown-water. No cat should have to endure what he did in the Dark Forest. And few cats could have come away from it unscathed. You must take care of him, Squirrelflight, and take care of yourself. Thunder-Clan has always been such a strong Clan, and Bramblestar a noble leader, but you have both been through so much. I truly hope you can reclaim that."

For a moment Squirrelflight stared at him as if she wasn't sure how to respond. Flamepaw, too, wasn't sure what to make of the WindClan cat's words. His Clanmates had always made it sound as if the other Clans looked up to ThunderClan. But though Crowfeather wasn't hostile any longer, it didn't sound as if he looked up to them at all.

It sounds more like WindClan pities us.

Eventually Squirrelflight gave Crowfeather a brisk nod. "I appreciate your concern, Crowfeather," she mewed. "But Bramblestar doesn't need looking after. You're right, no cat should have endured what he faced in the Dark Forest, and I'm telling you that very few cats could have. I only wish every Clan could be lucky enough to have such a strong leader. As for you, Crowfeather," she finished, "don't forget about that prey."

Not waiting for a reply, she turned and led the way through

the trees, back toward the ThunderClan camp.

Following her and Sparkpelt, Flamepaw thought over what had happened. They had gotten the promise of prey that they wanted, and without having to fight for it, but somehow he didn't feel as triumphant as he had expected. He couldn't help suspecting that they had only made the situation more complicated.

CHAPTER 17

❧

Frostpaw shivered as she emerged from her den. The sun was not yet up, though a golden glow on the horizon told her it would rise soon. She padded across the stretch of pebbles to the stream for a drink, noting how chilly it was getting, Leaf-fall was in full swing, which meant leadbare wasn't far off. Her thirst quenched, Frostpaw was giving herself a quick grooming when Mothwing bounded down the bank and came to a halt beside her.

"Good, you're awake," her mentor meowed. "I've just chosen some cats for a patrol to go and find Reedwhisker, and I want you to lead it."

Frostpaw felt a jolt in her belly as if some cat had hurled a rock at her. "Me?" she exclaimed, staring at Mothwing. "Oh, no, I can't possibly!"

"Of course you can," Mothwing responded calmly. "You're the cat who had the vision of where to find him."

"But . . ." Frostpaw couldn't believe that her mentor had chosen her for the task. She wanted to feel proud, but instead every hair on her pelt was quivering with apprehension. "I'll join the patrol, of course I will, but I can't lead it!"

For a moment Mothwing sat looking at her with her head on one side. "Frostpaw, you're a medicine cat," she mewed at last, in a tone that didn't allow for any argument. "It's your destiny to take great responsibility for the well-being of your Clan, and there's no better time for you to start. I have every confidence that you can do it, so let's have no more nonsense. Come and help yourself to some fresh-kill, and then you can get going."

Her tail drooping, Frostpaw followed Mothwing back up the bank and hurried over to the fresh-kill pile. While she gulped down a mouse, she saw Mothwing cross the camp to where three cats—Curlfeather, Splashtail, and Gorseclaw—were waiting near the entrance. Mothwing said something to them, too quietly for Frostpaw to hear, but she heard Gorseclaw well enough, the white tom's voice carrying clearly in the chilly morning air.

"*Frostpaw* is leading us? Have you got bees in your brain, Mothwing?"

Mothwing's response was as icy as the breeze that flowed across the camp. "Frostpaw is a medicine cat who has had a vision of where we can find our new leader. And you'll need a medicine cat in case Reedwhisker is hurt. Who else should lead the patrol?"

"I thought you would, Mothwing," Splashtail meowed.

"Yes, that would work really well," Mothwing snapped. "Seeing that I don't have the faintest idea where to go." She spun around. "Frostpaw!"

Swallowing the last mouthful of mouse, Frostpaw swiped

her tongue around her jaws and bounded across the camp to her mentor's side. "I'm ready, Mothwing," she mewed, trying not to let her voice shake.

Mothwing gave her a brisk nod. "Off you go, then."

Frostpaw felt as if a tough bit of prey were sticking in her throat. All three warriors were looking at her; Curlfeather had a glow of affection in her gaze, but both Gorseclaw and Splashtail seemed doubtful, as if they were waiting for her to make a mistake. Her paws seemed frozen to the ground; she told them to move, but they didn't obey her.

"The last time we saw Reedwhisker, on that patrol," Curl-feather began in a helpful tone, "we were hunting near the greenleaf Twolegplace. We could start there. If you think that's a good idea, Frostpaw," she added.

Frostpaw silently thanked StarClan that her mother was part of the patrol. She swallowed hard.

"That's a great idea," she agreed. She tried to put some authority into her voice, but she thought she must sound like a scared kit. "We'll start by heading in that direction."

Frostpaw felt as if a whole flight of butterflies were whirl-ing around in her belly as she left the RiverClan camp at the head of the patrol. She could still hardly believe that Moth-wing had given her the responsibility; she just hoped that her mentor had been right to trust her.

Oh, StarClan, please let me find Reedwhisker, she prayed silently, and added to herself, *Alive.*

If only she could return to camp with the deputy, the cat who was overdue to become Clan leader, with some explanation of where he had been all this time, then River-Clan's troubles would be over. But Frostpaw couldn't quite make herself believe that it would happen.

Heading out into the territory, Frostpaw was comforted by the presence of her mother padding by her side, with Gorse-claw and Splashtail just behind. She was sure that whatever lay ahead of them, the three warriors would make sure that nothing could go too badly wrong.

Though she tried to seem confident, Frostpaw was aware that she didn't know the territory nearly well enough. After she had been made an apprentice, Mothwing had taken her on a tour of the borders, and they went out nearly every day to gather herbs. So Frostpaw knew the best places to find horsetail and marigold—but she had no idea where the deep, shadowy place she had seen in her vision might be.

"I wonder if Twolegs could have taken Reedwhisker," she suggested to her mother as they turned toward the greenleaf Twolegplace.

Curlfeather gave her whiskers a thoughtful twitch. "I've heard of that happening," she responded. "Does it fit with what you saw in your vision?"

"I don't think so." Frostpaw shook her head uncertainly. It was becoming harder to remember exactly what she had seen up at the Moonpool, but the place in her vision had seemed wilder and more desolate than anything to do with Twolegs.

Though I thought I heard Twoleg voices in the distance, she reminded herself. *That might mean we're heading in the right direction.*

Frostpaw led her patrol along the edge of the lake until they had almost reached the halfbridge. Hesitating for a moment, she wished once again that she knew the territory well enough to guide the patrol. There had been no sign of the lake in her vision, so the obvious choice was to veer away from the waterside toward the RiverClan border that ran for many foxlengths alongside the first dens of the Twolegplace.

"This way," she meowed with a wave of her tail, hoping she sounded confident.

But as Frostpaw headed for the border, she realized after a few paw steps that Splashtail wasn't following.

"Why would Reedwhisker have gone this way?" he grumbled. "There's not much prey near the Twolegplace." He added, in a voice just loud enough for Frostpaw to hear, "Mouse-brained apprentice!"

Annoyance gave Frostpaw the courage to argue with a warrior. "Who's leading this patrol?" she demanded.

Splashtail shrugged. "Suit yourself. Don't blame me if it all goes wrong."

The ground was almost flat near the lake, but as the patrol moved farther from it, the slope rapidly grew steeper. Reaching the ridge, Frostpaw realized that she stood on the brink of a ravine, with ferns and bushes rooted in a rocky cliff. At the bottom was a winding path of sharp stones; Frostpaw guessed that in rainy weather there might be a small stream, but for now the rocks were dry.

Frostpaw's fur prickled as she gazed down into the ravine. A sick feeling swelled in her belly and rose into her throat; she had to choke it back. Her dark vision returned to her mind:

This was a shadowy place, just like the one Leopardstar had spoken of. And it was near the place where her mother had told her the patrol had been hunting.

"Do you sense something here?" Curlfeather asked.

"I think so." Frostpaw's voice was shaking, and she made a massive effort to steady it. "We should investigate the ravine."

To begin with, the warriors spread out along the top of the cliff, calling out Reedwhisker's name, over and over. There was no reply. With every heartbeat that passed, Frostpaw felt more and more worried.

Something terrible has happened. If Reedwhisker were alive and well, he would have come back to camp by now.

"This is no use," Gorseclaw meowed eventually. "We'll have to go down there."

Splashtail gave the cliff a doubtful look. "We could break our necks."

"No, it'll be fine," Gorseclaw told him. "I've hunted here before. When the stream is running, it's a good place for prey. And I know a way down. Follow me."

A few tail-lengths along the top of the ravine, a narrow path led down among the rocks, zigzagging across the face of the cliff. Gorseclaw took the lead; Frostpaw followed, with Curlfeather just behind her and Splashtail bringing up the rear.

"Watch where you're putting your paws," Curlfeather warned Frostpaw. "If you slip, I'll try to catch you."

I'm not a kit! Frostpaw thought, indignant at her mother's fussing. *I'm a medicine cat, leading a very important mission.*

All four cats reached the bottom of the cliff without mishap.

"We'd better split up and search," Frostpaw suggested, slightly embarrassed to be directing experienced warriors.

"Good idea." Gorseclaw gave her an approving look, making her feel better. "We'll call out if we find anything."

The patrol headed off in different directions. Frostpaw plodded along the dry streambed, her pads soon feeling sore from the sharp stones. Not far away she could hear her mother calling, "Reedwhisker! Reedwhisker!" Frostpaw couldn't feel hopeful enough to call out the deputy's name. A cold stone seemed to have settled in her belly; she was sure the deputy was dead.

Ahead of Frostpaw the ravine narrowed, the cliffs on either side drawing together into an impassable barrier. She realized she would have to turn back. At the same moment, she heard a bone-chilling wail rise up behind her and recognized Gorseclaw's voice.

Instantly Frostpaw whirled around and began racing back the way she had come, with no thought now about her sore pads. Splashtail and Curlfeather appeared from the undergrowth as she ran, and the three cats sped together along the ravine bottom until they reached Gorseclaw.

The white tom was standing at the top of a tumble of rocks. When the stream was flowing, they would have formed a waterfall. He was staring downward; panting up to his side, Frostpaw followed his gaze. Stretched out at the bottom of the rocks was Reedwhisker's body.

"Oh, no!" Curlfeather exclaimed, her voice full of distress. "He is dead! I just knew it!"

"We should go down," Gorseclaw meowed. "Maybe he's just unconscious."

Frostpaw was sure that the white tom was wrong, and that the Clan deputy really was dead: his head was at a strange angle, as if his neck was broken. The last thing she wanted to do was go down there and check, but she knew that as a medicine cat it was her duty.

Slowly Frostpaw began picking her way down the tumble of rocks toward Reedwhisker's unmoving body. She heard her mother warn her to be careful, but she was concentrating too hard to respond. She could imagine herself slipping and landing beside Reedwhisker, dead like him or badly injured, and she had to brace herself and stop her paws from shaking.

"If only I'd had my vision sooner," she mewed, a hot wave of guilt washing over her. "Then we might have been in time to save him."

"It wasn't your fault," Curlfeather responded briskly. "There's nothing any cat could have done. It looks as if the fall killed him."

Frostpaw hoped that her mother was right, but her feelings of guilt wouldn't go away.

Finally Frostpaw made it to the bottom of the rocks and padded up to Reedwhisker's body. The black tom was lying with his limbs splayed out; his eyes were filmed over and his teeth set as if he were growling at an enemy. When Frostpaw stretched out a tentative paw and touched his shoulder, he was stiff and cold.

A moment later Curlfeather was beside her, brushing her

tail over Frostpaw's shoulder and giving her ear a comforting lick. "I'm sorry you have to see that," she sighed, then added, "Look at those scrapes along his back. That's where he must have hit the sharp rocks as he fell."

Frostpaw looked more closely, and saw several scratches running the length of Reedwhisker's spine, where the fur had been torn away to expose the flesh beneath. The scrapes had bled, though the blood was dry now.

"That looks almost like a badger's claws," she mused.

"Nonsense, that's nothing like a badger," Curlfeather meowed. "The fall must have killed him. We should bring him back to his Clan."

Stepping back, she saw that Gorseclaw and Splashtail had also joined her at the bottom of the slope. Both of them stood with bowed heads, and when they looked up, Frostpaw saw grief and apprehension in their eyes.

"I'll carry him on my back," Gorseclaw declared. "Splashtail, Curlfeather, you can walk with me and help balance him."

Frostpaw watched while her Clanmates lifted the deputy's body onto the white tom's back. Her mind was spinning as she tried to work out what the future would hold for RiverClan.

It was Splashtail who put words to her misgivings. "What happens to RiverClan now?" he asked. "How do we know which cat should be leader?"

"That's up to StarClan," Gorseclaw replied. "They will decide."

Every hair on Frostpaw's pelt began to quiver with nervousness. *Mothwing can't make contact with StarClan. That means it's up to me to speak with them and tell my Clan who their choice is for leader.*

Together the three warriors managed to haul Reed-whisker's body up the narrow path to the top of the ravine, with Frostpaw following. Her paws felt heavy, as if her body were echoing her reluctance to return to camp and face the overwhelming responsibility that had been laid upon her.

When they reached the top and set out across the territory, Curlfeather beckoned to her with a flick of her ears. "I can tell you're nervous," she mewed quietly to Frostpaw, "but you don't need to be. StarClan helped you find Reedwhisker, didn't they? You're going to be a great medicine cat, and you should trust your instincts." She whisked her tail around to touch Frostpaw's shoulder. "You'll know when StarClan has chosen the new leader," she promised.

Frostpaw felt encouraged by her mother's words and her reassuring touch, but her task still loomed ahead of her like a massive tree that she was being forced to climb.

"I hope you're right," she responded to Curlfeather. The faces of her Clanmates seemed to swim in front of her, each one a loyal and talented cat. *Where will I even start? How will I know which cat StarClan has chosen?* "I'll do my best," she resolved.

CHAPTER 18

Sunbeam lay curled up in her nest in the warriors' den, her tail wrapped over her nose. She felt too depressed even to stretch out a paw, much less leave the den and try to join a patrol.

I know I'm moping, she admitted to herself. *And I can't go on like this forever. But if ever a cat deserved a bit of a mope, it's me, right now.*

It wasn't every day that the cat you were hoping might one day be your mate did something so totally mouse-brained behind your back, then immediately told you that you weren't right for each other.

What's wrong with me? she asked herself.

Lightleap had told her that she wasn't in love with Blazefire, but that didn't mean Blazefire hadn't fallen in love with *her.* Sunbeam found it hard to believe that it was a coincidence Blazefire had decided that the two of them wouldn't be good as mates just after he had started spending a lot more time with Lightleap.

Does that mean I'm boring? Sunbeam wondered miserably. *Maybe I should volunteer to go into the Dark Forest, then get too scared and feel bad about it? Would that make me a more attractive mate?*

Sunbeam gave herself an inward shake. She knew she wasn't

being entirely fair to Lightleap. *But then, nothing about this is fair!*

She looked up at the sound of a cat brushing through the low-hanging branches that guarded the den. She opened her eyes to see her brother Spireclaw picking his way around the empty nests to join her.

"How do you feel?" he asked. "Are you okay?"

"Oh, yeah, sure," Sunbeam replied, a sarcastic edge to her tone. "Everything is sunshine and daisies right now, thanks for asking."

Spireclaw let out a sigh and settled himself beside her with his paws tucked under him. Sunbeam wasn't usually especially close to him, but he had caught her just after Blazefire had told her they would never be mates. Struggling with misery and anger, she had told Spireclaw the whole story about Blazefire and Lightleap. His kindness had been like a warm pelt wrapped around her, and now his eyes were full of sympathy.

"I'm sorry, I really am," he murmured. "Love is complicated."

Sunbeam couldn't suppress a snort. "What would you know about it?" Her littermate had never shown the least interest in any of the ShadowClan she-cats.

For a heartbeat Spireclaw did not meet her gaze, and at once Sunbeam felt guilty for snapping at him. "I shouldn't have said that," she mewed. "I know I shouldn't take it out on you, but I'm so angry and sad right now, I couldn't help it. Maybe I shouldn't be around any cat for a while."

"But you can't hide in here forever," Spireclaw objected,

sounding brisk and practical. "Is it actually making you feel any better?"

Sunbeam had to shake her head. "No, it's not," she admitted.

"So get out there," her brother urged her. "Go and live your life. Show those mouse-brains that they can't upset you. You'll feel so much better."

Spireclaw was being just as annoying as usual, but Sunbeam couldn't deny there was sense in what he said. "Okay," she responded, the word breathed out on a sigh. "I'll try, if it'll make you happy."

"Good." Spireclaw leaned over to nudge her shoulder with his nose. "Cloverfoot is sorting out hunting patrols. She'll be glad of another set of paws."

With a massive effort, Sunbeam stood and shook the debris from her nest out of her pelt. *Spireclaw is right. I need something to take my mind off all this.*

Slipping through the branches out into the open, Sunbeam spotted Cloverfoot surrounded by a group of warriors as she arranged the patrols.

Sunbeam bounded over to her. "Can I join?" she asked.

"Sure you can," the deputy replied. "Here, you can go with Snowbird and Whorlpelt."

Snowbird gave Sunbeam a friendly nod as she padded over to join the patrol, limping slightly as she always did. As the white she-cat turned to lead the others out of the camp, Sunbeam noticed that along with the other two warriors, Gullswoop was coming with them, too.

Oh, no, not her!

Gullswoop didn't speak, and Sunbeam certainly wasn't about to discuss Blazefire with her, but she could feel her Clanmate's sympathetic gaze resting on her as they padded into the forest. It stung, as if a whole nestful of ants were crawling through her pelt.

Ranging a few paces ahead of the patrol in her efforts to avoid Gullswoop, Sunbeam concentrated on her hunting, and managed to catch a mouse as it scuttled for cover among the roots of a tree.

"Great leap!" Whorlpelt exclaimed.

"Yes, you're a brilliant hunter," Gullswoop added, still with that infuriating look of sympathy in her eyes.

"Thanks," Sunbeam mewed through gritted teeth. *If she doesn't stop trying to cheer me up, I'll . . .*

The hunt continued: Snowbird and Whorlpelt brought down a squirrel with a neat bit of teamwork, and even Gullswoop stopped staring at Sunbeam long enough to catch a blackbird. *Spireclaw was right,* Sunbeam thought. *I do feel better out here, instead of lurking in the den.*

"This is going well," Whorlpelt commented. "We should have a nice full fresh-kill pile tonight."

Skirting a clump of stunted pine trees, the patrol emerged into a clearing that was half covered by a sprawling bramble thicket. Flaxfoot and Hollowspring were standing beside it, staring into the mass of tendrils with a disgusted expression on their faces.

"What's the matter with you?" Snowbird asked, bounding

forward to join her Clanmates.

"We caught a couple of pigeons," Flaxfoot explained, as Sunbeam and the others padded up. "At least, Hollowspring caught his, but I was stalking mine along that tree branch up there." He gestured with his tail at a long pine branch that stretched over the cats' heads. "I caught it all right, but my claws snagged in its wing feathers, and it fell into the brambles here." He let out a sigh of exasperation. "The thicket is far too dense for us to go in and get it. It was a good fat one, too."

"Clumsy furball," Hollowspring meowed, giving his Clanmate a friendly shove with one shoulder.

Sunbeam peered into the brambles. She could just make out the gray-and-white feathers of the pigeon, almost completely hidden by the tangled tendrils. "I'll go and get it," she announced.

"What?" Snowbird turned on her, a look of dismay in her eyes. "Absolutely not."

"You'll only hurt yourself," Whorlpelt added.

"Yes, and I'll feel like it was my fault." Flaxfoot rested his tail for a moment on Sunbeam's shoulder. "It's because I was careless that the stupid thing fell in there in the first place."

"The Clan won't starve for the loss of one pigeon," Snowbird pointed out.

"I said I would do it," Sunbeam hissed. She was desperate to do something, and she had no patience to wait for approval from her Clanmates.

Without any more delay, Sunbeam flattened herself onto her belly and crawled into the bramble thicket, trying to wriggle her way forward where the tendrils were thinnest. She could feel the thorns catching in her fur, but she kept going until she could grasp the pigeon's wing in her jaws.

But when Sunbeam tried to retreat, creeping backward and dragging the pigeon with her, the thorns dug deeper, raking through her fur and over the flesh beneath.

Maybe the others were right, she thought. *But it's too late to change my mind. I just have to get out of here.*

More determined than ever, she tugged harder at the pigeon, ignoring the countless stabs of pain from the thorns. The tendrils twined around her, almost as if they were alive and she were their prey. But finally she emerged, staggered to her paws, and turned to drop the pigeon in front of Flaxfoot.

"There you go," she meowed. "You're welcome."

Her Clanmates simply stared at her in dismay, jaws gaping. Sunbeam realized that she must look as if she had bees in her brain. Her pelt was scraped the wrong way, she was covered in scratches, and she had left enough of her fur behind in the thicket to line a nest.

"What?" she asked.

When there was still no response, she turned and padded away.

Almost at once she realized that Snowbird and Gullswoop had followed her, and were escorting her, one on either side.

"You're going straight back to camp," Snowbird ordered, in a tone that defied argument. "You need the medicine cats to look at those scratches."

"What about collecting our prey?" Sunbeam asked.

"Whorlpelt and the others will do that," the white she-cat responded.

"Yes, you've got to take care of yourself, after what you've been through the last few days," Gullswoop added, curling her tail around Sunbeam's neck. "You know you're only making things worse."

Her unwanted sympathy shattered the last of Sunbeam's patience. "Keep your tail to yourself!" she snapped.

"Sor-*reeeee*." Gullswoop sprang backward, sounding not sorry at all. "I was only trying to help."

Sunbeam ignored her. She stalked back into camp with her head held high. When she reached the medicine cats' den, she quite enjoyed the startled look Shadowsight gave her as he looked up from the herb store.

"What happened?" he asked. "Did a fox attack you?"

"No, she attacked a bramble bush," Snowbird told him, an edge to her voice. "She insisted on burrowing in to retrieve a pigeon that fell in there. Come on, Gullswoop. We're done here."

When her Clanmates left, Sunbeam sat down and waited while Shadowsight examined her, sniffing carefully at her scratches. By now they were really starting to hurt, and she could feel blood trickling through her pelt.

I wish I could have done something daring and reckless that didn't sting so much, she thought ruefully.

"You know, this is the most mouse-brained thing I've seen in moons," Shadowsight told her when he had finished examining her. "If you're unlucky, these scratches could become infected, and the infection could kill you. Do you really want to die in such an awful, embarrassing way?"

Shadowsight was usually so gentle that Sunbeam was startled by his fierce tone. "I didn't —" she began.

"Didn't think?" Shadowsight interrupted, glaring at her. "No, I can see that. In the future, remember that medicine cats have enough to do treating wounds that weren't deliberate, never mind sorting out mouse-brained cats who injure themselves for fun!"

Guilt swept over Sunbeam like a cold wind from the lake. "I'm sorry," she mewed.

"I should think so!" Shadowsight snorted. More calmly, he went on, "I know you're having a bad time, but injuring yourself is not the answer. Sit still, and I'll put some damp moss on your back to soothe the pain. Then I'll fetch some fresh marigold leaves and trickle the juice into those scratches. And for StarClan's sake, Sunbeam, don't ever do this again!"

When the medicine cat had left her with the cool moisture from the moss soaking into her fur, Sunbeam sat in silence, relaxing as the pain ebbed. Then, for the first time, she remembered that she wasn't the only cat recovering in the medicine cats' den.

Blazefire!

The white-and-ginger tom was watching her curiously from his nest at the far side of the den. Between the shadows in the den and concentrating on her own injuries, Sunbeam hadn't noticed him before.

She stared at him, suddenly feeling stupid for having injured herself, not to mention how she must look with clumps of fur missing and moss sticking to her back.

"Those scratches must be really painful," Blazefire remarked after a moment. "Whatever possessed you to go into the brambles?"

"I don't owe you an explanation," Sunbeam snapped at him, turning her head away. "I don't owe you anything!"

"I know," Blazefire mewed quietly.

Silence fell; after a few heartbeats, Sunbeam couldn't resist glancing up at him again. "How is your leg?" she asked.

"It's too soon to tell," Blazefire replied with a sigh. "I can't move it. Shadowsight gives me poppy seeds for the pain, but they make me sleepy."

In spite of all that had happened between them, Sunbeam couldn't help feeling worried for him. "What will you do if your leg doesn't heal right?" She found it was hard to keep her voice steady. "You might have trouble walking for the rest of your life."

Blazefire gave an uneasy shrug. "I suppose I'll deal with that when and if it happens. But yes, when I'm awake, it does prey on my mind."

Sunbeam fought off a surge of irritation mingled with compassion. *I shouldn't care so much, but I do.* "Maybe you should have been a bit more careful," she told him.

Blazefire gave her injuries a long, thoughtful look. "I could say the same to you," he meowed.

Sunbeam almost let out a *mrrow* of amusement, until she remembered that things weren't right between her and

Blazefire. Instead she turned away.

"But you're right about one thing," Blazefire continued. "I could have been much more careful with you. I can tell you're hurting, and you don't deserve that."

Once again, silence fell.

After a few heartbeats, Sunbeam summoned all her courage to ask, "Do you love Lightleap now?"

"No!" Blazefire sounded surprised. "There's a lot I admire about Lightleap, but we're just friends. I hope you and I can be friends, too, Sunbeam."

Relief warmed Sunbeam to the tips of her claws, and the pain around her heart eased a little. Somehow she was better able to bear losing Blazefire if it wasn't because he was padding after Lightleap. "Maybe we can," she mewed.

After a while, Blazefire's soft, rhythmic snores sounded throughout the den, and Sunbeam was able to relax. *What would it be like to be Blazefire's friend again?* she wondered. *Maybe if he's just friends with Lightleap, there's hope for us in the future.*

Sunbeam was dozing when she was roused by the sound of another cat entering the den. She opened her eyes expecting to see Shadowsight, but the newcomer was her mother, Berryheart. Sunbeam braced herself for another scolding. To her mother, being a productive ShadowClan warrior was *a very big deal.* Her mother had left ShadowClan as a young cat to follow Darktail and his Kin, and she'd lost everything, including her kit, Needletail. It was only by chance that Tigerheart found Berryheart and Sparrowtail on his way back to the lake territories with Dovewing and their kits, and their family was

folded back into ShadowClan when it revived under Tigerstar's leadership. Sunbeam and her littermates had been born
on that journey. Berryheart told them often how important
it was to serve their Clan—to use good judgment, follow the
rules, and contribute to the prey pile.

I failed on two out of three this time!

Berryheart paused for a moment, gazing across at Blazefire's snoring form, then padded forward to sit at Sunbeam's
side. To Sunbeam's surprise, her voice was gentle.

"I don't blame you one bit for acting out like you did. That
family—all of Tigerstar's kin think they can do whatever they
like."

Sunbeam had never expected to hear that from her mother.
To Berryheart, respect for their leader was part of being a
good ShadowClan warrior. "What do you mean?" she asked.

"It's not important," Berryheart responded, obviously
regretting that she had said so much. "Just something that's
been on my mind."

But Sunbeam was desperate for something to distract her
from the pain of her injuries and the whole mess with Blazefire and Lightleap. "Please, tell me," she pleaded.

Thoughtfully, Berryheart licked a forepaw, then drew
it over her ear. "It's all this talk of changing the code," she
mewed at last, "when it's cats like Tigerstar and Dovewing
who will benefit the most. Obviously, I'm not Ashfur," she
continued. "He went much too far in his obsession with the
code. But sometimes I think too many cats aren't all that
trustworthy, and when that happens, the code is there to help

them do the right thing." She broke off suddenly. "I'm sorry—
I'm rambling," she finished.

"I think I understand," Sunbeam told her, giving her
mother an affectionate lick around her ear.

Her mother's sympathy felt nice. And Berryheart had given
her plenty to think about. Lightleap hadn't betrayed her by
becoming mates with Blazefire, in the way she had assumed
at first, but it had still been a betrayal to convince Blazefire
to take such a risk for no reason. And it was a betrayal of the
whole Clan to weaken it by encouraging a warrior to risk
injury. Could Lightleap still be called a trustworthy cat?

Sunbeam heaved a deep sigh. *Should I have been a better friend to
Lightleap? Should I have made her understand how important the warrior
code is? She seems ready to set her paws on a dark path. Was there anything
I could have done to make a difference?*

CHAPTER 19

❧

As Flamepaw leaped from the end of the tree-bridge and trudged up the slope toward the center of the Gathering island, he could feel every hair on his pelt bristling with a mixture of rage and misery. He wasn't sure he wanted to be around his own Clan-mates, let alone cats from all the other Clans.

When he had been chosen to come to the Gathering, his first thought had been to refuse. But Sparkpelt and Lilyheart wouldn't take no for an answer, so all Flamepaw could do was grit his teeth and hope it would be over quickly. Bile rose in his belly and a bitter taste filled his mouth as he remembered his second failed assessment and how he would be ridiculed yet again for not having his warrior name.

I'll keep my eyes open for those apprentices from last time. I'm not sitting anywhere near them!

He cast a hopeful glance up at the sky, but the clouds that had covered it earlier had cleared away, and the moon floated serenely above the trees. There was no sign that StarClan might be angry and draw the Gathering to an early close.

All Flamepaw wanted was to go off by himself and brood about how unfairly his Clan was treating him. The sooner the

Gathering was over, the sooner he could do that.

He pushed his way through the bushes in the paw steps of his Clanmates and flopped down in a shadowy spot as far away from the others as he could get. He didn't want to join them in greeting friends from other Clans and settling down to exchange gossip.

I don't have any friends.

Tigerstar, Harestar, and Leafstar were already perched on branches in the Great Oak; Bramblestar swiftly crossed the clearing and leaped up to take his own place. Only the River-Clan cats were missing.

Time dragged on; several cats were beginning to shift uneasily and cast glances in the direction of the tree-bridge. The leaders in the Great Oak were obviously consulting one another. Finally, as Harestar rose to his paws to begin the Gathering without them, a waft of RiverClan scent came from the lake, and the first of their cats began to appear from the bushes.

"About time!" some cat exclaimed loudly.

But as the RiverClan cats found places for themselves in the clearing, Flamepaw noticed that Mistystar wasn't with them. Their deputy, Reedwhisker, was missing, too; the cat who leaped up into the Great Oak to join the leaders was Mothwing.

Weird, Flamepaw thought, *and so not fair! If a Clan leader can't be bothered to show up to a Gathering, why do I have to be here? I'm not even a warrior yet.*

At least, Flamepaw reflected, Mothwing didn't seem any

happier to be there than he was himself.

"Mistystar and Reedwhisker can't be here tonight," she announced with a nervous nod to the Clan leaders. "River-Clan is dealing with an outbreak of whitecough." An anxious rumble greeted her words from the cats in the clearing, and Mothwing hastened to add to what she had said. "We have it under control, and everything will be fine. There's nothing to worry about."

Alderheart rose from where he was sitting with the other medicine cats. "Do you need any help, Mothwing?" he asked. "I could come over and bring some extra catmint with me."

"Thank you, Alderheart," Mothwing responded with a polite dip of her head, "but it isn't necessary. We'd rather cope with it on our own, and we have plenty of catmint from the gardens in the Twolegplace."

Alderheart dipped his head in return and sat down again.

Flamepaw thought that Mothwing looked grateful when Harestar stepped forward on his branch and announced that the Gathering would begin.

"Bramblestar," the WindClan leader meowed, "would you like to start us off with news from ThunderClan?"

Gazing upward, Flamepaw saw his Clan leader give a start, as if his mind had been somewhere else altogether. His eyes were unfocused as he rose, and a few heartbeats passed before he spoke.

"Everything is fine in ThunderClan."

Harestar tilted his head to one side. "Maybe it's because of that tasty shrew WindClan sent over," he suggested.

Crowfeather, who was sitting on the roots of the Great Oak with the other Clan deputies, let out a *mrrow* of laughter, echoed by more of the WindClan cats. Bramblestar simply blinked in confusion; clearly he had no idea what all that was about.

Flamepaw cast a curious look at Squirrelflight. *Has she still not told Bramblestar about our trip to WindClan to remind them about the rules over borders?*

From the filthy look Squirrelflight gave Crowfeather, he guessed that she had not. Now she jumped to her paws and announced clearly, "Prey is running well in ThunderClan. We have all we need to eat."

Harestar narrowed his eyes at Squirrelflight with a curious tilt of his head. He seemed to realize that she was covering for her Clan leader, drawing attention away from his bewilderment. Turning to Bramblestar, he asked, "Is there any other news from ThunderClan?"

Flamepaw was aware of cats from the other Clans turning to look at him. This was the moment he had dreaded, because if he had been made a warrior, this was when his leader would announce it. But Bramblestar just shook his head and stepped back.

Fixing his gaze on the ground, Flamepaw dug his claws into the earth. He wanted to lash out at some cat, to screech at Bramblestar or Squirrelflight about the unfairness of it all. But even in his tumult of emotions, he knew that would only make things worse.

Is this why Squirrelflight made me come? he asked himself. *Maybe she thinks I need a good shaming, as if I failed because I didn't work hard enough.*

Then he heard Squirrelflight clear her throat. "Thunder-Clan has no more news to report," she meowed, "but I'm sure we will soon."

Flamepaw bared his teeth in a snarl. *Yeah, Squirrelflight— that's so helpful!*

Tigerstar spoke next, launching into some complicated story about a new kittypet in the Twoleg den on ShadowClan territory, and Flamepaw was no longer the center of attention. But he could still sense that some cats were casting him pity-ing looks. His embarrassment and shame swelled within him until he thought it would consume him completely, but just when he thought he couldn't bear it anymore, Harestar raised his voice to make his own announcement.

"At the last half-moon, all our medicine cats went to the Moonpool and walked in dreams with StarClan, to pres-ent them our ideas about changes to the code. I'm sure each medicine cat has reported to their own Clan, but I have been chosen to make the announcement here at the Gathering."

He paused, letting his gaze travel around the clearing; every cat's attention was firmly focused on him. Even Flame-paw looked up and pricked his ears to listen.

"As you probably realize," the WindClan leader went on, "StarClan has approved our ideas, and so now I announce that from this moment, these changes will be added to the warrior code."

A murmur of many voices rose from the crowd of cats in

the clearing. Flamepaw half expected protests, especially from the warriors who had argued against the changes, but every cat seemed to realize that the time for protest was past.

"Because of this, I have another announcement to make," Harestar continued. "The WindClan warrior Fernstripe has decided to leave our Clan, and join ThunderClan to be with Shellfur. I'm not happy about the thought of losing one of our warriors, but we all agreed to this change in the code about relationships between different Clans, so I can't deny her request. They will face the challenges that the Clans have agreed to, and let that decide the outcome."

Once more a murmur rose from the cats in the clearing, part shock, part approval, but almost at once Leafstar's voice cut through it.

"I have also received a request, from Fringewhisker," the SkyClan leader announced. "She has asked to leave SkyClan and join ShadowClan because she wants to be with Spireclaw."

The murmur grew louder, and Flamepaw could feel excitement tingling in the air. He guessed that many cats had accepted the idea of the changes without thinking that anything would actually happen, and not realizing what upheaval this would cause in the life of the Clans. He hadn't expected that cats would want to take advantage of the changes, certainly not as soon as this. He wondered whether he would ever care enough about a she-cat to leave his Clan for her.

In the confusion, Berryheart of ShadowClan sprang to her paws and raised her voice to be heard above the tumult. "I know it was agreed that cats would be given a chance to follow their hearts to a new Clan," she began, "but I didn't think any cat would jump at the chance so quickly."

Leafstar gazed down at her with sympathy in her amber eyes. "I've spoken with Fringewhisker," she assured the dismayed she-cat, "and this wasn't a decision she came to lightly. As much as she loves SkyClan, she loves Spireclaw more, and she's willing to do whatever it takes to be with him."

Berryheart was obviously trying to hide her irritation, but she couldn't prevent her tail-tip from whipping to and fro. *Of course—she's Spireclaw's mother,* Flamepaw remembered. *This matters to her.*

Before Berryheart could say any more, Spireclaw leaped to his paws and faced her. "Fringewhisker is a great cat," he declared. "She'll be an asset to ShadowClan."

Berryheart turned her head to glare at him. "That's not for you to say," she snapped. "You haven't got the sense of a day-old kit."

"That's enough," Tigerstar broke in from where he sat on the branch of the Great Oak. "These arguments belong in our own camp, not at a Gathering."

Spireclaw looked embarrassed and dipped his head to his Clan leader before he sat down again. But Berryheart still remained on her paws.

"I understand how Fringewhisker could want to change," she went on curtly. "Any cat would be lucky to be with my son Spireclaw. But I have to ask: Are cats being too quick to give up on finding love within their own Clans? And if cats are that eager to change Clans for love, how long will it be before they start finding other reasons to change? How long before there's so much change that there are no real Clans anymore?" She paused, the anger draining from her voice to be replaced by deep uncertainty. "I love the pride of ShadowClan. I love the way we do what we want and we don't need to rely on any other Clan. Leaving my Clan to follow Darktail was the biggest mistake I ever made. It means everything to me that I am now a true ShadowClan warrior, and it frightens me to think that I might be in danger of losing that."

At Berryheart's words the noise died into an uneasy silence. With no comment from the Clan leaders, the cats in the clearing began to break up into small groups, discussing what the ShadowClan she-cat had said in lowered, intense voices.

Flamepaw stayed where he was, thinking over what he had just heard. If ShadowClan could change, he thought, then so could ThunderClan. *Would it matter to me?* he asked himself. *If ThunderClan weren't ThunderClan anymore? Do we even have anything that makes us special—or did we throw it away like a piece of crow-food when we thought Ashfur was our leader?*

"That's just typical ShadowClan!"

The exclamation distracted Flamepaw from his thoughts; he turned his head to see a group of senior warriors from his own Clan. The speaker was Thornclaw; his tabby fur was bristling as he glared at Berryheart.

"Who do they think they are?" he continued. "Talking like they're the best Clan in the forest!"

"Well, every Clan thinks they're the best Clan," Whitewing

mewed, laying a calming tail-tip on Thornclaw's shoulder.

"Yeah, but when we say that, we're right!" Bumblestripe grumbled. "But we won't be, not for long, if the other Clans steal all our best warriors."

"And send us the lazy ones and the troublemakers," Thornclaw agreed.

Flamepaw edged even farther into the shadows, disgusted with his Clanmates and hoping that he could avoid talking to them or any other cat. Looking around, he could see that he wasn't the only one. At the far side of the clearing he spotted the brown-and-white tabby she-cat he remembered from the previous Gathering—the ShadowClan warrior who had told him he didn't look like a Flamepaw. She looked just as miserable as he felt, staring fixedly at her own paws.

I wonder what's going on with her.

But Flamepaw's attention was distracted from the she-cat by whispering voices much closer to him.

"What's wrong with him?"

"Why hasn't he been made a warrior yet?"

"Well, we could just ask him."

Looking up, Flamepaw saw a group of young cats eyeing him curiously. He didn't recognize them, but from their skinny forms he thought they must be from WindClan.

Flamepaw certainly wasn't going to answer their questions. Rising to his paws, he slunk along the line of the bushes until he came to a narrow gap leading to a spit of land hidden by shrubs and looking out over the lake. It was a peaceful spot to sit and brood, until he heard the shrubs rustling as another cat pushed their way through.

"This spot is taken," he snapped without looking up. "So just beat it, okay?"

"You don't own this spot," an annoyed voice informed him. "I have as much right to be here as you do."

Flamepaw turned his head to see the brown-and-white ShadowClan she-cat, her expression furious and sad all at once. "I'm sorry," he mewed, letting out a sigh. "I just wanted to be alone."

"So did I," the ShadowClan cat responded. "I didn't know this spot was here, but it's perfect for hiding out." She sat beside him and tucked her paws under her. "It's Flamepaw, isn't it?"

Flamepaw nodded. "I don't know your name."

"I'm Sunbeam. Though, to be honest, I feel like I should be Raincloud right now."

"What is it you're hiding from?" Flamepaw asked her. "I thought you looked kind of upset when they were talking about leaving your Clan for love." *Maybe that's her problem?* "Did it have anything to do with . . . well, that?" he asked hesitantly.

"Was it so obvious?" Sunbeam asked, giving her chest fur a few embarrassed licks. For a moment Flamepaw thought she wouldn't reply, as if she didn't want to share her feelings with a complete stranger. Then she gave a tiny shrug and continued, "I thought I was going to be mates with Blazefire, but now he's backed out, and he's hanging around with the cat who was my best friend all the time. They say they don't want to be mates, and I believe them, but I've still lost my friend *and* the cat I love, all at the same time."

"That's tough," Flamepaw murmured sympathetically.

"And that's not all," Sunbeam went on. "Now I've just found out that my brother Spireclaw has been secretly padding after Fringewhisker from SkyClan, and he never told me. And my parents are *furious* about it—especially Berryheart."

"It could be worse," Flamepaw suggested. "Spireclaw could be the one to leave his Clan and go to hers."

"I know," Sunbeam sighed. "But if Fringewhisker comes to us, Spireclaw will be too busy with her to think about me, and my parents will be too angry to talk. I feel so alone."

"I'm not surprised. That's just awful." Flamepaw felt anger gathering inside him again, not for himself this time, but for the ShadowClan she-cat who had been so badly betrayed. "Maybe we should do what Fringewhisker and Fernstripe are doing," he suggested, only half joking. "Look for a cat in another Clan to fall in love with, and leave our own Clans behind."

Sunbeam let out a snort. "I doubt my mother would be okay with that," she meowed. "It's bad enough that Fringewhisker is going to try to join ShadowClan to be with Spireclaw. You heard what Berryheart said just now—you know she's our mother, right? I'm sure she doesn't want to have SkyClan kin. Not that there's anything wrong with SkyClan, but obviously our mother would rather Spireclaw found a mate in our own Clan, just like I wanted to be mates with Blazefire. But I guess neither of us will get what we want."

Flamepaw shot her a sympathetic glance. "It's Blazefire's

loss," he declared. "I don't know you very well, but you seem like a great cat."

"Thank you." Sunbeam looked up at him, blinking gratefully. "That's kind of you. So why are you here?" she added after a moment. "What is your problem?"

"I failed my assessment," Flamepaw confessed. "For the second time. I really don't think it was my fault, but Squirrelflight still persuaded my mentor to fail me." He flexed his claws in frustration. "It's so unfair! I know I have what it takes to be a warrior, but here I am, still stuck as an apprentice." Putting it into words just made the pain bite more sharply; Flamepaw wondered how he could go on enduring it. "If I fail again," he confessed, half surprising himself, "I don't think I'll want to be part of the Clan at all."

"That's so wrong." Sunbeam's voice was understanding, but she wasn't fussing over him like a mother cat whose kit had a thorn in its paw. "I'm sure you'll pass next time, and you'll be able to put all this behind you." She paused, then added, "But you have every right to be angry now."

Flamepaw gazed at her. No cat in his own Clan had said this to him. *They all act like my problems are my own fault.* But here was a cat from a different Clan, a cat who really saw him, who knew what he was going through. *It feels so great to be understood, but she's a ShadowClan cat, so I might not get to talk to her again.*

His throat felt choked up, but he managed to whisper the words. "Thank you."

CHAPTER 20

The full moon rose high above the hills, casting its silver light over
the tough moorland grass, as Frostpaw headed to the Moonpool with Splashtail by her side.

"Are you sure you want to do this without the other medicine cats?" he asked her gently.

More than anything, Frostpaw wanted to answer, "No,"
and race back to the safety of her den in the RiverClan camp.
The thought of what she had to do weighed on her as heavily
as if she were trying to carry a fox on her shoulders, but she
knew there was no way she could turn back.

"I have to," she replied with a sigh. Duskfur, Curlfeather
and Mothwing had decided that if she went to the Moonpool during the Gathering, there wouldn't be much chance of
another cat seeing her and wondering why she was going. And
there was so much confusion in RiverClan, with no single cat
in charge, that she hadn't felt she had the right to argue. "I
have to do this for our Clan."

"You're right, but it's tough," Splashtail agreed.

"Well, until we work out how we can choose a new leader,

we can't let any cat in the other Clans know what's going on," Frostpaw continued. She looked at Splashtail, wondering if she should comment on how supportive he'd been toward her lately. They'd been friends since they were young, but it still stung to think of how he'd insulted her on the patrol to find Reedwhisker. *Maybe that helped him realize that I* am *capable,* she mused. "It's up to me to speak with StarClan and find out who our new leader should be. Only . . . what if I can't do it?" All the fears Frostpaw had tried to banish came rushing back; she felt as if she were trying to stay on her paws in raging floodwater. "What if StarClan does send me a message, but I get it wrong? I'm only an apprentice, and what I say could affect the Clan for seasons."

Splashtail laid his tail across her shoulders in a comforting gesture. "You should have faith in yourself," he told her. "You're a bright, talented medicine-cat apprentice, and Star-Clan wouldn't guide you wrong."

Grateful for his words, Frostpaw could only hope that he was right. In any case, she had no choice but to try. *Besides,* she told herself firmly, *our Clan is full of worthy warriors who want to see RiverClan succeed. I'm sure that whoever I choose will step up to the challenge.*

Finally Frostpaw and Splashtail scrambled up the rocky slope and halted beside the line of bushes that barred the entrance to the Moonpool hollow.

"You'll have to wait here," Frostpaw told Splashtail. "I have to do this part alone."

"Sure." Splashtail sat down and wrapped his tail around his paws. "Good luck, anyway. I'll be right here waiting for you if you need me."

Frostpaw dipped her head in thanks, feeling warmed by her friend's support. She pushed her way through the bushes, then paused briefly at the top of the spiral path, her breath catching in her throat at the beauty that lay before her. She had never seen the Moonpool beneath a full moon before. The waterfall seemed like liquid light, and the surface of the pool glittered as the moving water broke up the reflection of the moon and stars.

Then Frostpaw gave her pelt a shake. *I can't stand here gawking like a kit when their eyes first open. But oh, StarClan, I'm so glad that I've seen this!*

Shivering with a mixture of wonder and terror, she began to pad down the spiral path, feeling her paws slip into the paw marks of those cats from so long ago. It felt strange to be there on her own. Mothwing or Alderheart should have been taking the lead, or Jayfeather grumpily finding something to complain about. Instead, it was only her approaching the pool in the vast silence and shimmer of the night.

Frostpaw sat at the edge of the Moonpool and concentrated on quieting her mind so that she could commune with Star-Clan. Closing her eyes, she took a few deep breaths, calling out with her thoughts to the spirits of her warrior ancestors. When she leaned forward and touched her nose to the cool water, she was sure she could hear a whisper of something in her ears. But she couldn't quite make out the words.

The moments slid by as Frostpaw remained immobile, straining with all her senses to pick up some message—any message—from StarClan. At one point she heard a faint sound coming from somewhere above her, but it wasn't repeated, and finally she accepted that it must have been a bird or some small animal scuffling about.

After what felt like moons, Frostpaw had to sit back, slumping in disappointment. *Does StarClan have nothing to say? Or do they just have nothing to say to me?*

She wondered what she would tell her Clanmates when she got back to camp without any word from StarClan. What would they think? Would Splashtail be the only one who still had faith in her abilities as a medicine cat?

Worry was coursing through Frostpaw from ears to tail-tip, but there was nothing more she could do. She rose to her paws, stiff from crouching by the water for so long, and began the slow climb up the spiral path to rejoin Splashtail.

But on her way upward, Frostpaw spotted something white in the grass beside the path. *What could that be?* She padded up to it and looked closer, realizing that it was a feather. A curled feather.

Frostpaw bent her head to sniff at the feather, then tasted the air, but all she could pick up was the scent of wild thyme that was growing all around. She gazed at the small scrap of white again, and wondered if she could discern a faint frosty glitter at the very edges.

Suddenly Frostpaw understood what she was seeing; her chest felt tight and her breath came short in her throat.

StarClan doesn't only speak in dreams and visions . . . they guide us through signs, too. And this is a sign! StarClan has spoken to me after all.

And the sign could not have been clearer. StarClan had placed a curled feather in exactly the right place for Frostpaw to find it. The only cat it could refer to was Curlfeather. Frostpaw's mother was meant to be the next leader of RiverClan!

For a few moments Frostpaw stood rigid, as if she were a cat made of ice. Partly she felt surprise, but mostly she was transfixed by a huge sense of relief. Curlfeather was so capable; she would guide RiverClan just as she had guided Frostpaw and her littermates ever since they were born. *I won't have to feel so responsible anymore, because I know I can trust Curlfeather. Oh, StarClan, thank you for making everything all right again!*

Excitedly, Frostpaw bounded up the path away from the feather and wriggled through the bushes to find Splashtail patiently waiting for her.

"Well?" he asked. "Did you get the answer you were seeking?"

Frostpaw nodded vigorously. She wanted to spill it all out, to tell her Clanmate about the wonderful thing that had happened, but she knew she wasn't supposed to do that. "I have to tell Mothwing first," she explained. "And then she'll announce it to the Clan."

To her relief, Splashtail didn't press her to tell him. "That's okay," he mewed. "We'd better head out before it gets any later."

Frostpaw thought that her paws would drop off by the time she leaped over the stream and climbed the bank into the RiverClan camp. By this time the sky was paling toward dawn; apart from Podlight, who was on watch, there were no cats out in the clearing.

"They'll be sleeping off the Gathering," Splashtail remarked, with a massive yawn. "I'm ready for sleep myself."

"Thank you for coming with me," Frostpaw meowed, touching his ear with her nose. "I'll see you later."

Frostpaw hurried across the camp and leaped down onto the stretch of pebbles outside the medicine cats' den. Mothwing was just emerging, blinking and shivering in the chilly morning air.

"I did it!" Frostpaw announced excitedly. "StarClan has told me who the new leader should be."

Mothwing twitched her ears and shook her head to dislodge a scrap of moss. "So? Who?"

"Curlfeather!" Frostpaw announced proudly.

She had expected praise from her mentor; instead, Mothwing looked surprised and a little doubtful. "Curlfeather . . . ," she murmured. "I'm not sure I was expecting that."

"You thought it should be some other cat?" Frostpaw asked anxiously. *What other cat would be a better leader than Curlfeather?*

"No, I just . . . No." Mothwing sounded uncomfortable. "Are you sure that's what StarClan said?" she continued after a couple of heartbeats. "They can be a bit vague sometimes. You're not interpreting what they said in a way that makes your mother leader?"

"No!" Frostpaw was indignant that Mothwing would even suspect her of something so terrible as intentionally misinterpreting StarClan's intentions in Curlfeather's favor. "StarClan didn't speak to me at all. They left me a sign instead—a curled feather beside the path that leads down to the Moonpool. You can't get much clearer than that, can you?"

Mothwing still shook her head dubiously. "You wouldn't know this, but my brother, Hawkfrost, once left a moth's wing outside the RiverClan medicine cat's den so he would choose me as his apprentice. Since I found out about that, I've always felt we shouldn't put too much faith in signs."

Frostpaw's heart began to pound, in horror that any cat would dare to fake a sign, and hurt that her mentor suspected her of lying. "Do you think I put the feather there? Or that I'm making it all up?"

"No, of course not," Mothwing assured her quickly. "I believe that you're sincere. But I think you should sleep on it. You should be sure before we tell the rest of the Clan, that's all."

Frostpaw hesitated, struggling with anger. *Mothwing doesn't speak to StarClan, so I have to do all this on my own. And she's still telling me I'm doing it wrong!* But she couldn't bring herself to put any of that into words and quarrel with the mentor she still respected, in spite of everything.

"Okay," she agreed at last. "I'm so exhausted now, I'm ready to see if StarClan will send me a dream."

She headed into the den and curled up in her nest. Worn out by the long journey, she relaxed and let sleep enfold her like a dark pelt.

Almost at once, Frostpaw found herself beside the Moon-pool again. But this time, the ground by the pool and all the sides of the hollow were covered in curled white feathers. As Frostpaw gazed, entranced, they took to the sky and became birds, whirling around her head like a blizzard.

A clear voice spoke from the sky. "Have faith in yourself, Frostpaw."

Half rousing from her dream, Frostpaw let out a satisfied sigh. "You can't have a clearer answer than that," she murmured, burrowing deeper into her nest.

CHAPTER 21

❧

"Push!"

"Come on, Fringewhisker!"

"You can do it!"

Sunbeam looked on as Fringewhisker, a brown-and-white she-cat from SkyClan, struggled to push a fallen tree branch out of the ShadowClan camp. The youngest ShadowClan warriors were jumping up and down with excitement, loudly urging her on. Obviously, Sunbeam thought, they were caught up in the moment, not giving any thought to what this actually meant for the Clans. *If they had really thought about welcoming a SkyClan cat into the Clan, they wouldn't be so enthusiastic. SkyClan has only lived by the lake for a few seasons. What do we really know about them?*

Cheering loudest of all was Sunbeam's brother Spireclaw, but he knew exactly what this meant. It was the first ever trial of strength to decide whether a cat would be allowed to change Clans. If Fringewhisker succeeded in this test, she would be accepted into ShadowClan and could become Spireclaw's mate.

The branch was a heavy one; it had taken three or four warriors to drag it into the camp for the trial. Fringewhisker had to summon all her strength to move it, especially as there was an upward slope from the center of the camp to the barrier of bushes that surrounded it.

Most of the Clan was out in the clearing to watch. Tigerstar stood at the front of the crowd; his expression showed nothing of what he was thinking. Hawkwing, the SkyClan deputy, who had come with Fringewhisker to witness the trial, was easier for Sunbeam to read. His gaze was full of disapproval; he clearly wanted Fringewhisker to fail, or to come to her senses.

Fringewhisker had managed to push the tree branch to the top of the slope. There were a few tricky moments as she maneuvered it past the line of bushes, shoving it through until it disappeared, but then Sunbeam could hear it bumping down the slope on the other side.

Panting, her eyes shining with triumph, Fringewhisker turned back and bounded into the center of the camp. Tigerstar stepped forward to meet her.

"Fringewhisker has succeeded in completing this challenge," he announced.

The younger ShadowClan cats exploded into cheering, while Spireclaw raced forward to touch noses with the cat he loved.

But not every cat was happy with the outcome. Sunbeam spotted her mother, Berryheart, with a small group of the older cats, all shaking their heads as if something terrible had happened. Sunbeam eased closer so that she could hear what they were saying.

"This is dreadful," Berryheart muttered. "I never thought I'd see such a thing."

"What's so dreadful about it?" Tawnypelt asked.

"Well, *you* might not think so." Berryheart looked the tortoiseshell she-cat up and down, and Sunbeam remembered that Tawnypelt had been born in ThunderClan, the sister of its leader Bramblestar. "But I always imagined Spireclaw with a ShadowClan she-cat—I even had a few in mind. They would have made beautiful ShadowClan kits together. But now," Berryheart continued with a lash of her tail, "I'll have half-Clan kin whose mother will always have one paw back in SkyClan. And all because of this stupid sham of a test!"

Tawnypelt seemed to stifle a hiss and stalked off. Sunbeam watched her go, remembering that Tawnypelt had joined ShadowClan long before she was born, from ThunderClan. *She must not like all this half-Clan business,* she mused.

"Berryheart," Sunbeam's father, Sparrowtail, mewed, "maybe we should let this—"

But Snowbird interrupted.

"Why do you think it was a sham?" she asked.

Sparrowtail looked pained as Berryheart let out a disapproving snort. "To begin with, it was way too easy. Even the youngest apprentices know how to clear debris out of the dens. What's so hard about pushing a branch out of the way? And did you see what Fringewhisker did before she started? She broke off some of the smaller branches and twigs that would have slowed her down, so the branch was smoother and was easier to roll."

But that's not cheating, Sunbeam thought as Sparrowtail got to his feet and walked away. *That's just common sense. Maybe we should be glad to welcome a bright warrior like Fringewhisker into our Clan.*

"The last bit of the challenge was on flat ground, at the top of the slope," Berryheart went on. "And once she got it through the bushes, it rolled down the other side on its own. This whole idea is mouse-brained!"

"If that's true," Grassheart mewed, looking puzzled, "then why would Tigerstar go along with it? Is he biased in some way?"

"How do I know what goes through his head?" Berryheart demanded with an angry shrug. "Maybe he just wants to steal a warrior from SkyClan. Maybe since Rowankit and Birchkit were born, and they're so small and fragile, he would like another fully grown warrior to help protect them. Who knows? But I'll tell you one thing: I doubt Tigerstar will be so cool about it when a *ShadowClan* warrior wants to leave. Then he'll see what damage switching Clans like this can cause."

Murmurs of agreement came from the cats around her. "But what can we do?" Snowbird wondered.

"The warrior code forbade this for a reason," Berryheart responded. "Maybe the Clan just needs a reminder."

A reminder? Sunbeam backed away out of earshot, not liking the sound of that at all. The way her mother was talking sounded like a cat planning to make trouble for the Clan. And after all they had been through with Ashfur, Sunbeam thought Tigerstar ought to know about it right away, so that he could nip it in the bud.

But can I inform on Berryheart like that? Sunbeam asked herself. *She's my mother, for StarClan's sake!* She remembered how she had told the truth about Lightleap, and how badly that had gone. If she had kept her jaws shut, she wouldn't have quarreled with her best friend, or been in trouble with her Clan leader.

Besides, the last thing Sunbeam wanted was to get Berryheart into trouble, especially if she was wrong. Her mother might be just venting, without really intending to do anything.

Sunbeam remembered how Blazefire used to tease her about being too caught up in the rules. *But if Berryheart does do something, and I knew about it but kept my mouth shut, how will I feel?*

From the first day Sunbeam had been an apprentice, she had been taught that loyalty to Clan was even more important than loyalty to kin. If Berryheart was planning something that would be anything like Ashfur's evil plots, then Tigerstar needed to know. Telling him was the right thing to do. What he did with the information was up to him.

Taking a deep breath, Sunbeam braced herself and looked around for Tigerstar. Soon she spotted the Clan leader standing to one side, gazing proudly at the young cats who were gathered around Fringewhisker, congratulating her on her success.

It's the perfect moment to speak to him.

Sunbeam padded up to her Clan leader and cleared her throat. "Do you have a moment?" she asked shyly.

"Of course," Tigerstar responded, dipping his head. "I always have time to talk to my warriors. What's on your mind?"

The words Sunbeam wanted to say were poised on the tip of her tongue, like birds about to take off from a branch. But when she spotted her mother at the other side of the camp, then glanced at Spireclaw as he happily praised Fringewhisker, her throat dried up and the words remained unspoken.

If I tell Tigerstar what I heard, what will happen to Berryheart? Will he punish her? Exile her? And what about Spireclaw? If Tigerstar thinks our mother is a traitor, will he think the same about him?

Sunbeam could imagine Tigerstar punishing Spireclaw by refusing to accept Fringewhisker into the Clan. *And would there be any good reason for it?* she asked herself. *What do I really know, anyway?*

Berryheart hadn't been making specific plans when Sunbeam overheard her. If she voiced her suspicions to Tigerstar now, with no more evidence than her mother's disapproval of changing Clans, she would only sound silly. *I don't want to be in trouble with him again!*

Tigerstar was still waiting for her to speak; his whiskers had started to twitch impatiently. "Well?" he prompted her. "Spit it out!"

"Oh . . . um . . . I just wanted to go on the next hunting patrol," Sunbeam mewed desperately.

Tigerstar stared at her as if she had just sprouted another head. "That's it?" When Sunbeam only nodded, he continued, "Okay, fine. Just let Cloverfoot know."

"Thanks, Tigerstar," Sunbeam choked out.

"Is everything okay with you?" Tigerstar asked. "I know you've had a tough time lately." He hesitated, then added awkwardly, "If you need to talk . . ."

Sunbeam quailed inwardly at the thought of unburdening herself to her Clan leader, who wasn't known for his patience. "No, it's fine, Tigerstar," she assured him hastily. "Thanks all the same."

She bounded away, feeling utterly ridiculous, and only hoping that her leader didn't think she was a mouse-brain.

Sunbeam headed for the fresh-kill pile, hoping a juicy mouse might make her feel better. But almost as soon as she settled down to eat, Berryheart appeared at her side. "Are you okay?" she asked.

Sunbeam looked up, alarm pulsing through her. *Did she see me talking to Tigerstar? Does she know what I was planning to tell him?*

"I'm fine," she managed to reply. "Why?"

Berryheart leaned close to her. "I'm quite aware of what you're thinking," she murmured. "I'm your mother, and I know you better than you know yourself. I saw your face when you were listening to me and the others talking, and it seemed to upset you."

Sunbeam felt all her muscles tense as she waited for her mother to accuse her of informing on her to Tigerstar. But to her relief, Berryheart said nothing more, only standing with her head tilted expectantly for a response.

"After all the Clans have been through," Sunbeam responded with a weak nod, "I just want every cat to get along."

Berryheart gave her a sideways, sardonic look that made Sunbeam feel like what she had just said was naive.

"I want that, too," Berryheart meowed. "But if you really

heard me and some of the others out, I'm sure you would agree with us about what's best for the Clan. After all, you want ShadowClan to be as strong and united as possible, don't you?"

"Of course I do."

"Then why don't you join the discussion next time?" Berryheart suggested. Her voice was pleasant, but somehow it sent a shiver right down to the tips of Sunbeam's claws. "We're only trying to preserve the ShadowClan we all know and love—surely you agree with that?"

Sunbeam nodded mutely, feeling more uncomfortable with every heartbeat.

"Then join us," Berryheart mewed. "You might like what you hear."

CHAPTER 22

❧

Stalking forward on moss-soft paws, Flamepaw hardly dared to breathe. He skimmed over the forest floor, careful not to make a sound, his senses alert for any change in the breeze, any crackling dead leaf that might give him away to his prey.

Somewhere nearby, he knew, Lilyheart and Squirrelflight would be keeping an eye on him, but he hoped that the rabbit he was tracking couldn't see him. He had watched it leave its burrow, nose twitching as it tried to sense something succulent to eat. He had flattened himself in the long grass while it hopped forward and plunged its muzzle into a clump of bright green leaves. Then he began to work his way around to the mouth of the burrow.

Thank StarClan I'm pretty skinny, he thought. *I'm just the right size for this.*

Flamepaw reached the opening and turned around to back tail-first into the tunnel. When he was far enough from the entrance that he couldn't be seen, he settled down to wait patiently. Before long he could hear the shuffle of the rabbit's paws on the earth floor, and the crunching of one last crisp leaf.

Then the sounds stopped. Flamepaw couldn't see anything in the darkness of the burrow, but he guessed that the rabbit had caught his scent. It was too late, though. Powering forward, he slammed into his prey and fastened his teeth into its neck.

The rabbit fought back, pounding Flamepaw's side with its wide, flat paws; Flamepaw held on, sinking his teeth in even further and shaking the rabbit until it collapsed into a limp heap.

"Thank you, StarClan, for this prey," Flamepaw gasped.

Getting the rabbit out of the burrow was harder than he had expected. It was heavy, and too big for him to squeeze past in the narrow tunnel. He had to push instead, panting with the effort until he managed to thrust it out into the light.

Lilyheart burst out of a nearby clump of fern, her eyes sparkling with excitement. "That was clever!" she exclaimed. "Such a good idea, and brilliant stalking!"

"Thank you," Flamepaw responded. Her praise warmed him, but his heart started pounding unpleasantly as he asked her the inevitable question; he was almost too afraid to listen to the answer. "Does that mean I pass?"

Lilyheart glanced over her shoulder, and Flamepaw spotted Squirrelflight lingering beside the nearby trees. Slowly the Clan deputy padded over to join them, and stood for an endless moment eyeing Flamepaw and the lifeless rabbit.

"Great StarClan, Flamepaw," she meowed at last. "You do have to find weird ways of doing stuff, don't you?"

Far from pounding, Flamepaw's heart felt like it might

stop. *Is she telling me that I've failed my assessment a third time?*

Squirrelflight relaxed, a gleam of humor in her green eyes. Then she nodded. "I'd call that a pass, wouldn't you, Lilyheart?"

"I would," Lilyheart agreed. "Well done, Flamepaw. I knew you would get there in the end."

Flamepaw wanted to jump up and down, squealing with excitement, like a kit playing moss-ball. But he knew that warriors didn't behave like that. Instead, trying to be dignified, he dipped his head to his mentor and his Clan deputy. "Thank you," he mewed.

"Flamepaw, I hope you know I was only hard on you because I've known all along what you were capable of," Squirrelflight told him. "I didn't want you to settle for anything less. Now you've proven that you'll be a smart, brave warrior, and a credit to ThunderClan."

Flamepaw repeated his thanks. Part of him would have liked to argue that he felt he had proved his worth during his previous assessment, but he pushed the thought away, just happy to be a warrior at last.

"You'd better get back to camp," Squirrelflight continued. "Lilyheart and I will bring your rabbit. It's too big for one cat to manage."

Flamepaw wanted to stay calm and self-controlled, but his paws were itching with pride and relief, and by the time he reached the stone hollow, he was speeding through the trees, eager to share his news with all his Clanmates. He shot through the thorn tunnel and burst out into the camp.

"I did it!" he yowled. "I passed!"

His sister, Finchlight, who was outside the nursery playing with Spotfur's kits, looked up, then raced across the camp to join him.

"Congratulations!" she purred, nuzzling his shoulder. "Tell me all about it."

"Well," Flamepaw began, "there was this enormous rabbit. . . ."

As he told the story, more of his Clanmates padded up to offer their congratulations. Jayfeather was one of the first, giving Flamepaw a curt nod. "About time," he rasped.

"A big rabbit, eh?" Cloudtail passed his tongue over his jaws. "The Clan will eat well tonight."

"Good job, youngster," Lionblaze praised him, his amber eyes glowing. "You'll make a fine warrior."

Seeing how pleased they were gave Flamepaw a warm feeling from ears to tail-tip; he had been afraid that no cat in the Clan, except his sister, cared whether he passed or not. He felt happier still when he saw his mother, Sparkpelt, shouldering her way through the crowd and gazing down at him with approval in her eyes.

"So you passed!" she meowed. "I'm so proud of you, Flamepaw."

"Thank you," Flamepaw responded, feeling closer to her than he had in a long while.

"I knew you could do it," Sparkpelt continued. "After all, you're a descendant of Firestar. Being a skilled hunter is in your blood."

Flamepaw suddenly felt his chest tighten, as if he couldn't get enough air. He was tired of being told he had to set his paws on a certain path because Firestar was his ancestor. Besides, he hadn't passed his assessment because of which cats he was related to. He had passed because he had worked so hard.

Did Sparkpelt really not notice how much time I spent practicing? Building up my strength, learning as many fighting and hunting techniques as I could? And all that while I was doing my apprentice duties as well? All the apprentice duties, because I was the only one.

Flamepaw wondered when his mother would give him credit for his efforts, instead of pointing to the skills of some long-ago kin he had never even met. The answer seemed to be never.

They even sort of named me after Firestar, though my pelt is black.

His kin seemed to think they were honoring him, but Flamepaw felt as trapped as a mouse kept prisoner under their claws. Or as if he walked through his days under an enormous shadow—a shadow cast by the great leader Firestar.

"The sun is going down," Sparkpelt continued, seeming to be unaware of what Flamepaw was feeling. "We'll have to hold your warrior ceremony tomorrow." She gave Flamepaw's ear a swift lick. "I'm sure you can't wait!"

Flamepaw tried to recapture his earlier excitement, but it was hard. He felt that he was becoming a warrior in a Clan that only valued him because he was Firestar's kin, refusing to see the cat that he was. *This will be my last night as an apprentice— but I'm not looking forward to tomorrow.*

* * *

"Let all cats old enough to catch their own prey gather here. beneath the Highledge for a Clan meeting!"

Bramblestar's voice rang out across the camp; Flamepaw, who had been waiting outside the apprentices' den, nervously flexing his claws, rose and moved into the center of the camp.

The sun had just cleared the tops of the trees above the stone hollow. The dawn patrol had returned, and though Squirrelflight had arranged the first hunting patrols, she hadn't sent them out yet.

Instead, the Clan began to assemble. Cloudtail, Bright-heart, and Brackenfur slid out of the hazel bush that formed the elders' den and found a sunny spot where they could relax. Spotfur and Daisy were sitting together at the entrance to the nursery, while Spotfur's kits play wrestled in front of them. Alderheart greeted Flamepaw with a wave of his tail as he emerged from the medicine cats' den, followed by Jayfeather. The Clan warriors formed a ragged circle with Flamepaw at its center. Squirrelflight and Lilyheart took places side by side at the front of the crowd.

Flamepaw's heart began to thump. *It's really going to happen!*

Sparkpelt bounded up to him and gave his head and shoulders a few swift licks, while Flamepaw wriggled away in embarrassment. "I'm not a kit!" he protested.

"This is the most important day of your life," Sparkpelt pointed out calmly. "It's no time to look scruffy."

Flamepaw heaved a deep sigh, then stood still while his mother finished her grooming.

Meanwhile Finchlight padded up and touched noses with him. "I wonder what name Bramblestar will give you," she mewed. "Maybe something about the prey you killed to pass your assessment? Or maybe it'll have to do with your long whiskers?"

Flamepaw had no idea what warrior name Bramblestar had in mind for him. He didn't even know what name he wanted, except that he wished he weren't stuck with *Flame*.

Finally Bramblestar made his way down the tumbled rocks and joined Flamepaw in the center of the circle. Flamepaw met his gaze and saw a glow of approval in his leader's amber eyes.

"One of the most important tasks a Clan leader carries out is the making of a new warrior," Bramblestar began. "And the cat we honor today has waited a long time for this ceremony." Turning to Lilyheart, he continued, "Has your apprentice learned the skills of a warrior, and does he understand the demands of the warrior code?"

Lilyheart dipped her head. "He has, and he does."

"Then I, Bramblestar, leader of ThunderClan, call upon my warrior ancestors to look down upon this apprentice. He has trained hard to understand the ways of your noble code, and I commend him to you as a warrior in his turn." The Clan leader turned a wide-eyed gaze on Flamepaw, and continued. "Flamepaw, do you promise to uphold the warrior code, and to protect and defend this Clan, even at the cost of your life?"

Flamepaw lifted his head. All his hard work, all his struggles, even his two failed assessments, had been worth it for this moment. "I do," he replied.

"Then by the powers of StarClan I give you your warrior name," Bramblestar went on. "Squirrelflight tells me that you showed extraordinary patience and ingenuity in your last hunt, just like Firestar. To honor that connection, from this day forward Flamepaw will be known as Flameheart, and we welcome him as a full warrior of ThunderClan."

Flamepaw stared at his Clan leader, his mouth gaping in shock. He couldn't believe the name his Clan leader had given him. It was bad enough that *Flame* was part of it, when he was a black cat. But now Bramblestar wanted to burden him with Firestar's warrior name, too. *Will they ever appreciate me for who I am?*

Meanwhile, yowls of approval broke out from the assembled cats. "Flameheart! Flameheart!"

Flamepaw gathered every scrap of his courage and held up his tail for silence, raking the crowd with a grim gaze. Bramblestar could not have spoken words that would have hurt him more, to speak of his kin at a special moment which that should have been for him alone. He felt as though his heart had been pierced with icy claws.

But that just makes it easier to do what I'm going to do now.

His Clanmates had begun to realize that something was wrong. Their joyful chanting grew ragged and uncertain, until it died away altogether. Every cat was staring at Flamepaw in confusion.

When the stone hollow was silent, Flamepaw drew himself up. "Flameheart will not be my name," he announced.

Gasps of shock ran through the crowd. Flamepaw could guess why: As far as he knew, no cat had ever refused their warrior name—certainly not at their naming ceremony.

Squirrelflight was the first cat to speak, her green eyes snapping fury. "What do you mean?" she demanded. "How dare you reject your name!"

It was hard for Flamepaw to face her without flinching. After all, Firestar had been Squirrelflight's father; he couldn't blame her for being angry.

Before he could respond, Bramblestar turned to his deputy and waved his tail at her in a calming gesture. Then he looked back at Flamepaw.

"If you don't want to be named Flameheart, what name do you want?" he asked.

"I don't know yet," Flamepaw confessed. "I just know that I want something that reflects the cat I am, not some cat from the past that you all wish me to be." His anger overflowed, and he spat the words out. "I'm not Firestar! I don't even look like him, in case you haven't noticed. I will think of a perfect name for myself and let you know."

Cats were exchanging bewildered glances, clearly not knowing how to react. But Flamepaw thought he saw a glimmer of understanding in Bramblestar's eyes. No cat spoke to Flamepaw, except for his mother, Sparkpelt, who broke away from the crowd and bounded forward to his side.

"You're being disrespectful and mouse-brained," she hissed. "This is no way to endear yourself to your Clan."

"That's not fair!" The protest came from Flamepaw's sister,

Finchlight. "Flamepaw was humiliated when he was made to take his assessment three times, even though every cat knows he deserved to be a warrior long ago. So the least you can do is let him choose his own name!"

"Warriors do not choose their own names!" Squirrelflight retorted icily, her dark ginger fur bristling.

Growls and loud meows rose from the assembled Clan as every cat began to join the argument. Seeing how angry he had made Sparkpelt and Squirrelflight, Flamepaw began to wonder if he had gone too far. Desperately, he clung to his conviction that he was right, but it took all his strength to ignore the turmoil around him and keep his gaze fixed on Bramblestar.

His Clan leader still stood calmly in the midst of the turmoil, holding Flamepaw in his quiet attention. At last he raised his voice, and his Clan fell silent.

"We will compromise," he announced. "Flamepaw, I will give you a name that more accurately reflects your appearance and demeanor, but still honors your ancestor. That is the way of this Clan, and—like it or not, Flamepaw—we see some of Firestar's qualities in you." He raised his tail as Flamepaw opened his jaws to protest. "You're right that your pelt doesn't bring fire to mind," he continued. "Just like your father, Larksong, you are as black as night. So from now on, Flamepaw, you will be known as Nightheart."

CHAPTER 23

"So, Frostpaw, did StarClan send you a dream last night?" Mothwing looked up from grooming herself as soon as Frostpaw emerged from her den, blinking in the pale dawn light.

Frostpaw paused for a moment before replying. The last shreds of her dream still clung to her, and she was reluctant to surrender the wonder in exchange for an ordinary day in the RiverClan camp.

But it's not an ordinary day, she reminded herself. *It's the day we get our new leader!*

"Well?" Mothwing asked, an edge of impatience in her tone.

"Yes, I had a dream," Frostpaw replied at last. "I was back at the Moonpool, and the whole ground was covered with white, curled feathers. It was so beautiful!"

"Hmm . . . So Curlfeather is to be our new leader." For a moment Frostpaw thought that Mothwing sounded almost disappointed, or perhaps doubtful, as if somehow she wasn't pleased that StarClan had sent the dream.

She can't be jealous of me, surely! She never seemed jealous of Willowshine because she could speak to StarClan and Mothwing can't.

When Mothwing next spoke, she sounded as brisk and

capable as always; Frostpaw thought she must have been imagining things.

"We'd better make an announcement to the Clan, so you and Curlfeather can set off for the Moonpool."

Without waiting for a response from Frostpaw, Mothwing bounded past the opening of their den, up the bank, and through the bushes into the center of the camp. Frostpaw followed more slowly, stifling a groan at the thought of the endless stretch of moorland she would have to cross for the second day running.

By the time Frostpaw emerged from the bushes, Mothwing was standing on the Highstump. "Let all cats old enough to swim gather to hear my words!" she yowled.

The dawn patrol, with Podlight in the lead, was about to leave, but turned back at the sound of Mothwing's summons. More warriors—Curlfeather among them—pushed their way out of their den, yawning and blinking sleep out of their eyes. Mosspelt crept from the elders' den, flopped down at the entrance, and began to wash her ears.

As soon as Mothwing spotted Frostpaw, she leaped down from the Highstump. "Up you go," she meowed, angling her ears to tell Frostpaw to take her place. "You ought to make the announcement."

Frostpaw shrank back. "Mothwing, I can't . . . ," she protested.

"Nonsense, of course you can." Mothwing's tone was sharp, but her amber eyes were warm and encouraging. "It was your sign."

Knowing there was no point in arguing, Frostpaw scrambled up onto the Highstump and gazed down at her Clan. She was acutely conscious of the faces of all her Clanmates, raised toward her, each gaze firmly fixed on her.

Please, StarClan, help me do this.

"Cats of RiverClan," she began, then realized that her voice was too high-pitched; she was almost squeaking like a kit. She swallowed and began again. "Yesterday at the Moonpool, StarClan sent me a sign, and last night they confirmed it with a dream—a dream of white, curled feathers. Their meaning is clear: Curlfeather will be the new leader of RiverClan."

For a few heartbeats the Clan stood in silence, as if they needed time to take in what Frostpaw had just told them. Meanwhile Curlfeather turned a shocked look on her, one that gradually changed to an expression of pleasure and pride.

"Me?" she asked. "Really, me? Oh, thank you, Frostpaw. I swear by StarClan that I will do my best to be a true leader of this Clan."

But while she was speaking, some of her Clanmates turned to each other, exchanging uneasy glances. Doubtful murmurs rose from the crowd. *Suppose they don't accept what I told them?* Frostpaw thought anxiously.

"Are you okay with that, Mothwing?" Owlnose asked eventually.

The medicine cat dipped her head in reply. "I trust Frostpaw's instincts and her connection with StarClan," she meowed. "If she says StarClan has chosen Curlfeather, then Curlfeather will be our leader. Besides, StarClan must still approve her by giving her nine lives and her name. If they refuse, we will know Frostpaw was wrong."

The Clan seemed to relax at Mothwing's words, gathering around Curlfeather to congratulate her. Frostpaw's littermates, Graypaw and Mistpaw, nuzzled her proudly.

"If I can't be leader myself," Duskfur, Curlfeather's mother, declared, "then I'm glad it's my kit. You're a good warrior, Curlfeather, and we all trust you."

Murmurs of agreement rose from the assembled Clan, their doubts seeming to vanish like morning mist. Frostpaw sensed a feeling of relief that the problem of leadership had been settled at last. The camp was in disarray: The fresh-kill pile wasn't as full as usual, and the bedding in the dens had been allowed to get stale. A strong leader and an efficient deputy would soon take care of all that.

RiverClan will soon revive and be as strong as ever, Frostpaw told herself.

The sky was a clear, pale blue as Frostpaw and Curlfeather padded past the horseplace, but there was little warmth in the sun's rays, and every blade of grass was edged with frost. The leaves on the trees across the lake in ThunderClan territory had almost all changed from green to brown and gold.

Leaf-fall is really here, Frostpaw thought.

"I'm sure you'll be a great leader," she told her mother, "but I wish the whole decision hadn't been up to me."

Curlfeather flicked Frostpaw's shoulder affectionately with her tail. "The rest of the Clan seems happy about it," she mewed. "And you didn't choose me because I'm your mother, did you?"

"No!" Frostpaw stared at her in shock. "I wouldn't do that! I really did see a curled feather beside the Moonpool, and have the dream. I wouldn't lie to my Clan."

"Of course not," Curlfeather purred, seeming satisfied by Frostpaw's answer. "And I promise you that I'll do my best for the Clan, from today right to the end of my nine lives. I just wish that you seemed happier about it. If you saw the feather . . ."

"I did—but my decision was based on how I interpreted that feather." Frostpaw couldn't share her mother's confidence. "How can I be sure that I was right?"

"You should trust yourself more." Curlfeather's voice was bracing. "Your decision was based on more than that feather. It was your connection to StarClan that showed you the sign and helped you realize what it meant. And it was StarClan who sent you the dream."

"I suppose you're right, but—"

"If you need proof," Curlfeather interrupted, "I'm sure you'll feel calmer once I receive my nine lives from StarClan."

"I hope that's true," Frostpaw meowed. "More than anything, RiverClan needs stability and strength, and naming a great leader like you would help. I just hope it all goes well. The sooner you receive your nine lives, the better."

Privately, though, Frostpaw still had her doubts. She knew that ordinarily all a medicine cat had to do was escort the new leader to the Moonpool. But maybe this time she would need to do more. Curlfeather had never been Clan deputy, and as far as she knew, StarClan had never given nine lives to a cat in a situation like this.

Mothwing had told her how Nightstar, who had led ShadowClan back in the old forest, had never received his nine lives, because the former leader, Brokenstar, was still alive, even though he had been deposed for his savage mistreatment of his Clan. And StarClan had actually brought the second Tigerstar back from the dead because his Clan needed him to lead them. But none of that was the same as what RiverClan was facing now.

She let out a long sigh. "This is all new territory," she murmured.

Curlfeather gave her ear an encouraging lick. "Then I'm glad we're exploring it together."

Frostpaw and her mother reached the border stream between WindClan and ThunderClan territory, and followed it uphill until they found a place that was narrow enough to leap across. Soon they had left the trees of ThunderClan behind them and emerged onto the open moor.

A cold wind was blowing right in their faces, plastering Frostpaw's fur to her sides and making her eyes water. The tough grass felt chilly beneath her paws. The long trek to the Moonpool daunted her, yet she longed to reach it and have all this over with, so that she could return to her Clan with their new leader. *They'll all be so relieved that the problems are behind us. And then I can have a nice long nap, knowing the Clan is in capable paws.*

They were still trudging up the first moorland slope,

Frostpaw's legs tired from the journey of the day before. They had almost reached the top when she heard a terrifying baying sound.

"What was that?" Curlfeather exclaimed.

Frostpaw glanced over her shoulder to see three dogs burst out of the forest they had just left. For a couple of heartbeats she froze in panic at the sight of the huge creatures, their muscular bodies and brindled pelts, their jaws gaping as they howled. Then Curlfeather shoved at her sharply, almost carrying her off her paws.

"Run!" her mother yowled. "Back to the trees!"

Frostpaw gaped, staring at her mother in horror. *Is she telling me to run* toward *the dogs?*

"Go!" Curlfeather repeated. "We have to get off the moor."

Then Frostpaw understood. Here in the open there was nowhere to hide, nowhere to avoid the fearsome creatures that were already closer, letting out deep-throated barks as they followed the cats' trail. *And we're RiverClan cats, not WindClan; we don't have their speed.*

Putting out all her strength, Frostpaw raced back down the slope, her belly fur scraping the moorland grass. Curlfeather kept pace beside her. But the trees scarcely seemed to draw nearer, while the dogs had veered to intercept the fleeing cats before they could reach safety. For one horrifying heartbeat Frostpaw thought they would collide. She caught a glimpse of tongues lolling from gaping jaws, and rows of sharp teeth. Then she and Curlfeather were past, with a clear run to the forest, but with the dogs still hard on their paws.

Is this the end? Frostpaw thought. *Is there to be more tragedy for RiverClan? What will they do if they lose both of us?*

Curlfeather dodged around a clump of gorse bushes; Frostpaw followed, hoping that the thorny branches would slow the dogs down. Casting a glance over her shoulder, she saw that they had gained a little, but the dogs seemed to be eating up the ground with their long legs and flying paws, panting and drooling only a few tail-lengths behind. The stink of fresh-kill from their breath washed over her and caught in her throat.

Frostpaw felt as if she had been running forever, trying to force extra speed from her aching legs, but at last they reached an outlying oak tree, its branches spreading wide and close to the ground. Frostpaw leaped for the lowest branch, but her claws barely scraped it and she fell back, winded and shaking with terror.

"Climb!" Curlfeather yowled.

She thrust her shoulders under Frostpaw's belly and boosted her up the tree trunk. Frostpaw scrabbled frantically at the rough bark until she managed to reach the safety of the branch.

"Keep going!" Curlfeather urged her.

"Then follow me!" Frostpaw yowled in reply. "Save yourself!"

Turning back, she expected to see Curlfeather climbing up after her. But the dogs were already upon her; Frostpaw let out a wail of horror as she saw the lead dog sink its fangs into her mother's hindquarters. Her head swam and she felt as if the whole tree were tilting around her.

"Curlfeather!" she wailed. "No!"

Curlfeather was staring up at her, her eyes welling with love and emotion. "Keep RiverClan safe!" Her voice rose into a screech of agony. "And trust no cat!"

Then she disappeared under a tangle of snarling dogs.

Frostpaw squeezed her eyes tight shut, but she couldn't shut out the shrieks of pain from her mother or the snarling and snapping from the dogs. She was trembling so much that she nearly fell off the branch. Only the knowledge that she was still in danger helped her pull herself together.

Mouse-length by mouse-length, she managed to climb up to a higher branch. Then, seeing that it stretched out into the limbs of another tree, she crossed over, then crossed again into another. The ground, so far below, seemed to whirl around her; she froze, squeezing her eyes tight shut. *I can't move! I'm going to fall!*

But she could still hear the horrible sounds of her mother's dying screams somewhere behind her, and she knew she had to go on.

My mother gave her life to save mine. I won't let her die for nothing.

Frostpaw forced herself onward until she couldn't hear the dogs anymore. She tasted the air: Even their scent had faded. For a few heartbeats she stayed where she was, all her senses alert, until she was sure that she was far enough away from the dogs to make her way safely down to the ground. She had no idea where she was, except that she must be on ThunderClan territory; the scents of ThunderClan cats were all around her.

Please, StarClan, don't let them catch me trespassing!

For a moment Frostpaw wondered if she ought to go on to the Moonpool, until she realized that there was no point now. With a crushing sense of defeat, she knew that all she could do was go home and tell her Clan the terrible news of what had happened to Curlfeather.

There's no hurry, she thought drearily. *It's far too late to save her.*

Pausing to listen, Frostpaw could just make out the sound of running water; she headed in that direction and came eventually to the bank of the border stream. With a gasp of relief she leaped across, then followed it as far as the lake. Stunned and exhausted, she still found the strength to pad along the lakeshore until she passed the horseplace and regained River-Clan territory.

When Frostpaw stumbled into camp, her pelt shaking and scratched, her heart aching, the first cat she saw was Mallownose, standing alertly on guard. His eyes widened as he spotted her and he ran up to her side.

"Frostpaw!" he exclaimed. "What's wrong? What's happened?"

"Dogs!" Frostpaw gasped. "They attacked me and Curlfeather."

Mallownose stared at her in shock for a moment, then turned and called out across the camp. "Mothwing! Duskfur! Splashtail!"

The warriors he had named emerged from their den, followed by several of their Clanmates. Mothwing appeared from the direction of the stream and bounded across the camp to Frostpaw's side.

"What happened? Where's Curlfeather?" the medicine cat demanded.

Her voice trembling, Frostpaw told the story of how she and her mother had been attacked by dogs on their way to the Moonpool, and how Curlfeather had thrust her to safety up a tree at the edge of the forest.

"Just where is this tree?" Mothwing asked when Frostpaw had finished. "I have to find Curlfeather and look after her."

"It's too late," Frostpaw choked out. "The dogs killed her." Briefly she was back in the tree, looking down as her mother was overwhelmed by the dogs, and hearing her agonized shrieks.

Gasps of horror followed her words, with cries of protest and disbelief. Graypaw and Mistpaw moved to the front of the crowd, eyes wide, jaws open. In Frostpaw's mind, their voices blended with all the others' into a single wail of anguish. The whole camp seemed to tilt and whirl around her. She was vaguely aware of Mothwing and Splashtail supporting her as far as the medicine cats' den, where she collapsed into her own nest.

Just outside she could hear Mothwing and some of the warriors discussing how they could gather a patrol to find Curlfeather's body and bring it back to camp. Frostpaw curled up tighter in her nest, her eyes shut and her tail wrapped around her ears as she tried to block out the voices, and the rest of the world with them. She didn't want to believe that her mother was truly gone.

At the same time, Frostpaw kept hearing her mother's final

words, forced out in her shriek of agony as the dogs pulled her down. *Trust no cat!* What did it mean? Should Frostpaw not trust Mothwing? Should she not trust any of her Clanmates?

As Frostpaw was struggling to make sense of all of it, she felt something warm and soft slip into the nest beside her. When she opened her eyes, she nearly gasped—Mistpaw and Graypaw had snuck into the medicine cat den and were snuggling in on each side.

"Shhh," Mistpaw whispered. "No cat knows we're here. But we needed to be near you now."

Frostpaw licked her sister's ear gratefully.

"It's hard to believe." Graypaw mewed. "But . . . we're all we have now."

Frostpaw wiggled closer to her siblings, and at last she slipped into uneasy dreams. When she woke, she wasn't sure how much later, her littermates had gone. She could still hear Mothwing and some of the warriors talking outside the den, but she could tell by the red-gold light that the day was drawing to an end. She tottered to her paws and staggered out into the open.

Mothwing was sitting beside the stream with Mallownose, Duskfur, and Splashtail. Duskfur's eyes were dull with grief, and her tail drooped; she looked as if Curlfeather's death had aged her seasons in a single day. Graypaw and Mistpaw were sitting nearby with their mentors, Breezeheart and Icewing. They looked as lost and forlorn as Frostpaw felt.

When Frostpaw emerged, her mentor spotted her at once and padded up to her. "We have found your mother's body," she meowed gently. "Tonight we will sit vigil for her, and then bury her in the way of the Clans."

Frostpaw dipped her head in gratitude, but she was too deep in grief to find words.

"So what are we going to do now?" Mallownose asked. "Curlfeather was supposed to be our new leader."

"Maybe we should go on as we've been doing, with a group of cats to lead us," Splashtail suggested. "Mothwing, you could choose two or three of the senior warriors—"

"That's mouse-brained!" Mallownose interrupted harshly. "A Clan has always had one leader. We need to wait until Frostpaw can speak to StarClan again."

Frostpaw gazed at the brown tabby tom in dismay. "I can't go back to the Moonpool!" she wailed. "Don't make me!" Her muscles were limp with exhaustion, and her paws felt heavy as rocks. And the thought of the dogs made her belly cramp with terror.

"Mallownose, you're the one who's mouse-brained." Duskfur laid her tail gently over Frostpaw's shoulders. "We shouldn't ask that of Frostpaw. She just lost her mother!"

Frostpaw felt her fear ebb and she leaned gratefully into Duskfur's shoulder. A vast wave of relief enveloped her as Mothwing dipped her head to Duskfur. "No," the medicine cat meowed. "We can't put Frostpaw through that right now. I know that you won't want to hear this, but . . ." She paused and took a deep breath. "It's time to tell the other Clans. We need help."